FORGIVEN

PART 2
OF THE TRILOGY
BETWEEN THE MOUNTAINS
AND THE SEA

FORGIVEN

BETWEEN THE MOUNTAINS
AND THE SEA

RUTH SUTTON

HOAD
PRESS

First published in United Kingdom
by **Hoad Press** in 2013
2 Lowther Street, Waberthwaite, Millom, Cumbria LA19 5YN
www.ruthsutton.co.uk   ruth@ruthsutton.co.uk

ISBN–13: 978-0-9523871-8-3

A CIP catalogue record for this book is available from the British Library.

Prepared for publication by Aldridge Press
enquiries@aldridgepress.co.uk

Editorial: Charlotte Rolfe
Design: John Aldridge
Cover design: Kevin Ancient
Cover photos: John Aldridge
Text photos: 1, 31, 51, 136, 198, 257 John Aldridge; 60 Boguslaw Kupisinski | Dream-
stime.com; 106 Sergiy Zavgorodny | Dreamstime.com; 153 Menno67 | Dreamstime.
com; 218 Prentiss40 | Dreamstime.com; 248 Chris Leachman | Dreamstime.com; 283
Spbphoto | Dreamstime.com

Typeset in Bulmer 11.5/14.5pt

Printed and bound in UK by TJ International, Padstow

Acknowledgements

As with *A Good Liar*, the first book in this trilogy, I am grateful for the help provided by the staff and resources of the local history archives in Whitehaven. Details of many of the events stemmed from the pages of the *Whitehaven News*, and from the memories of my friends and neighbours.

For the background of coal mining during the period, particular thanks are due to Pamela Telford at the Haig Mining Museum in Kells, Whitehaven.

Invaluable feedback and support has been offered on first and successive drafts by Mick Shaw, Judy Coghill and my editor, Charlotte Rolfe. The final meticulous production was achieved through the skill and experience of John Aldridge. Thank you to all of them.

RS, Waberthwaite, April 2013

Author's note

Much of the inspiration for this trilogy has come from the landscape, people and history of West Cumbria where I now live. All the characters are fictional, and any resemblance to real people is purely coincidental.

Much of the action takes place within the real communities of Kells, Boot, Sandwith, and Seascale. The village of Newton, however, is a fictional community, combining the features of two or three villages close to where the Esk River meets the Irish Sea.

I have presented the voices, accents and dialect of some of the key characters in a way that I hope maintains authenticity while making them intelligible to the reader without a tedious glossary.

Chapter 1

1946. Early September, late afternoon. The air was thick, stifling. Jessie Whelan looked up from her desk in the empty classroom, knowing that something was about to happen. When she opened the outside door of the school, her hair rose from her scalp, galvanised by electricity crackling in the air. Almost at once, with the roar of an approaching train, the storm tore into trembling trees that moaned and thrashed in protest, torn leaves and branches sailing across the yard. Jessie fled back into the building and shut the heavy door with all her strength. Breathless, she peered through the rattling window. Beyond the blizzard of foliage, across the lane, a figure was crouching by the schoolhouse door. She saw it jerk, impaled by light and sound, before it straightened, turned and lurched towards the school.

At the gate the figure stopped, thwarted by the catch. Then it was through, a long coat clinging to the thin body that strode across the yard. The outer door burst open and wind tore through the room.

1

Someone called out, 'Miss Whelan? Are you there?' Jessie backed towards the furthest wall of the classroom as the stranger appeared in the doorway. He wore a beret, and a long coat, from which water dripped onto the floorboards. He wiped his thin brown face with his hand. Jessie noticed the round white collar.

'Who are you?' she asked, realising as she spoke that she already knew.

Another thunderous crash coincided with lightning that tore the sky above their heads. Jessie saw the man's mouth move but heard none of his words. She waited until the overwhelming noise abated, reverberating among the old stone walls of the village and the rocky fells all around.

'You must be Reverend Barker,' she said. 'They told us you would be here next week.'

The man nodded. 'Gideon Barker. And you must be Jessie Whelan.'

She was surprised. She was Miss Whelan to everyone except close friends. 'How do you know my name?'

'You are on my list of people to see,' he said. 'There was no answer at the schoolhouse, then I saw someone at the window, here.'

'The children will be back next week and I came across to do some work. Take off your coat, vicar,' she said. 'We'll go back to the house when it calms down.'

He hung the dripping coat over a chair, and took off his beret, revealing pale hair plastered to his head. His face was tanned but thin and drawn. Without the coat he looked like a bedraggled schoolboy; she wondered how old he was, where he had been.

'Sounds strange to be called "vicar",' he said, pulling up a small chair. The wet trousers clung to his legs. 'It was always "padre", out east. I got back home a couple of weeks ago and found the letter from the diocese.'

2

'About being the vicar here in Newton, you mean?'

'Aye. Didn't know anything about it. Orders go astray all the time. Didn't even know where Newton is. I'm from Sheffield. Bit different down there.'

More lightning lit up the north-facing window, and the thunder was less strident, a second or two later.

'The storm's passing over,' said Jessie. 'I was going to light a lamp, but we may not need it.'

He glanced round the room. 'No electric?'

Jessie laughed. 'No electric anywhere in Newton,' she said. 'Not yet. A few cars, one or two telephones.'

'Tractors?'

She shook her head. 'Most farmers round here don't like the idea, and where's the fuel going to come from when everything's rationed? Milligans just up the valley, they have a tractor. Much more noisy than the horses.'

'It's like another world,' he said.

Jessie felt uncomfortable, as if he disapproved of her, and Newton. 'The rain's eased off,' she said. 'We might as well make a dash for the house and I'll brew us some tea.'

She hoped that tea and cake and a comfortable chair in the small front room of the schoolhouse would soften the young man's mood, but it did not appear to do so. He seemed restless, staring out of the window that Jessie had opened. The storm had passed, and already the air was fresher.

'Can you smell the sea?' she asked.

'Can't smell much any more. They beat us. The Japs, in the camp.'

'I'm so sorry,' she said.

'Aye. Well, that was the war, out there. Everyone's war was different. What was it like 'ere?'

Jessie hesitated, still thinking about what he had said. 'Some of

3

the men went away to fight,' she said, 'and we even had some stray bombs, but nothing like those poor folk in the cities. And we've had the rationing and coupons of course, shortages of everything, queuing for food, all that. Nothing's changed much, really, since the end of the war.'

'Everything has changed,' he said, turning back to the open window. 'People here, people like you, Jessie, you won't understand that, not really. But for people like me, the war is here,' he tapped his hard tight chest. 'We served, we suffered. I've seen things in the camps, that you couldn't imagine.'

Jessie didn't know what to say and said nothing. He was like a child from a wretched home, set apart by memories of violence. She watched his narrow back, silhouetted against the window. The sky had cleared, and a thrush was singing somewhere outside.

'Tell me about this place,' he said. 'Here we are, miles from anywhere, mountains over there, sea over here. Farms, fields, poverty, except for those folk at Skeffington Hall yonder. They're doing alright, I'll bet.'

He wants me to react, she thought. 'We are isolated, that's true,' she said. 'But actually it's not just green fields and feudalism. Further north there are pits and factories, just like in Yorkshire. And south of here there's Barrow, with ships and steel. That's where I was born. Barrow was hit badly, Mr Barker, and we all did our bit, digging the coal, making the uniforms, building the ships. Hundreds of evacuees from the north-east came, the children were in our school. Our previous vicar's son, Andy Leadbetter, he was a gunner with the Canadian air force. And my nephew John Pharaoh, he wanted to join the navy but he wasn't allowed. "Reserved occupation" – he had to stay in the pits.'

Gideon Barker wasn't listening. 'This isn't where I thought

they would send me. I wanted Yorkshire, where I'm from, the city, real problems …'

Jessie dealt with her mounting irritation by clearing their cups and plates. He followed her into the kitchen. Before he could say any more she turned to him. 'I think you need to understand, Mr Barker,' she said, choosing her words carefully, 'that we are real people here, too, with strengths and doubts like everybody else. We may be a little behind the times, but sometimes it feels as if the war is still going on. Rationing, shortages, everything run from London. The men are only just coming home. Our Mr Crompton, the other teacher, he was demobbed only a few weeks ago. I haven't spoken to him yet. He was in the navy, in the Atlantic I believe.'

'I heard that,' he said.

'Alan Crompton and I worked together here before the war,' Jessie went on. 'It could be difficult for him, coming back.'

'How long have you been here?' he asked.

'Since 1925. I was very lucky to get this job, and the school-house, and to hold on to it during the thirties.'

'Twenty years,' he said. 'And you live alone at the schoolhouse? No family?'

She shook her head. 'My mother died many years ago, and my sister went to New Zealand. There's just my nephew, John. He works in Whitehaven.' She hesitated. 'He has his own life. And you, Mr Barker?'

He ignored the question.

'So, you're sitting pretty Miss Whelan, I would say,' he said, not looking at her. 'In charge at the school, pillar of the community, nice house all to yourself.'

Jessie asked herself if this was jealousy, or just rudeness: either way, the man was insufferable.

'You may see it that way,' she said quietly. 'All I see at present is

5

that the children return next week and I have to be ready for them, and to welcome back Mr Crompton, of course. I'm sure you and he will find much to talk about.' She moved towards the door.

'I'll have to get back to the vicarage,' he said. 'Got some people moving in there. Too much space for me. Thanks for the tea, Jessie. And the chat.' She had opened the front door with an unmistakeable gesture of dismissal, but he paused and looked back at her.

'It was my faith that kept me going, all those years,' he said. 'Sometimes I can hardly remember the man I was before, but I will find him again. It'll just take a little time. Sorry if I'm a bit, you know, sharp.'

Jessie smiled but said no more as she closed the door behind him and leant against it. Sharp or not, what had he been trying to say? It sounded like disapproval, that she should move over and leave her job and the house to someone more deserving. And what would her friend Agnes Plane, wealthy, well-connected Agnes Plane make of him? Jessie couldn't help but smile at the thought of the confrontation to come. Agnes had wanted a village party, to mark the anniversary of the end of the war, but the parish council had scorned the idea. 'Nowt to celebrate, nowt to celebrate with,' they'd said, so the party would be at Applegarth, not the village hall, and Jessie knew that the new vicar would be invited. She would have to warn Agnes about him, but she still wanted to be there when they met for the first time. Agnes knew more than most people about the post-war world through her work in London at the Ministry of Supply. Gideon Barker wouldn't be able to browbeat her, but Jessie would enjoy seeing him try.

The following morning a letter arrived at the schoolhouse. Jessie recognised the writing on the envelope and felt a familiar twist in her stomach. It was from John Pharaoh, the man she called her nephew. Even after all this time, ten long years, any word from him made her anxious. When they had settled on the public lie, to keep their secret and protect Jessie's job and home, lying had seemed so easy. It should have been even easier as time passed, she thought. but instead, her sense of unease grew. She wondered how much longer he would let her deny that he was her son, that she had given him away to strangers when he was four days old and lied about it ever since?

She opened the letter, feeling the fear in her clumsy fingers.

Dear Jessie,

Agnes has invited me to her birthday party next week, but it will be easier for both of us if I don't come. I have a new job, by the way, in the wages office at the Haig Pit. It's a step up, and closer to the house in Sandwith.

I hope you are well,

John

New job, his own home. No mention of a girlfriend. She wondered how John would keep their secret when he had a wife and children of his own? She hated not knowing when the axe would fall. Maybe it would be better to just tell people, herself. When the secret was out, she would have to resign; if she didn't they would sack her, and she couldn't let that happen. And what about Matthew? He liked her, she knew that, but he was the doctor, respectable Dr Dawson. How would he react to the news that she was a liar and a fraud?

John's letter lay on the kitchen table, taunting her. She crumpled it up and threw it away.

The party would certainly be easier without John. Relieved of that anxiety, she could enjoy Agnes's hospitality, and catch up with friends she hadn't seen for a while.

* * *

'Have you seen Matthew, dear?' Caroline Leadbetter asked as she was taking off her gloves. 'He set off from Cockermouth ahead of us.'

Jessie smiled at Caroline's eagerness. 'He's in the kitchen, talking to Agnes.'

'He was so looking forward to seeing you, Jessie, he told me so himself. He looks well, don't you think? Handsome even, for a man his age.'

Jessie nodded in agreement. He is a handsome man, she thought, more than she remembered from those years ago when he and his wife lived in the village, before the war.

'And here he is,' said Caroline. 'I'll leave you two to catch up. Can you hear Lionel anywhere?' She squeezed Jessie's arm and was gone.

'Hello, Jessie,' said Matthew, 'Have you got a drink? Can I get you something?'

'I'm fine, thank you,' she said, picking her glass from the hall table.

'I'm going to have a look at the new raised beds outside that Agnes was telling me about, while it's still light. Come with me?'

Why not, she thought. They slipped out of the front door together, and round the side of the house.

The warmth of afternoon sun was still trapped in the enclosed garden. Jessie and Matthew inspected the raised beds and considered what might grow well, and who would manage the project.

'Agnes feels she's done enough at the Ministry. She hasn't said it in so many words, but she never expected the demands to be as great, or long-lasting. This is her home, and she's full of plans for the house and the garden when she finally has time to spend on them. It's frustrating for her to have this lovely home and not have enough time to enjoy it. Nellie looks after the house, and Mr Barnett does the garden. They're both very conscientious, but it's not the same as doing things yourself, seeing the fruits of your own efforts.'

Matthew nodded. 'You must feel that about the school – the fruits of your own efforts, I mean.'

'I do in a way,' she said. 'You know the best time for me was when the evacuees were here. They were a challenge, but it was a challenge I needed. Since they went, it's felt rather flat. I should be happy to coast along until I retire, but I don't feel like that.'

'Sounds as if the new vicar may be your new challenge,' said Matthew, 'from what Agnes was saying. She's invited him to the party, but no sign of him yet.'

'I do hope he comes,' said Jessie. 'We could have sold tickets!'

'Is he so difficult?' he asked.

'Not difficult, just very different. And whatever happened to him during the war, it's left him bitter, wanting to change everything. He's only been here a few days, and he's managed to upset everybody, apparently. The only person who seems to like him is Alan Crompton, the other teacher at the school, the one who's just come back. They were both overseas and treat each other like brothers-in-arms, standing together against a common foe. Or that's how it feels anyway.'

'Who's the common foe?'

'Anyone with a big house, or a big job, or who wasn't in the forces, apparently.'

Matthew nodded. Jessie felt he understood.

'Have you ever thought of giving up, doing something else?' he asked.

'I have, actually, but in a vague way, nothing specific. I'll be fifty later this year, Matthew. I could stay at the school another ten years, fifteen even, but then what? Sometimes I find myself wondering if that's all there is. I've even thought of emigrating … but that's too drastic.'

'There are other things here a woman of your talents could do, I'm sure,' he said. 'What are you interested in?'

'That's the problem. I don't know. I know there's more to life than teaching. I read a lot, but I've never really travelled. Even talking to the vicar and Alan Crompton has made me realise what they've seen over the past few years. I know much of it was awful, but they've seen places I could only dream of. I've just been to London a few times with Agnes. And I know more about music now than I did, but it's just bits and pieces, nothing substantial. In some ways my life has been on hold, for years, and I want to start learning again.'

She waited, remembering, aware of his close attention. 'Would you believe I worked in a factory, making shells, in the first war? The other girls thought I was the brainy one, because I'd been to college. But I'm not using my brain enough now.'

'There's time,' he said.

'And the new vicar may be just the push I need,' she said. 'I'm trying to see his arrival in Newton as an opportunity.' She laughed. 'That's quite a challenge, in itself.'

A flock of finches fluttered round the sheltered garden, settling in the hedge like random jewels before skittering away. Jessie realised that she was telling Matthew things she hadn't shared with anyone else, not even Agnes. She turned towards him.

'How are you settling, in the new house?' she asked. He was such easy company; she wished he lived a little closer.

'It's quite a change, on my own for the first time in years,' he said. 'But after Joan died, the link with Newcastle was broken, really. And when Ann went off to college in London, it just seemed right to come back here. They'll need family doctors in this area when the new health scheme starts – if it starts.'

Jessie nodded. 'Cumberland's too quiet for you, maybe, after the city.'

Matthew turned to look at her. 'Perhaps it is. But I can see attractions here … You haven't changed at all, Jessie. The same warmth, your hair, and that smile, just as it was.'

She felt herself blush and turned away.

'We'd better go in,' she said, noticing faces in the window turned towards them. He followed her glance.

'Caroline's funny, isn't she? She seems determined to find me a "companion", as she calls it. I want to explain that I'm quite content as I am, but that would be too direct. Everything is hinted at, nothing explicit. Quite hard to deal with sometimes.'

'That's exactly it,' said Jessie. 'I've been aware of it ever since I moved here. People don't say things directly, and I've always found it difficult. So it's not just me, you feel it, too.'

"All the time,' he said. 'We should start a club, you and I. We could call it, Plain Speakers United'

They both laughed. Jessie waved cheerfully at Caroline who was watching them through the window.

'Come on,' she said. 'We've teased her for long enough.'

* * *

Much later, lying still sleepless in her bedroom as the first bird-song heralded a new day, Jessie went over the conversation with Matthew in the garden. Agnes had been hinting that the two of them seemed made for each other, and maybe she was right. But further back in her mind, buried deep but not deep enough, Jessie could not forget Andrew Leadbetter, the only man who had ever known this room, this bed. For a short while, ten years before, he had been her lover, and still she could not forget the risks and excitement of their affair. Two young men haunted her past and threatened her future, John the son, and Andrew the lover. She could not give in to them now.

Chapter 2

'When's the Big Walk, miss?' asked George Tyson in the school-yard one morning. He was nearly as tall as his teacher.

'Is it your turn already, George?' said Jessie. 'How old are you now?'

'Twelve, miss, nearly thirteen. Me and the others'll go first time this year, then again next year, before we leave. So when are we going?'

'I'll have to ask Mr Southward about the weather,' she said. 'He's usually right about it. If he says we've got a fine few days coming up, we'll do it then. Have you got some strong shoes to wear?'

'I can borrow some, miss.'

'You get that organised and I'll talk to Mr Southward.'

George ran off, excited, to tell the others.

It was several years since Jessie had first taken the older children on the Big Walk, when she realised that some of them had never been up to the high ridges that they could see from the school, never seen Morecambe Bay on the other side of the hill. For some of the children Newton and the flat coastal strip on which it lay was their whole world. They needed to look down at it all from a high place, and Newton Fell was the easiest place to get them to. They looked at maps, but that wasn't enough. The Big Walk was part of her effort to get all the children to see a little of the wider world. Every year for the past decade or so her friend Agnes had donated some money to the school, just enough to take the older children on a couple of trips. On one occasion they went north to Whitehaven on the train, to look round the busy town, up to St James Church and down to the harbour. She taught the children about the slave trade that made Whitehaven rich: it was a dismal story, and not part of what she was supposed to teach, but the children never forgot it. On another day they took the train to Barrow, round the edge of Morecambe Bay, across the viaducts, and then across the bridge to Walney Island and the furthest point of the Furness peninsular. They needed a long summer day, with time to walk along the wide shore from Biggar Bank to the southern tip of Walney, looking out into the shipping channel and across to Piel Castle. Blackpool Tower peeked above the horizon, and Jessie told the children how as a girl she had been on the paddle steamer that plied across from Barrow to Blackpool. Shore, sky and sea merged into each other out there and they would spot geese, ducks and seabirds, noting everything in their little books. The children had no idea that this was where their teacher had walked as a young woman with her first love, Clive Whelan, lying with him in the dunes under the sky.

The children called the excursion to the top of Newton Fell the Big Walk, as it was further and higher than many of them had ever walked before. For one or two, it was a more familiar experience. The older boys sometimes followed the hounds on foot, as was the custom in this part of Cumberland, wherever the fox would lead them. For them the Big Walk was relatively tame and predictable, and Jessie would put them in charge of the younger children as they picked their way up to the ancient rocks on the summit. If the day was well chosen and the air was clear, they could look right round, at the peaks of central Lakeland to the north, then out to the west across the Solway Firth to Scotland. Below them lay the Irish Sea, and between it and them the flat green coastal plain dotted with grazing sheep and cattle, where they lived. Newton lay on the southern side of the estuary; the road that followed the river led first to Ganthwaite and then on to Boot, along the green flat floor of the Esk valley, chequered by stone walls.

After the Big Walk every year Jessie gathered the children around the map of Lakeland that hung on the wall of her classroom. They marked out the route they had taken and what they had seen, connecting the reality of their experience with the two dimensions of the map. Did it make a difference, she wondered. Did it make any of them wonder what lay beyond, in the rest of England? She wanted to make them curious, to make their feet itch with the possibilities of a larger world, beyond the confines of their village where they knew every tree, every chimney stack, every gatepost.

Jessie heard young voices and looked out. Children from Mr Crompton's class were running into the yard, dressed in vests and shorts, despite a brisk wind and drizzle blowing in from the sea. Mr Crompton was with them and Jessie saw to her surprise that he too was in vest and shorts, with a whistle in his mouth that he blew insistently when he wasn't shouting. The children jostled into rows facing the teacher and jumping with varying degrees of skill and enthusiasm. Alan Crompton pulled one of the larger boys out of the line and made him stand at the front, facing the others. The boy began to jump awkwardly, raising his arms above his head while his teacher stood behind him, poking at his legs with a long stick. Some of the children stopped and began to laugh, until another of them was pulled out to the front and the laughing stopped.

Why was he doing this, she wondered, right outside her room? Was he trying to make a point? She had asked him not to take his

14

children out for exercise in all weathers, but here they were again. This was the same man who'd found the mildest of children hard to manage when he first started at the school ten years before; the same man who had blushed and stammered whenever Lionel Leadbetter had spoken to him.

He had always struggled to control the children, she remembered, and seemed to have decided that fear and humiliation was the answer. Maybe that was what the navy had taught him. He even looked different now: wiry rather than thin, his face harder than before, brown and lined. He'd been in Atlantic convoys they said, for five dangerous years, and his compassion seemed to have been lost at sea. For some of the parents and the older boys, this new, regenerated Mr Crompton was a hero; to Jessie, he was a bully.

At the end of the day Jessie spoke her mind. It did not go well. She hadn't expected his obvious disdain for her.

'Maybe you've been here too long, Miss Whelan,' he said. 'The school is too soft, I believe, and so are the children. We learned a lot from being away these past years. These children need discipline, and that's what they'll get, from me at least. The last war may be over, but the next isn't far away, you mark my words. Those Russians …'

'What are you suggesting, Mr Crompton?' she said, wondering who he'd been talking to.

'I'm suggesting, Miss Whelan, that times have changed and we need to change, too. All of us. The old, soft ways got us into the last war, and who knows how long the peace will last? We need to stay tough, and that's what I'm doing to these children. If I had the chance I'd have the whole school out there.'

'Remember how the last war ended,' said Jessie quietly. 'It didn't matter whether those poor Japanese children were tough or not.'

Alan Crompton said nothing, but looked at her with the same defiance.

'Have you talked to the vicar about this?' she asked.

'Mr Barker and I talk about a lot of things. I'm sure he would agree with me about the need for our children to toughen up.'

'Indeed,' said Jessie. 'Maybe I need to talk to the vicar myself. Of course, you may take your children out for exercise, but not in the pouring rain, and I don't expect you to single out any children for public punishment. Is that clear?'

'I fought for my country,' he countered, his neck flushing. 'You have no idea ...' He looked away from her, out towards the sea. 'We all need a fresh start, or –'

'That may well be,' she interrupted, raising her voice. 'But bullying children will not be part of it.'

He stared at her, then down at his feet, moving slightly.

'You've been here for many years,' he said, without looking up.

Jessie waited.

'That's an important job in this community,' he went on.

'Yes, it is,' she said.

'People expect the headmistress to be, well, above reproach, don't they?'

Jessie suddenly felt a little dizzy.

'What are you trying to say, Mr Crompton?'

He looked at her. His oiled hair flopped forward over his face and he pushed it back.

'I know about you,' he said.

She held his look, steadying herself.

'It was years ago,' he pushed on, 'before the war, but I know ...'

'Mr Crompton,' said Jessie, pulling herself up to his height, and holding on to the edge of a table. 'I have no idea what you're hinting it, and I'm not sure I want to know. We're here to talk about your treatment of the children, and it will go into the record –'

'Oh, but it won't,' he said, 'not when you hear me out.'

'Are you threatening me?' she asked, wanting him to continue, but dreading what he might say.

Alan Crompton hesitated, but only for a moment. He took a deep breath and said, 'I know about you and him.'

Jessie's mind raced, trying to find a connection to any of the people who knew about John.

'For heaven's sake,' she said, 'what are you talking about? I have better things to do.'

'I noticed, but I didn't say anything. Didn't dare then, but now it's different. I watched you together, I saw him at your house, at night.'

'What?' she demanded. 'Who did you see?'

'Leadbetter,' Alan Crompton's face was red.

'The vicar?' said Jessie, with as much incredulity as she could muster.

'No, the son, Andrew. I saw you together, I know about you.'

'What? Where? Andrew Leadbetter went away to Canada years ago.'

'It was just after I started here,' he said. 'When the vicar was talking about building the new school. I saw Andrew at your house one night, in the dark.'

'For goodness' sake,' she said, sitting down. Her legs suddenly felt weak. 'I know you've had a dreadful few years, and it must be hard coming home, taking orders from a woman, as you see it, but you cannot go around saying things like this.' As she talked, the words came more freely. 'Andrew Leadbetter and I had a meeting or two, at my house, about the new school, but that was all. Since then he has served his country bravely, in the Canadian air force. What are you implying is an insult to us both, and makes you appear weak and spiteful. I suggest you keep this nonsense to yourself.'

Alan Crompton looked down at his feet. He seemed smaller now, like a boy in trouble not a man in control. Jessie had seized the moral high ground, and pressed home her advantage.

'I have no idea what brought this on, Alan. I'm prepared to believe that it's just part of what you may be going through. But you know how much damage can be done by loose talk in a village like this, and I am sure you will be more careful in the future. I will not make a note about you going against my expressed wishes regarding the children, for now, but I expect that to be the end of the matter. Is that understood?'

There was silence, save for the wind whining in the window frame. He opened his mouth, but she put up her hand to stop him.

'Enough,' she said. 'You've said quite enough already.'

Without speaking, and without looking at her, he turned smartly on his heels and left the room, shutting the door behind him with more energy than was required. Jessie waited for a minute or two, hardly breathing. He was a weak man, and he was trying to intimidate her like he did the children. She was fearful and furious all at once and felt the tears pricking her eyes.

* * *

Later, talking to Agnes, Jessie tried to make light of what had happened.

'He looked so silly, standing there with his little moustache wobbling up and down, and his nasty hair in ridges on his head. He must have combed it specially before he came to see me.'

'You are his superior, after all,' said Agnes.

'And he hates that, I know. All those years at sea must have left their mark. And I told him so, gave him a way to back down, but I honestly think he's going to carry on. Did I tell you the phrase he used, about me as the headmistress? I had to be "beyond reproach". Sounds like something out of the Bible.'

'Or out of the vicar,' said Agnes. 'That's where it's coming from. You know how close the two of them are. They may feel it's them against the world, and a world full of women at that. My mother told me it was the same after the first war, the men wanted to put the clock back, get the women back into the kitchen where they belong.'

'I think Crompton wants my job,' said Jessie. 'He wants my job, and the schoolhouse, and thinks he can bully me into moving out.'

'And Barker will back him up,' said Agnes. 'One more thing to talk to the Bishop about.'

They sat for a moment, each thinking her own thoughts.

Agnes spoke first. 'He's right about "beyond reproach". It's still true, even now.'

'About me, you mean?'

'Yes, dear, I'm afraid so.'

'But he doesn't know about John, or that would have been thrown in my face straight away. It was Andrew he mentioned. And that was, well, nothing really. It happened and was over, and so long ago.'

Agnes looked across at her friend, watching her carefully.

'I never understood it,' she said, her voice quite soft. 'I still don't. I know you were lonely. We all get lonely at times, but … not that. Not with … someone like him, Jessie.'

Jessie sat up suddenly. 'I remember what you said that day. We were in this very room. You said you were disgusted. I've never forgotten that.'

Agnes pulled a small handkerchief from the pocket of her cardigan. 'Don't let's talk about it now, I shouldn't have …'

'No, Agnes, we need to. We never did at the time, with everything else going on. But that word, it's stayed with me ever since. *Disgusted.*'

'It was the shock,' said Agnes. 'I guessed something was going on, but I never thought, not for a minute, that you and he …'

'That we'd been to bed together? Come on, Agnes, say it. It was a mistake, maybe, but it wasn't evil. We were both unattached, no one else involved.'

'But he was so young,' said Agnes.

'Yes, I know, and my friend's son, and he had girls all over the county. I knew all that. That was part of it, why I wanted him.'

Agnes shook her head.

Jessie went on, remembering the turmoil of those weeks with Andrew. 'He was young, and handsome and he had lots of women and he chose me. I was flattered, can't you see that?'

Agnes shook her head again. 'You could have said no.'

Jessie got to her feet. 'Don't say any more. Just leave it. I hoped you'd back me up, against Alan, and the vicar if it comes to that. If you can't, fine. But don't rake all that stuff up again.'

She picked up her coat from the back of a chair by the door. 'I'm going home now. Don't judge me, Agnes, please. You have always supported me about John. Don't back away from me now.'

Agnes watched her friend, her dear friend, walking quickly up the drive and out of sight. The only thing she wanted, the only thing she had ever wanted, was for she and Jessie to live in this house, together. John would be a son for them both, and they would love him as much as they loved each other. But the years had passed and the dream had never come any closer, until now. If Jessie didn't have the schoolhouse, she could move into Applegarth. It wasn't too late.

Chapter 3

THE ENVELOPE ON THE WORN CARPET by the front door of the schoolhouse had Jessie's name on it. She looked at it, her mind a blur – anything unexpected made her nervous now. For weeks she'd feared that things were about to unravel, and sometimes the anticipation made her feel quite sick. She picked up the envelope and examined it carefully. The postmark was Cockermouth. Matthew? He had written to her, after the party, saying how much he'd enjoyed seeing her, and hoping to see her again, but he'd not mentioned anything specific. Maybe he wanted her to suggest something. So much for plain speaking.

But this was Caroline Leadbetter's writing. Something might have happened to Andrew. Did they know, she wondered? Had they ever guessed about their son? Surely there would have been some sign, however discreet they tried to be. She must have been deranged. In a way she had been. Part of her had wanted him so badly, even while the respectable part had known that it was madness and that it would never work. And then, there was that night, when it all went wrong. She willed herself not to think about it. 'Beyond reproach'.

Perhaps it wasn't about Andrew at all. She tore open the letter and skimmed through it. It was about Lionel. Caroline's hand-writing was less tidy than usual.

I'm sorry to tell you, Jessie, that Lionel has been taken ill. We were with friends in Lamplugh on Saturday evening. In the middle of dinner he suddenly stood up, opened his mouth to say something and then just collapsed. He'd been holding the tablecloth – terrible mess everywhere. We carried him to the car, what a blessing there were people there to help. The hospital said he'd had a stroke. I think I knew that already. He couldn't speak, or move his left side. His mouth was drooping, all the classic signs.

They sent me home, and the Stallards stayed with me at the vicarage overnight. Such kind people. Now they've gone and I have to let people know. I've sent a telegram to Andrew in Toronto, just in case. You know what it's like between him and Lionel, but he might want to come and I think Lionel would want to see him. With all his friends in the air force he might be able to get here quickly, if he wants to.

Could you telephone me when you get this? Sorry to burden you with all this, Jessie. I know how busy you are.

In haste,
Caroline

It was a shock. Lionel Leadbetter had always seemed larger than life: big man, big voice, big reputation in the village and beyond. But his plan in 1937 to rebuild the school at the parishioners' expense had been a step too far. Lionel had expected all the villagers to pay for it, or give their work for nothing, and that was never going to happen, not with money so tight. In the end the diocese had stepped in but things were never the same. After the war started they'd given him a new parish in Cockermouth, and he'd only just retired. Gideon Barker was as tight as Lionel had been … 'unbuttoned' – that was the word. And now the big man was very sick, by the sound of it. She needed to talk to Caroline.

She took the Applegarth key off its customary hook in the schoolhouse pantry and let herself in shortly after eight. The house was cool, and smelled of polish. Nellie Kitchin must have been in to clean as she did every week, whether Agnes was there or not; the regular payments were a lifeline to Nellie and her family now that her Bill was gone. Agnes left ration coupons in a drawer for her, not knowing as everyone else did that Nellie sold them for the extra cash.

Jessie looked at the telephone crouching on the hall table, shiny and black with a round face and big ears. She still didn't like it. Agnes had installed a telephone before anyone else in Newton, but then she was always first with the new things, always had the latest model of car, and fashionable clothes. Caroline's telephone number was in the book in the hallstand drawer. Jessie dialled the operator and repeated the number carefully. There was a short pause before she heard it ringing.

'The Leadbetter home,' said the familiar voice.

'Caroline, it's Jessie.'

'Oh, my dear, thank you so much for calling. I know you don't like the telephone.' Caroline's voice sounded nervous, and she was talking so fast that Jessie struggled to take in what she said. She gathered that there was some improvement, but Lionel was still unable to speak, and it would be a while before they knew how long it would take … Caroline's voice faltered.

'Is there anything I can do?' Jessie asked.

'Come up to the hospital when you can. They say he needs to see people, be reminded who he is and so forth. And can you tell Agnes? I don't know how to contact her in London. Just tell her what's happened but not to worry, and not to come back specially. The girls will help, and so many friends, and maybe Andrew too. I've asked him to come, but you know how things are between him and his father.'

23

Jessie could hear that Caroline was starting to cry.

'I'll track Agnes down, dear,' said Jessie. 'You get some rest. This must be so hard for you. I'll get the bus up to the hospital tomorrow after school. I'll see you then.'

Jessie replaced the receiver carefully on its cradle and sat on a little chair in the darkness of the hall. She hadn't seen Andrew since that night in 1937, just after Christmas, when he'd bolted for Canada. He'd written to her but she hadn't replied, except once after his accident. She'd sent him a note then, just a few words to wish him well. When a reply came, thanking her, it had been written by someone else. What would he do, she wondered. War changes everything, and Andrew had been lucky to survive. Maybe family feuds feel different when life is so fragile.

For the next few days, prompted by her visit to Lionel and conversation with Caroline, Jessie could not get Andrew out of her mind. Memories of him suffused her house. As she lay in bed she felt his weight beside her, on her, and the warmth of his body. She remembered the night that had finished it, when he was drunk and forced himself on her. Some of the details had faded but the feeling of shame and humiliation had not. She'd forgiven him too quickly, she knew that now, but it was so long ago, and she had to forgive herself.

It was nearly two weeks after Caroline's letter, and quite late in the evening, when Jessie heard someone knocking on the back door of the schoolhouse. She knew immediately that it was Andrew. No one else ever came to the back door. He had always done so, to avoid being seen. She found it hard to breathe. Another knock, louder this time, and his voice, 'Jessie, are you there?'

She ran both hands through her hair, pinched her cheeks, took a deep breath and opened the door. Andrew Leadbetter stood at the bottom of the steps. His hat was pulled down over his face, but she knew it was him.

Jessie stood back, and he stepped up and past her, a bag over his shoulder. She smelt tobacco on his clothes. 'Come through,' she said, as normally as she could manage, leading the way into the small front room and closing the curtains before turning up the lamp.

'Don't,' he said. 'Leave it.'

'Someone might see us from out there,' she said, aware of the village all around her.

Andrew put down his bag. 'I don't care about that. I want to tell you – before you see me.'

'Tell me what?'

'About this,' he said, taking off his hat and turning the right side of his face towards her. Even in the low light she could see the scarring, the glossy skin pulled tight, the eye slightly askew.

'It looks better than it did,' he said. 'That's why I didn't come before, when we were stood down. The treatment took a long time. My hands as well. Look.'

He took off his gloves and held up his hands, turning them to show her the damage, before he sat down on a small chair and looked at her.

Jessie sat down, her hand to her mouth. She remembered his hands and his fingers, strong and confident on her body. Now they were claws, gnarled and bent.

'What happened?' she said. 'Caroline never told me.'

'I told her not to say anything. When I went home to Canada last year I wanted you to remember me as I was before, not like this.'

'I do remember,' she said. 'I remember too much.'

Andrew looked away. 'I was young and stupid. I don't drink now, I swear to you, not since then. I know what I did to you.'

They sat in silence on opposite sides of the room. The oil lamp hissed.

'It's cold in here,' she said. 'Keep your coat on. I'll light the fire.' Fussing with the coals in the grate gave her a few minutes to slow down her heart.

A short while later the fire was beginning to warm the room. Andrew took off his big coat and hung it on a hook behind the door. She noticed the white scarf that he unwound from his neck.

'I've seen those scarves in pictures of air force men,' she said. 'Can I feel it?' The scarf was luxuriant, smooth and warm from his skin.

'Silk,' he said, watching her. 'We all wear them, for the cold.'

'It feels wonderful,' she said, putting the soft fabric to her cheek. The smell of him, ingrained into the fibres, jolted her memory but she said nothing more, handed the scarf back to him and escaped into the kitchen. When she returned with tea for them both, Andrew pulled on his gloves to protect his hands from the heat, and they sat facing each other on either side of the fireplace.

'Tell me what happened,' she said.

He looked at the fire, seeing a city in flames. 'It was early in '45, last year. We were coming back from a raid on Dresden. Bombed the poor bastards to hell. Took a hit, one engine and the landing gear shot away, but we were OK. Fuel was leaking, so we had to find a strip. When we found one, another plane had landed just ahead of us, slewed right across the runway. We hit it. I was rear gunner. Fuel and fire everywhere, couldn't get the hood off. They smashed it in the end and pulled me out, but not before ...' He held up his gloved hands.

'I ended up at East Grinstead, where they took the burns cases. Dozens of our lads were there. They did special surgery at the hospital, remaking faces, noses, hands. Most of them were much worse than me. I was lucky. Stayed in London for a while before they sent me back. Had to learn to write with my other hand. It was bloody difficult.'

'You should have told me.'

'Why? I didn't want you to feel sorry for me. Didn't want your pity.'

Jessie looked across at him. 'When Caroline told me you were in bombers I thought I'd never see you again.'

'I never forgot you,' he said, fumbling for something in his coat pocket. He held out a scrap of paper towards her. It was a photograph, creased and repaired with tape. She took it from him and held it towards the light; it was an image of herself, younger, smiling, holding a puppy in her arms, hair blowing across her face.

'Mother sent it,' he said, 'early on, before the war. They were in the picture too, Mother and the old man, but I cut them out and kept it. I carried it with me right through, inside my flying jacket, on every raid. The other guys had their wives and their kids. I had you.'

Jessie stared at the picture. Then she handed it back to him. He looked so tired.

'Sit still,' she said, kneeling down to untie his shoes. He didn't move. 'Stretch out while I make some food. When did you last eat?'

'Hours ago. I'll just close my eyes for a while.'

As she watched, his taut, scarred face relaxed. He folded his gloved hands on his chest and slept.

The smell of food woke him and they ate in silence. As soon as he had finished, he stretched out again and fell instantly back to sleep. It was late. She went upstairs and lay on her bed, but didn't get undressed. When she woke with the grey light of dawn, Andrew was standing in the doorway of her bedroom, looking at her. She sat up with a gasp. He didn't move from the doorway. She couldn't see his face clearly.

'I'll make us a drink,' he said, and turned away. She listened to his footsteps on the stairs and wondered how long he had been there.

She heated water for Andrew to wash and shave, and fried some scraps of bacon with two eggs from Nellie's hens and two slices of bread. They sat down together at the small table in the kitchen.

'Does anyone know you're here?' Jessie asked.

He smiled his new lop-sided smile.

'Still worried about that?'

'Of course. Newton's the same place it always was.'

'No one knows I'm here. I told Mother I'd get to Cockermouth sometime today. Managed to hitch a ride with an old buddy who was taking a plane to Scotland. He dropped me at Prestwick and I got the train down here. I can be at Mother's today as expected, and no one any the wiser.'

'You were very tired,' she said.

'No sleep on the way over. Up and down for refuelling, nowhere to get comfortable. Noisy too. I feel better now. Bit stiff though. I think I ended up on the floor.'

'You could have had the spare bed.'

'Too tired to be bothered. Can't take the stairs two at a time like I used to.' He looked at her. 'You've hardly changed at all, Jess. Still so beautiful.'

'I'm nearly fifty, Andrew, and I look it.'

'No, you don't. And if you did, it wouldn't make any difference to me. I love what I see, I always have.'

'Don't say any more,' she said. 'It's not real, Andrew. None of this is real.'

He said no more, and they ate in silence. She noticed how he held his fork in one hand, like Americans did in films. But it was his left hand. The right hand, and the right side of his face were the most damaged. When he turned the other side of his face

28

towards her, it looked just the same as before. The same handsome face she'd loved, the same tall strong body.

'Do you know the train you need to get?' she said, determined to keep the conversation light. She could feel herself thinking about the time before, the time they'd spent together in her room upstairs. 'Your father's still very ill. I saw him the other day. He looked frail – "reduced" your mother called it.'

'I'm not here for him,' said Andrew. 'I'm here because Mother asked me to come. The old man and I have nothing to say that's not been said a dozen times before. If he's recovering, I won't stay. Work's busy. I want to get back.'

Nothing had changed: still the same old resentment towards his father, even after all that had happened.

'Tell me about Canada,' she said. 'You don't have to leave just yet.'

They talked for a while, about his job in Toronto, about his apartment.

'They've been very good to me, about this,' he said, raising his hands. 'I'm good at what I do, Jess, and they help me to do it. You could come over too, really. Not to look after me, for yourself. Come and see how we could live. It's a fresh start, away from the rationing and the misery of it all.'

Jessie said nothing, her mind a jumble of possibilities.

He hesitated, looking at his watch.

'Shall I come back here, before I go home?'

'No,' she said, without hesitation. 'It was good to see you. But I couldn't …'

'I know, you need time,' he said. 'But I want you to think about it. England's finished. This place is dead. America, Canada, Australia, that's where the future is. People can live over there, not just exist. I have a good life, despite everything. I want that for you, too.'

He took her hand and held it tight. 'All your life you've struggled, Jessie, but it doesn't have to be that way. I still love you. You loved me once, and you could again. Think what we had, what we still have.'

He leaned across the narrow table and kissed her. The feel of his mouth was intense, but she turned her face to one side. 'It's no good,' she said. 'I can't think with you here.'

'Take your time,' he said. 'When you want to come over, just tell me and I'll send the money for the ship. Anytime. I've left the address in the other room.'

Andrew took his big coat from the hook on the door and put it on. Jessie picked up his bag, but he took it from her and set it down on the floor again. Then he put his arms around her and they stood together, her face buried in his shoulder. She felt the same strength she'd always loved, and feared she would never find again. Then he picked up his bag and was gone.

CHAPTER 4

AT EXACTLY TWENTY MINUTES PAST SEVEN John Pharaoh shut and locked the front door of his house in Sandwith, turned to the north and walked up the hill out of the village along the windy ridge towards Whitehaven and the Haig pit in Kells where he worked. He'd been there only two weeks after several years at a different pit in the town. He felt more at ease now that the new routines were starting to take shape.

John hadn't heard from Jessie; there'd been no reply to his letter. He tried not to think about her, and any expectation of warmth had cooled long ago. Instead he took pleasure in the present. He could smell the sea and salt that carried on the wind. Reaching a gap in the hedge to his right, he looked across as he always did to the hills, but there was little of the familiar skyline to see today. Instead of blowing away on the westerly wind, the cloud simply renewed itself and held a stubborn line that blotted out the peaks.

As he reached the outskirts of Kells the streets were quiet: too early for the children heading to school, and too late for anyone on the first shift. It wasn't just his starting time that distinguished John from most of the workers at the pit, his work clothes were different, too. John wore shoes, not clogs, a hat rather than a cap, a jacket and tie. His hands were smooth, not hardened and scarred. His strength came from the rock climbing that was his passion, not from hewing and hauling coal.

John kept himself to himself. He could afford to live alone, in a house of his own choosing, only because Enid and Arthur Pharaoh, his adopted parents, had died and left him their savings and a house to sell. The Sandwith cottage was just far enough away from his work to keep the two separate, and he could pay for it outright. The village wondered about that, but he didn't care what they thought. He'd always felt himself an outsider, even in his own family. His climbing friends were all the company he wanted, and women had always worried him, except Hannah, who was old enough to be his mother. He'd often wished that Hannah was his mother, rather than his Enid who'd adopted him and lied about it, or Jessie, who'd given birth to him, and lied about it ever since. His life was built on lies, and the pretence wearied him.

At the Haig John managed the wages office, but last week Arthur Curran, his boss, had given him charge of the Bevin Boys too, young men conscripted into the mines in a desperate attempt to keep the pits running for the war effort. They worked in the screen shed, where John had never even set foot. He was afraid that the dust in there would make him cough.

'Why me, Mr Curran?' he'd asked. 'Isn't there someone who knows more about it?'

'Not much to do, lad. They'll be gone soon, when we can spare them,' Arthur had said. 'You've made a grand start 'ere, and Bevin lads' gaffer has gone off again, so you can do it. Just keep an eye on 'em. They're pretty useless, just need keeping out of t'way. Screen lasses tell 'em what to do. You just 'ave show your face every now and then. I've told Geordie Flett you'll be over there today.'

It was not what he wanted to do, but he hadn't been in this job long enough to object. The screen shed would be cold and dirty, and full of noisy women who were shunned by most folk. He left it as long as he could, and then put on his coat and walked across the yard.

Inside, when his eyes adjusted to the light, John found Geordie Flett, the gaffer, standing on an iron gantry in the draughty shed. John's height and the low ceiling didn't allow him to stand straight, and he rested his elbows on the rusting rail in front of him, looking down.

Below, standing in groups around the long tables, were about twenty women, and the lads he'd come to find. Each woman's face was framed by a scarf like a nun's wimple holding back her hair, topped off with a beret. There were gaps in the windows and the floor of the shed, and the air was chilled by wind straight off the sea. Each strong body was shrouded by a heavy coat pulled tight against the cold and the dirt. Coal dust started to blacken John's pale face, catching the back of his throat and making his lungs itch. The noise was deafening.

Geordie was trying to tell him something. Some of the words fell victim to the noise in the shed, until John moved closer, bending his head so that Geordie could shout into his ear.

'Yon Bevin lads are driving a clear,' said Geordie, pointing down at two men wielding large shovels, 'They shovel waste down t'chute so the lasses have space to work. One o' the lads fell down th'hole last week, silly bugger. We 'ad to pull 'im out by 'is feet. Lasses thought it were grand!'

There was a rumble and the gantry vibrated beneath them.

'Load coming in,' said Geordie without turning his head. 'Can

33

you feel it? Big stuff goes on yon table and gets smashed up. 'Ave to get rid of slate so it don't spit sparks all over t'place.'

'Who smashes it up?'

'Screen lasses. That's what we pay 'em for.'

'How do they do it?' said John, standing up to avoid the cloud of coal dust, and scraping his head on the low ceiling.

'They're bloody strong, them lasses,' Geordie shouted back. 'Share the work, help each other, like men down in't tunnels. Women used to work underground, tha knows. Parliament stopped it, the women wanted to carry on. So they ended up 'ere, doing men's work, but up top.'

As if to reinforce the point, two of the women picked up hammers and spikes, swinging at the great lumps of coal on the table.

'Proper miners didn'a trust the Bevin lads,' Geordie shouted. 'Thought they were conshies, like, trying to get out of fighting. Gave 'em a hard time, so bosses put the lads to work in 'ere.'

John thought about his war work. He'd wanted a uniform and action in the navy but he hadn't been allowed to sign up. Instead he was in a reserved occupation, which meant staying where he was, keeping the pits going. He looked around: the noise, the dust, the cold. He couldn't imagine working in a place like this, hour after hour, day after day. John told Geordie who had sent him and why, and got out as quickly as he could.

Back at his desk an hour later, a sudden silence made him stop, pen poised over the page. He sat quite still, his head cocked like a blackbird listening for the scratch of a worm under its feet. Arthur Curran put his head round the door, a sandwich in his hand.

'Screens have stopped, but wheel's still turning. Just started me bait.' He waved the sandwich. 'Get back over there and see what's what. I 'ate it when things go quiet. Allus means trouble.'

Back John went across the cobbled yard, breathing the salty

air off Saltom Beach far below, filling his lungs before the dust hit them. When he opened the door of the screen shed, blackened faces turned towards him.

'Ush up,' cried one of the women. 'Listen.'

Everyone stood motionless. They heard a faint scratching, and another sound, like a baby crying in a distant room.

'It's an animal,' said a voice.

'A cat?'

'Nay, a dog, or a fox mebbe.'

'Where?'

'God knows. Under t'floor somewhere. 'Ush up again,'

They waited, scarcely breathing. Around them the dust settled slowly. A few long seconds passed. The same sounds, but louder now, and longer.

'It's moved! Under Maggie's table.'

John watched as one of the women dropped to her knees, cleared away some of the waste and put her ear to the bare floor, holding her other hand high to prolong the silence in the shed. She shuffled forward and to the side, clearing a path for herself as she went, then pressed her ear to the floor again.

'I can 'ear it. Sounds like a dog.'

Maggie Lowery got to her feet, looking up at the gantry where Geordie was standing.

'What's under t'floor, Geordie?' she called.

'Nowt. Rock. Shed were just put on't ground, and that were rough like, up and down. Mebbe a drainage tunnel. Daft bloody dog must have pushed in and can't get out. Tek a while to die under there.'

'Who says it'll die? We can get it out.'

'Nay lass, we're not shutting th'ole bloody line down for a bloody dog, or whatever it is. Once we're going again you won't even 'ear it.'

A furious noise greeted this announcement, a cacophony of swearing that John struggled to decipher.

Geordie looked sideways at him, for support from a fellow gaffer, or protection from the furies below.

John hesitated. 'How long would it take to get it out?'

'God knows,' said Geordie. 'Depends where it is.'

The screen lasses didn't wait for bosses to make up their minds. They were already moving the tables to one side when they heard the rumble and vibration, signalling the imminent arrival of another load of coal.

'Fuck,' muttered Geordie, pushing past John to the door at the far end of the gantry. 'Wait!' he shouted, waving his arms at the men about to tip the load of coal onto the screens. They stopped just in time, before the load crashed through onto the heads of women and lads now systematically tearing up the floor.

'Wait,' echoed Maggie, assuming leadership of the operation. 'Shut up, all o' you.' She put her head down to the hole in the floor.

'Over there more,' she cried, and they responded immediately.

By now the screen shed was filling up with onlookers as the early shift came up, crowding onto what remained of the floor. Word got round about what was happening. More men surrounded the outside of the shed, pulling at rocks and weeds with their bare hands. John did the same, overcome with a sudden urge to be part of it, not to stand aside as he did sometimes, watching life happen around him.

More than two hours later, after part of the railway and fifty feet of drains had been dug up, they found the dog, wedged into the end of a pipe, its back legs scrabbling ineffectually as one of the Bevin lads pulled it gently free.

The crowd cheered. John and Geordie the gaffer slapped each other on the back. Women hugged. Men shook hands. After years of war and struggle, it felt like a real victory, a happy ending. Maggie wiped a tear and smudged white across her face.

John cried too, surprising and embarrassing himself. It was only a dog, he told himself. Lost, and now found and comforted, likely to be taken home and fed, cared for, loved.

Chapter 5

MAGGIE LOWERY HAD BEEN WATCHING the new man all day, as he came and went on the gantry above the screens, and then as he worked alongside them to free the dog. He must be new, or she'd have noticed him before. Wages office, they said. Good with money then. Might even be honest. Looked a bit spindly, too tall to be a miner. Most of the men she knew worked down the pits. They were strong as bulls, short and broad, like her dad before his accident, but now you'd never know how strong he'd been. Even when they lifted him out of the wheelchair his legs were too weak to hold him up.

'Who's big lad, next to gaffer?' she asked Gladys who was working alongside her.

'New, likely. Not seen 'im before.'

'Ask your Eric tonight, 'e might know.'

'Fancy 'im then?'

'I like tall men.'

'Your Isaac wasn't tall.'

'I know,' said Maggie.

Stopping the line to find the dog made it a very unusual day in the screen shed. When the excitement was over, the lasses sat round the stove in the bait room where they took their break and talked about lost dogs. There was an air of satisfaction verging on

38

triumph about their success in finding this one, but what pleased them most was their success in stopping the line when the boss had said 'No'. Just this once, they had made something happen.

'If we'd not said 'owt, Geordie would have kept us going. Poor little bugger would've starved to death, right under us feet.'

''E's scared of us, that Geordie, allus 'as been. Stands up there looking at us, but he's scared to come down 'ere.'

'In case we eat 'im,' said Annie, taking a large bite of pie. 'That tall new lad up there today. E'd be a mouthful,' she went on, pastry crumbs dropping onto her coal-sodden coat. 'Start at 'is big feet and keep going. Tek a while but might be worth it.'

They all laughed, the Bevin Boys loudest of all because talk of man-eating made them nervous. Not far away, across the yard, John Pharaoh was sitting quietly at his desk holding a carefully made sandwich in his long clean fingers, mercifully unaware of the discussion in the screen shed.

Even after three years on the screens, every muscle in Maggie's back and shoulders ached as she walked home with her mother at the end of their shift. She'd started the job for the money, which was more than in the laundry or the canteen, but now it wasn't just the money that kept her going. There was something about the screens and the women who worked there. They were special; 'dirty clothes, dirty minds' some said, but she'd never been around a group of women who laughed so much. Could be cruel, vicious even, if someone didn't fit in. She remembered how they'd tested her out when she started, and was glad her mother had been around to keep a check on things. She'd heard all sorts of stories about the screen lasses, and they were mostly true.

'Your turn or mine?' she said to her mother as they turned the corner into North Row, and walked down the hill towards the sea.

'Nay, you go first, Maggie love. Your reward for getting that dog out. You'll be ganging down t'street later?'

'Nay, not tonight,' said her daughter. 'Want to finish that book. Anyway I'm buggered. All that crawling around on t'floor. Look at me 'ands. Worse than ever.'

Maggie looked hard at her wretched hands, ingrained with dirt, calloused and scarred. That was a sure sign of a screen lass; you had to wear gloves when you were out or people might guess, and turn their backs.

The McSherry's house was on West Row, overlooking the Irish Sea, where the terraced houses stood close to the cliff top, each with a small garden in front, then a strip of field and a steep drop to the wide tumbling sea that washed the rocks below. Nothing much grew, buffeted and burned by the salty air, but when most food was rationed and scarce anything you could grow was a bonus. Potatoes and beets and onions, they all helped to eke out the miserable portions from the butcher, and you could rear a few chickens if the fox or some hungry kids didn't get them. It was more work for the two women, but they enjoyed it. Maggie loved the feeling of air and sky above her head, and the sea so close. She would stand sometimes, just watching, noticing the movement of the water below, the colours and light, constantly changing. Some days she could see the coast of Scotland to the north-west, Galloway and Kintyre. To the south the top of St Bees lighthouse peeped above the cliff. At night the flash of that lighthouse, and others across the Solway, would pierce the darkness for an instant, disappear and then come again, a slow rhythm warning of rocks and danger.

The routine when Maggie and Violet arrived home was well-established. One or the other would get first go at the big bowl of hot water that had been warming on the range for them, leaving just enough for the second. They bathed in the privacy and quiet of the kitchen, easier now that Judith was older and didn't need watching. These days she was out most of the time after school, playing among the flapping washing lines on the green behind the houses, or up and down the narrow streets with the other kids, watched by whoever happened to be close by, or no one at all.

Maggie unwrapped herself in front of the range, standing on newspaper to catch the worst of the coal dust that infested her clothes. She took off everything except her underwear, leaving her hair till last, and finally let the auburn curls fall to her shoulders before wrapping them up again in an old cloth. Later she would brush long and hard until her hair gleamed. Short hair would be easier, she knew, but she loved her hair just as it was. It was part of her disguise away from the pit: no one would guess that she was a screen lass, not with hair like that.

She washed herself with a bit of precious soap and a cloth, putting one foot at a time into the big bowl, to rinse her pale feet and legs. The water darkened. When she had to wash after her mother, sometimes she wondered if she was dirtier after she finished than before she started, but it was 'good, honest muck,' as her dad said. It always felt wonderful to let the warm water sluice down, taking with it some of the ache of the day.

She'd grown stronger over the years, no question. Maybe the stronger body helped to fade the faint stretch marks at the side of her breasts and above her hips. Her breasts were fuller than before Judith, but the rest of her was much as it had always been. Not bad. Isaac had liked it, but then he was mostly in too much of a rush to have a good look. The recollection of him was beginning to fade, like the stretch marks. It was years since he went off to North Africa with the army and never came home again. Killed at El Alamein. They never found his body.

She had missed him for a while, but not now. They were too young when they married, both of them. Maggie knew by the end of a brief honeymoon that Isaac was just a lad who had no idea about women, or anything else much except rugby, drinking and his mates. They got married because that's what you did. The best thing in the whole dismal business was Judith; once she arrived Maggie didn't really care about the rest. Now that her friends' husbands, those who survived, were coming home from the war, she acknowledged an inescapable relief that Isaac wouldn't barge back into her life. But she kept that to herself.

Judith knocked at the kitchen door.

'Are you done, Mam? Granny's moaning. She says she'll take off her clothes out here unless you hurry up.'

'Tell her I'm done,' said Maggie, wrapping an old green dressing gown around her. 'Don't let her take her clothes off or we'll all be turned to stone.'

Frank McSherry was sitting in the small front room with the paper. His bed was against the wall, and the wheelchair in which he sat was pushed hard against it, leaving just enough space for the door to be opened.

'We 'ave to do summat about this door, Dad,' Maggie said as she had done many times before, since the front room became her father's bedroom. 'It needs to open outwards, into the passage. That'd work better.'

'Aye, mebbe,' said her father, 'but that was my job, so who'll do it now? No McSherry man pays someone to re-hang a door, and folk have better things to do.'

'You can tell me what to do, and I'll do it. Women can do things like that, think what they did in t'war.'

Frank looked at his daughter in her green dressing gown, her flaming hair wrapped under a grey cloth. 'Look at you,' he said. 'If you held your arms out and put a fairy on your 'ead you'd look like a Christmas tree. And if we 'ad another man in t'family, that'd help. You're a good-looking lass, Maggie. Been a widow long enough now. Judith needs a dad and you need a proper 'ome, not lodging with your mam and me.'

'Mebbe so, Dad. But I don't want just anyone. That was the problem last time. Thought I ought to be wed, all that. I was too young, and so was 'e. I'll fix the door, you just tell me what to do.'

She felt a cold draught round her ankles. 'Wind's got up. Southerly. I can feel it. Allus makes the front door whistle.'

'God knows why we 'ave to live in the windiest spot in Cumberland,' said her father, going back his newspaper. 'If your mam weren't so stubborn we'd've shifted years ago. Even round the corner would be something, away from wind straight off t'sea and under t'door.'

'She'll never shift,' said Maggie. 'They'll carry 'er out of 'ere in a box first. Did she tell you about the dog?'

'Aye. What a carry on. Bet Geordie was mad.'

'Too scared to say so, though.'

'You women'd scare anybody,' said Frank. 'Should've sent you lot in on D-Day. Bloody Nazis would've run away.'

The disputed door opened and Judith stood, raising her hand to herald an important question.

'When's tea? I'm starving.'

Maggie pulled the child towards her and sat back on Frank's bed.

'No tea for you unless you tell me summat you learned at school today, summat interesting.'

'Oh no,' groaned the child. 'Do I 'ave to?'

'Come on,' said Maggie. 'One interesting thing.'

'Mr Huntley were going on,' Judith began, after a pause to think back over the day.

'Was going on,' Maggie corrected her.

'Mr Huntley was going on about somebody running all the pits, everywhere.'

'Did he say who?' asked Maggie.

'National something,' said Judith.

43

'No sign of 'em 'ere yet,' said Frank, looking over the top of his paper. 'Still same old bosses 'ere. Won't feel much different when National Coal Board does come, I reckon. Your work won't change, Maggie. Someone 'as to dig the black stuff out like I did, and then sort it. Won't find yon bosses getting their 'ands dirty, whoever they are.'

'It'll be better, Dad,' Maggie said, looking carefully at Judith's hair. 'Has to be. They're talking about pit-head baths, more safety, all that.'

'Safety,' snorted Frank. 'These pits'll never be safe. Tunnels out under t'sea, miles from t'shaft, no proper ventilation. Death traps, allus were, allus will be.'

'So why do we work in them?' asked Maggie, knowing the answer.

'Money, love,' said her father. 'It's a job.'

'Can I work with you and Gran, Mam, when I'm older?' said Judith pushing herself off Maggie's knee.

'Over my dead body,' said Maggie. 'You'll carry on at school, like I would've done if I'd had me 'ead screwed on better. No getting married for you. Look after yourself, do the studying, get a good job, keep your 'ands clean, not like mine.'

Maggie pointed at the jar of Vaseline standing on the shelf over the fire. 'Come on,' she said, holding out her ravaged hands. Judith stretched for the jar, unscrewed the lid, scooped some out and took her mother's hands one at a time, rubbing in the soothing gel with her soft chubby fingers.

It was the following Saturday when Maggie saw the new lad again. She had pushed her dad's wheelchair along to the rugby field to watch the match. The ground was rough and muddy and she was struggling with the chair when she heard a voice behind her.

'Can I help you with that?'

She let go of the wheelchair and turned around. It was him, the big lad she'd seen in the shed. He was standing just behind her, not too close, and smiling down at her. She noticed his height and his wide-brimmed hat, and the red scarf at his neck. He was a good-looking chap, no mistake, a bit stylish. Didn't see much of that in Kells.

'I'm sure you can manage,' he said, 'but it looks awkward.'

She was about to argue, then decided against it and stood back, yielding the handles of the chair to John with a slight nod of her head. Her hair was pulled back, but wisps were escaping in the wind and she tried to tuck them back into place while the young man manoeuvred the chair to the edge of the pitch. Frank McSherry turned to see where the extra impetus was coming from. Once the chair was settled, John stood back and moved away, but only a yard or two.

The two guardians of the wheelchair stood side by side, watching as the torrent of men flowed past them down the field.

'Don't know why we bother,' she said, without looking across. 'Too cold to be out, but 'e hates being cooped all day, and at least there's a bit o' sun.'

'Wind's swung round,' said John, watching clouds passing far over their heads.

This was her chance. 'You from round 'ere?' she asked.

'Ehyup, lass,' said her father, as the rugby ball fell out of the rushing sky towards them. John stretched out his arms instinctively and the ball fell into his hands. The referee blew his whistle, a player snatched the ball out of his hands and the game continued.

'Tha' should play cricket, lad,' said Frank. 'Grand catch, that. Would've 'it me right on the 'ead. '

He twisted round in his seat towards John, and stretched out his hand. 'Frank McSherry,' he said.

'John Pharaoh,' said John.

'From round 'ere then,' said Frank, recognising the name.

'No, not the Whitehaven Pharaohs,' said John, 'Barrow, then Ulverston.'

'What's tha doing up 'ere?' said Frank.

'I live up here now, working at the Haig,' said John, pointing vaguely towards the north.

'Office?' said Frank.

Maggie stepped behind John and shook her head furiously at her father.

'What's up wi' you, lass?' Frank squinted into the low October sunlight. 'And this is my lass, Maggie. Margaret for best.'

John turned. 'Nice to meet you, Margaret.'

'Charmed, I'm sure,' said Maggie, echoing the politeness. She couldn't work out whether John was really posh or just putting it on. She liked it anyway. At half-time John offered to buy the Bovril, but it was cold and the home team were getting beaten. Frank wanted to go home and Maggie was definitely ready to take him. She and John pushed the heavy chair to the relatively flat surface of the street.

'I can manage from here,' she said. 'Thank you, Mr Pharaoh.'

'John, please,' he said, smiling at her. 'And do let me walk with you. It's on my way home.'

'Where …?'

'Sandwith.'

'Right,' she said, recalling that there were some tidy little houses in Sandwith.

It wasn't far to the corner of North Row. When they reached it, John stopped and bent over the chair to speak to Frank. 'I'll leave you now, Mr McSherry, if that's OK. Can you manage?'

He wanted to speak to Maggie, but now he wasn't sure what to call her. Maggie sounded too casual but Margaret wasn't right either. He was never sure about these things.

Frank relieved him of the decision. 'Nay, lad, you'll come in for a brew. That's the least we can do as thanks for the 'elp. That's right, Maggie?'

'Aye, Dad, but let me run on and tell our Mam. Tell 'er someone's coming.'

'Go on then,' said her father. 'Tell 'er it's not the bloody king.' He turned to John. 'Women, eh. Never work 'em out. You married, lad?'

'No,' said John. 'I never ...'

'Very wise.'

This brief exchange was all the time Maggie needed. She ran to the house, pushed open the front door, and called to her mother.

'Dad's asked somebody in, Mam. A man from work, he was at the rugby. E's posh.'

Violet McSherry came in from the back yard, wiping her hands on a large grey cloth by the back door. 'What d'ye mean, posh?'

'He works in t'wages office at pit. He was in the shed the day we found the dog, standing on the gantry with Geordie. You'll know 'im when you see 'im. Doesn't recognise me, thank God. Don't tell 'im, Mam, please. Talk about summat else, but don't mention work. Please.'

The front door opened again, and they could hear John coaxing the wheelchair over the step.

'I'm back,' called Frank to his wife. 'Get kettle on, love, we got company.'

Maggie mouthed 'Please' at her mother. 'Judith!' she called up the narrow stairs. 'Come down pet, and meet somebody.'

A small child came slowly down the stairs, with one hand pressed against the wall. Auburn-haired like her mother, with a floppy bow to one side of her head, and a grave blue-eyed expression, she gazed at the stranger standing by the door.

'Say hello to Mr Pharaoh, Judith,' said Maggie.

'Hello,' said Judith.

'Your sister?' said John.

Maggie laughed. 'My daughter. She's nearly seven now, aren't you pet. Doing well at school.'

'Clever, like her mam,' said a woman from the doorway of the backroom.

'This is the wife,' said Frank. 'Vi, this is John Pharaoh. Met 'im at rugby and he 'elped Maggie push me 'ome. Asked him in for a brew.'

'Tea, Mr Pharaoh?' said Violet, reaching for the best cups off the top shelf.

'Steady on, love,' said Frank. 'No need for best china. John lives round 'ere, can't be that posh.'

'In Sandwith, Mam,' said Maggie, with emphasis. 'Get up Judith, and help your gran. We'll need a few plates, and fetch the cake tin down. That wind's made us hungry.'

They were sitting drinking tea, eating Violet's attempt at shortbread, and making safe conversation about nothing very much when there was a loud crash from upstairs. They all ducked as dust rained down from the ceiling above their heads.

'Bloody 'ell,' Frank shouted, covering his head with his hands. 'Thought war were over.'

'Mam,' wailed Judith, and Maggie pulled the child to her, brushing dust from her hair. John jumped to his feet.

'Upstairs,' said Violet, and John took them two at a time.

When he came back into the kitchen, John was carrying something wrapped in a cloth that had once been white but was covered in dust and bits of plaster.

'Something's come through the ceiling upstairs,' said John. 'Landed on one of the beds. Real mess. Plaster all over the place.'

'That's our bed, Mam,' said the child, turning her face into Maggie's shoulder and sobbing. 'Where will we sleep now?'

48

'I told you!' Violet shouted at her husband, taking the bundle from John and brushing away some of the dust and plaster. 'I told you no good would come of it. You and your schemes. Now what've we got, a bloody great 'ole in the bedroom ceiling and dust all over.' She stopped and looked at John, then at Maggie.

'You might as well know, Mr Pharaoh ...' she said.

'John, please,' said John.

'Well John, you might as well know, but this is between us. For God's sake don't tell anyone.'

'Tell them what?' asked John, still mystified.

'About this,' she said. 'The ham. It were hung up in the loft, out of sight. We got it off Frank's cousin up Ennerdale, under the counter like. Saving it for Christmas, and now look at it.'

'Give it 'ere,' said Frank. 'Look at rope, it's eaten through. Bloody mice. Ate through rope and the damn thing crashed down through t'ceiling. Could've killed our Judith.'

Judith wailed more loudly.

'Hush, Dad, for pity's sake,' said Maggie, putting her hands over Judith's ears. She'll 'ave nightmares for weeks if you carry on. You don't 'ave to sleep with her.'

'Well,' said John, 'I've heard of flying pigs, but this takes the bacon.'

'Takes the bacon,' said Frank, hitting his hand on his knee. 'That's a good one. Did you 'ear that, Mother?'

They all laughed, as much at Frank as at John's joke.

John and Maggie went up to the ravaged bedroom to clear up the mess. Maggie wasn't sure what to say, but John took a chance. 'Judith's father?' he began.

'El Alamein,' said Maggie, without looking up. 'We'd only been married a year. He never saw Judith.'

'I'm so sorry. How do you manage?'

'We manage. Me sister offered to take Judith in but I said never.

She were still a babby and wouldn't've known any different, but I couldn't. I couldn't just give 'er away.'

'No,' said John. 'Of course you couldn't.'

They cleared as much of the mess as they could. Maggie noticed that John had gone quiet. Maybe he was shocked about the ham and was wondering what to do. When they went downstairs again he seemed uneasy, saying that the dust had got on his chest. Maggie watched him carefully. Maybe he was sick.

Within a few minutes John had put on his coat and hat, thanked them for the hospitality and left the house. As the door closed behind him, the McSherrys looked at each other.

'Well, 'e's a strange one,' said Violet. 'One minute cracking jokes, and the next scuttling off home with 'is tail between 'is legs. What 'appened upstairs? What did you say to 'im? I thought you liked the lad.'

'I do like 'im,' said Maggie, shaking her head at her mother as Judith sat listening attentively to their conversation. 'Something must've upset 'im, but it wasn't me.'

'Nice lad, that,' said Frank. 'Not many like 'im round 'ere, our Maggie. Worth a second look, I'd say.'

'Dad,' said Maggie. 'Give o'er.'

Judith looked at each of them, wondering.

CHAPTER 6

JOHN WALKED QUICKLY AWAY from West Row, back towards Sandwith, breathing in the cool air and letting his mind settle. What Maggie had said about her child had hit him like a blow to the chest. She could never have let someone else raise her child, she'd said, not even her own sister. He slowed his pace a little, and thought about Maggie. That hair – he imagined it loose, falling onto her shoulders, and pushed the thought away. They were probably laughing at him now, her and her mother. Not Frank, he was alright. But the women – like those women in the screen shed – they seemed to laugh at everything. He liked Maggie. Maybe she could like him, too. He could ask her to take a walk with him, maybe. Nothing too serious, not at night. Or the pictures – a matinee – but that might be too public, too obvious. If she said no, it would be hard to backtrack. But maybe she might say yes?

Sitting alone at the little table in his kitchen, his supper steaming on the plate in front of him, he thought about her again. Why not?

Too many times over the years he'd thought of asking to see a girl again, but backed away, afraid of being laughed at. He wasn't good-looking, but he wasn't ugly, and he had a decent job and his own house. That had to count for something. He liked her. She was straightforward and strong, like Hannah. And she was beautiful. There must be men lining up for her; maybe the child would put them off. But how to do it? He could call in, casual like, on his way home from work one day. Frank would be there, and he could see how the land lay. If there were other people around when he asked her out, maybe she would be polite, even if she said no.

It was a few weeks before John summoned the confidence to put this plan into action. Winter was coming. The trees along his route as he walked to work in the mornings were raining brown and orange leaves, which the rain turned to a slippery mess under his feet. The wind blew sharp and straight from the north-west most mornings: he felt the prickle of rain on the side of his face as he turned into West Row one afternoon around five. The light was already fading. He knocked on the front door and waited. A voice called from inside. 'Door's open, come away in.'

John did as he was bid, and found Frank McSherry coming backwards in his wheelchair towards him. Frank turned round enough to see who it was and smiled as John tried to help him in the small space.

'Why it's Mr Pharaoh from Ulverston,' said Frank. 'Shut door lad, afore wind blows it open again.'

'Call me John, please,' said John, 'and I've not lived in Ulverston for a few years now. Have an aunt and uncle there but don't see them very often.'

'No family with you, then,' said Frank, pointing at the armchair by the meagre fire.

'Can I help with the fire?' John asked.

'Only if you can rustle up some more coal, lad. We've used all the lasses' allowance until end o' week. Got some that fell off back of a lorry you might say, but it's poor stuff, mostly dust.'

'It's hard, isn't it,' said John, 'not having enough when we're practically sitting on it, all those seams, running out to sea.'

'Bloody is,' said Frank, 'but bugger all to do about it. Seems to go on and on. And now bread's rationed too. Who'd've thought it, eh?'

The two men sank into silence for a moment. John knew he had to speak.

'Is Margaret at home, Mr McSherry?' he said, as casually as he could muster.

'Margaret? Oh, Maggie. Aye, she's home, out back somewhere. Try back door, she was getting washing off t'green.'

John opened the back door and looked across the green. Maggie was walking towards him, carrying a large basket, as spots of rain splattered at an angle on the outhouse wall. She saw him, and stopped. John closed the door behind him and walked across to her, taking the basket out of her hands without a word. He didn't know what to say, and the rain was getting heavier. She ran past him and held the door as he struggled into the tiny back room.

'Just in time,' she said. 'I could see rain coming. Thanks. It was 'eavy. Just put it down in t'corner there.'

When he straightened up she was looking up at him.

'Did you want summat? Mam's down in town with Judith.'

'It was just …' He stumbled over the words, despite having rehearsed them as he walked to the house. 'I wondered whether … if … you'd like to come for a walk with me at the weekend. Tide's going to be low in the afternoon and I like to go to Fleswick Bay, to the rock pools.'

Her face brightened.

'I love those pools,' she said. 'And it's a grand walk, looking

53

right out to th' Isle of Man on a good day.'

'Will you come then?' he said, amazed how easy this seemed to be. 'On Saturday, maybe, or Sunday?'

'Sunday's better,' she said. 'About one?'

'Grand,' said John. 'Well, I'll see you then.'

Maggie saw him through to the front door, as Frank watched. 'Good work, lass,' he said as she turned, smiling, towards her father. 'Told you he was a good 'un. Nowt too forrard, polite like. A real gent.'

'There must be a catch, Dad,' said Maggie. 'He still doesn't know where we work.'

John was early and nervous on Sunday afternoon. He waited on the main road for a while to calm down and appear at the agreed time, feeling, or at least looking, more confident. Maggie seemed so assured – what would she think if she knew how much he struggled with simple things like meeting people and making conversation? He so badly wanted the afternoon to go well, and the weather was certainly doing its best. The sun shone, the sea was flattened by an offshore wind, and the sky was on the blue side of grey, as it often was in November.

Maggie opened the door immediately after his knock. She was wearing a dark blue jacket and trousers, with strong shoes. That had been his other dread, apart from not having anything to say. If she had been wearing silly shoes, they would never manage the walk round the headland. But what could he have said? Her hair was covered by a bright green scarf, tied at the nape of her neck, which allowed her hair to stream out from underneath, curling onto the shoulders of the coat. He wanted to touch it.

'Have a nice walk,' Violet McSherry called from the back of the house. 'I'll put Judith to bed if you're out late.'

'We won't be late,' said Maggie, frowning at her mother's words.

Once the door was closed, and they were alone, they stood for a moment looking out at the sea, sheltered from the unusual easterly wind.

'No noise from the sea today,' said Maggie. 'Calm, and low tide, and t'wind tekkin' sound away. Most of the time you can hear it up 'ere.'

'Must get pretty wild in the winter.'

'It does that. You can taste the salt on the air, on your face. Hard to get the front door closed, and we have to pile stuff against it to stop the draught. Dad wants to move, but Mam never will.'

'I thought we'd walk to Sandwith along the lane for a start,' John said, 'to avoid the quarry. I know the way from there. It's a bit rough in parts but you'll be right in those shoes.'

He shortened his stride, knowing that most people struggled to keep up with him if he didn't. He was quiet, trying to think what to say, when Maggie started to talk. Nothing very significant, just about where Judith went to school, what her teacher said about her. Hannah had told him that women like men who listen to them, so John listened very carefully and asked the occasional question. In the shelter of the lane down into Sandwith the air was still and surprisingly warm. Maggie unbuttoned her coat. John took his off and tied it round his waist by the arms.

'Is this where you live?' she said, looking at the neat row of cottages along the edge of the green beyond the pub.

'Yes,' he said. 'The little one in the middle of the row. Blue door.'

'On your own?'

'I like my own company.'

'Where were you, growing up?'

'In Ulverston. When my mother died, I sold the house and moved up the coast, to the quarry in Eskdale.'

'That's a long way off the track.'

'I wanted to be nearer the mountains, for the climbing. And I like the little railway, you know, la'al Ratty they call it.'

'I went on that once, on a school trip,' said Maggie, smiling at the memory. 'Must've been just before I left. I could have stayed on. School wanted me to, but Dad's accident, you know ...'

'What happened?'

'Roof fall, underground. Him and another bloke were caught. T'other feller died, poor bugger. Dad were lucky. Took a while to dig 'im out. E'll never walk again but he's still 'imself, like. '

'Nice bloke,' said John. 'Straightforward, I like that. Find it hard sometimes when people ... when they aren't what they seem.'

'Do you rent the house?' she asked, as they passed it.

'No, I bought it,' came the quiet reply.

Maggie made no further comment and they turned right in the middle of the village along muddy lanes towards the lighthouse and the sea. Gulls were wheeling round the cliffs below them.

'All sorts of birds nest and breed down there in the spring,' said John. 'You have to lie flat on the edge to get a proper view.'

But today they kept walking, turning south along the cliffs. They passed the lighthouse, and the rounded shape of Black Combe rose out of the coastal plain far beyond. Then the path turned inland along the side of a steep gully, and they were looking down onto a curiously ridged beach, where rounded pebbles gave way to undulations of sandstone and long shelves of rock pierced by many deep pools. They scrambled down the steep path and across the rocks above the ebbing tide. The pools were straight-sided, created by nature but looking man-made, adorned with crimson groping sea anemones, bright green seaweeds and transparent shrimps.

'Isn't it grand,' said John, congratulating himself on providing such a rare spectacle for his new friend.

'We were down 'ere all the time as kids,' said Maggie, as if she'd heard his thought. 'No good if the tide was in. Just another beach then. But we could play in the caves, read names carved on the rocks. Paradise for us kids.'

John thought about his lonely childhood in the silent Ulverston house.

'I was adopted,' he said, suddenly, looking straight ahead to avoid seeing her reaction. He hadn't planned to tell her. It just bubbled up and out before he had time to think. 'When I was a baby, a few days old. My mother … gave me away.'

Maggie stopped, thinking about how this could happen.

'Didn't they want you?'

'My father was dead … he never knew. They weren't married.'

'When?' asked Maggie.

'It was 1917, in the first war.'

'Things happen like that in wartime. Isaac knew I was having Judith, but he never saw her.'

'But you didn't give her away.'

Maggie was quiet for a moment. They were standing still now, facing each other but not looking. 'So the woman in Ulverston, the one who died …'

'She was my adopted mother.'

Maggie looked at him in the fading sunlight. He'd taken off his hat and held it in front of him in both hands. She saw his long face, the way his hair fell over his eyes.

'You don't 'ave to tell me any of this,' she said. 'We all 'ave things we keep to ourselves.'

'Not you, though,' said John.

'Me, too,' she said, pushing the tell-tale hands further into the pockets of her jacket.

Lamps were lit in some of the windows when they walked back through Sandwith.

'Would you like to see my house?' he asked.

'Lead on,' said Maggie, controlling her curiosity. How did he

57

live, this strange self-contained man? She'd never lived alone and couldn't imagine doing so. Did he make meals, just for himself, or live on bread and dripping? Did he have a proper bed? A big bed? John unlocked the blue door in the middle of the row and stood back. Maggie stepped slowly into the small front room. There wasn't much in it: a chair, a small table with a lamp, a granite fireplace. The fire made up, ready to be lit. Curtains at the windows. Who made those, she wondered? It was neat, and clean, as far as she could tell without running a finger along each surface as her mother would have done.

'Who looks after th'ouse?' she asked.

'I do,' he said. 'I enjoy keeping the place tidy. Come in the kitchen. That's tidy, too.'

'I'm being nosey, aren't I?' she laughed. 'Never seen an 'ouse where someone lives on their own, except really old people, you know.'

"Now you want to know how old I am?"

'No!' she said. 'Don't mind me. Just like me mam. Nosey.'

'I'm nearly thirty,' he said, 'Imagine that!'

'I'm not far off that meself. Our Judith'll be seven next birthday.'

'Shall we have a brew?' asked John. 'There's even some cake in the tin.'

'Did you make that, too?'

'Believe it or not, I did,' he said. 'Hannah taught me, when I was ill one time with nothing to do.'

Hannah? He'd mentioned her before, but there were too many questions, and that one remained unasked.

They drank tea and ate gingerbread, sitting at the tiny table in the kitchen. He pulled up a stool to sit on as Maggie had the only chair. She was quiet but her mind was racing. There must be something wrong, something she couldn't see. A nice-looking man with a good job and his own house, never married, or at least no wife around now. Maybe he didn't like girls. Some men didn't, she knew that. But he had asked her out, and here they were. He hadn't done anything, not made a pass or even looked as if he wanted to. She couldn't work it out. Thank God she hadn't mentioned anything about it to Gladys. With any luck no one would know and she could avoid the questions until she was ready. Maybe it would never come to that. He was just being polite. Or he was lonely enough to take her for a walk but not enough for anything more. And he didn't know she was a screen lass. That might change everything. She daren't tell him, not yet.

'Another piece?' His voice cut across her thoughts. 'Or do we need to get going? About twenty minutes or so back to your house, and we could be there before dark.'

They walked back to Kells with just enough light to see their way. Neither of them said anything for a while. Before they reached South Row and turned left down the hill, he stopped and she stopped too.

'Can we do this again? Go for a walk, or you could come for tea sometime? Bring Judith if you like.' He had more to say but nothing more came out. She waited just long enough for him to think that she didn't want to see him. His head buzzed.

Then she smiled at him. 'Yes,' she said. 'I'd like that.'

'Saturday afternoon?' he said quickly, before she could change her mind. She didn't know what was happening, but it didn't seem to matter.

He left her at the door, saying he had to get back. She waited, but he didn't touch her. Maggie stepped into the room where her mother and father were sitting, listening to the radio.

'Well?' said Violet.

Maggie shrugged her shoulders and went upstairs to check on Judith.

Frank looked across at his wife. 'Leave it, Vi,' he said.

59

Chapter 7

John walked home in the dark. The moon rose from behind the grey outline of hills to the east, flattened and orange at first, like a setting sun. He had tried to stay calm when he was with her, to help the words to come out the way he wanted them to. But now with no words to worry about, the jumble in his mind spilled over. The hair, that pale skin and light green eyes. And the shape of her: a girl's face, a woman's body. And there was something less obvious about her; he felt she could see through him, understand him, but not judge him. She didn't pose, or tease him. Everything about her was real: the husband who died, the child, Frank and Violet, even the house looking out over the sea. It was all real, alive.

He'd wanted to touch her, but he didn't dare, in case it all disappeared. The last time he'd tried to touch someone, she'd pulled away, but he didn't know why. He'd thought she wanted him to touch her, but she hadn't. It was down in Bransty, when he was in digs there. He'd met her in a queue at the pictures, with her friends, and they'd all gone for a drink afterwards. He'd bought her a drink, and they'd sat together, away from her friends. He'd walked her home, and then he tried to hold her, that was all. But she pushed him away, and stomped into the house without saying anything. He'd seen her again, with the same group of girls, but she'd whispered something to them and they all laughed. He blushed even now to remember it. And still he didn't know. What did they want, these girls?

But Maggie was different. She'd been married, had a child. That must make a difference, surely. She reminded him of Hannah, straightforward, more like a man, and he always found men easier to deal with. He dreamed about her that night. She was naked, and so was he, but he was trying to cover himself, to hide away. She walked away from him, through crowded rooms where people were watching him, not her. He lost her in the crowd. He woke stiff and finished it, sweating and ashamed.

John put his mind to his work with more focus than usual for the rest of the week, and managed to keep Maggie out of his thoughts, but not out of his dreams. He wondered how he would face her on Saturday with those images so powerful in his mind. And where would they go? It was on Friday evening, when he was walking home, that he knew where he would take her. Too far to walk, and the Ratty wouldn't be running for passengers again until the summer, but he had the bike and just enough fuel to get them there and back. He would take a risk and show her something about himself. If he kept on sharing little bits of himself, one at a time, maybe she would get used to it, and wouldn't just walk away like the others, without telling him why. Hannah and Fred would ask lots of questions, but they wouldn't show him up. They would like Maggie, and he thought that she would like them.

He revved the engine of the bike outside the house in West Row on Saturday afternoon before he parked it. He had thought about the afternoon, and the plan made him confident. They would drive up to Boot, taking it slow. He remembered his first motorbike ride, clinging on to Andy Leadbetter's coat and thinking he was going to be sick all over it. The memory caught him unawares. What if she hated it, or wouldn't go on the bike? Too late now.

Maggie was upstairs when she heard the motorbike revving outside the house, and her father's wheelchair was blocking the narrow passage as she clattered down the stairs. She watched Frank stretch to open the door, back the wheelchair up the passage and turn with practised ease into the front room. John pushed open the door and stood on the step. He took off the leather helmet he wore on the bike to stop his hair blowing in his face and shook his hair free.

'Come in, lad,' shouted Frank. 'Can't 'ang about at door in this 'ouse, not with that wind coming off the sea.'

'It's not bad today,' said John, smiling at Maggie as he spoke to the unseen voice.

'It's allus bad,' the voice replied.

Maggie pulled John into the passage and squeezed past him to push the door shut. 'We 'eard you coming,' she said. 'Not much noise like that up 'ere, specially not with petrol rationed.'

'Saved mine up,' he said. 'Too far to walk where we're going today.'

'Oh, so you've decided have you?' she said. 'Hear that, Dad. John's got plans, a mystery tour. On a motorbike. Maybe I'll be too scared to get on it.'

Frank's laugh was audible.

'She's scared o' nowt, that lass. Where are ye off to?'

Maggie pushed John into the front room. Light from the sky

and the sea flooded in, making John blink.

'Should see it 'ere at sunset,' said Frank. 'Colours like you wouldn't believe.'

'Have you seen the green flash?' John asked, looking out at the line of the horizon.

'When sun hits the sea, like? Aye, not often mind, but we've all seen it. Never worked out how it 'appens,' said Frank. 'Maggie finds out about things like that, reads books tha' knows. Never read a book, meself.'

'So where are we going?' Maggie wasn't used to being told what would happen, not standing in her own house. She wasn't sure that she liked it.

'The people I used to live with, before I came to Sandwith, they live up top end of Eskdale, place called Boot.'

'Where la'al train goes?' said Frank.

'Aye, up there. They live at the water mill. Getting on a bit, both of them, and he only has one leg – from the first war, and she's only got one eye.'

'You making this up?'

'Sounds daft, I know, but it's true. They're a bit, you know, eccentric, but they were good to me, and I get to see them when I can, to do chores they have trouble with.' He hesitated. 'And I think Maggie will like them.'

Maggie wondered what they would think of a screen lass coming to call. She would have to tell him soon.

'Wind from the south,' said John, 'and it's looking fair out to sea. We might have a decent afternoon.' Maggie thought for a minute, told John to hang on and disappeared upstairs again, coming back with a red shawl wound round her head.

'Hair in the wind,' she said. He nodded.

'Tell Mam I'll be back before Judith's bedtime,' she said to her father. 'Come on, John. Day's a-wasting, and don't go too fast.'

Maggie was less confident than she looked as she clambered onto the bike behind John. She hung on as he revved away up South Row towards the main road. At first she pressed her head into his back and tried not to think about the speed they were going, but as they left the main coast road and turned east at the start of the flat valley floor she relaxed a little and took more notice.

It was sunny, and the cloud was clear of the fell tops on either side. She saw chasing patterns of light and shadow on the tree-covered slopes, and the sparkle of water in the streams. The noise of the engine enclosed them both and she moved her arms further round John's waist, feeling safe even when a bus came very close on a narrow bend. John pulled over and turned around.

'You alright back there?' he asked.

'Grand,' she said. 'Am I 'anging on too tight?'

'Bruises fade,' he laughed, and turned back to drive on. 'Not far now,' he shouted to her over his shoulder.

They passed the end of the railway and turned left up a narrow track. Just before a little bridge, John stopped the bike.

'We're here,' he said, pointing ahead to the other side of the bridge. Maggie could see a large building on the right and a smaller cottage on the left. A fast stream burbled under the bridge.

'This stream drives the water wheel, at the back there,' said John. 'Comes down off the fell with enough force to make the wheel turn, even when it's not rained much.'

'What's it used for?' she asked.

'Used to be grain, but not any more.'

'But it's turning, I can 'ear it,' she said. 'Unless that's summat else creaking back there.'

'It's the wheel alright,' said John. 'It's driving a generator, making electricity for the cottage.'

Maggie was astonished.

'Electric? In th'ouse?'

'Aye, had it for years. Couldn't work the mill, with Fred having only one leg, so they wired it up themselves. I told you, they're interesting people.' He looked at her. 'And they might ask a lot of questions,' he said. 'Personal things. I was a bit, you know, put out, the first time. They just like people, like to know all about them. Don't be offended.'

Maggie was alarmed. She had only a few minutes to decide what to say to them. She could already see a short woman coming round the side of the house, wearing layer upon layer of clothing, wrapped up like the lasses on the screens. The woman stopped and squinted at them, holding her head at a strange angle.

John called out to her. 'It's me, Hannah.'

'It 'ad to be you when I 'eard the bike,' she called back. 'So who's that with ye?'

John grabbed Maggie's hand and pulled her up and over the little bridge. He was smiling and Maggie tried to do the same.

Hannah stood at the front door of the cottage. 'Fred,' she shouted, pushing the door open. 'It's our John, wi' a lass.'

Maggie felt John's grip tighten. 'It's OK,' he said. 'They'll just want to know all about you.' Then he let go of her hand, and hurried towards the older woman, arms outstretched, bent and hugged her. Maggie followed behind, bracing herself.

'Come 'ere, pet,' said Hannah. 'Let me get a good look at ye.' She put one hand to Maggie's face, stroked down her cheek and held her chin. Maggie could see one fierce blue eye and the other hidden behind a half-closed lid.

'Lost the other one when I was a bairn,' said Hannah. 'Me dad said I'd never amount to 'owt. Me mam died 'aving me, and 'e never forgot.'

'I'm sorry.' It was the only thing Maggie could think of to say.

'This is Maggie, Hannah,' said John. 'Margaret Lowery, from Kells.'

A voice emerged from the room behind the door. 'Lowery, from Kells. What's your dad called?'

John and Maggie were standing at the door, peering into the gloom. Hannah was ahead of them, beside a chair from which the voice had come.

'Frank McSherry,' said Maggie, wondering what was coming next.

John walked across to the person in the chair, shook his hand and then turned towards Maggie. 'Maggie was married, Fred. Her husband was killed in the war. Maggie, this is Fred Porter.'

'Can't get up easy, love,' said Fred, looking up at Maggie. 'You're a brave one, tekkin' on our John and that bike.'

'We're not …'

'She's just a friend,' said John quickly.

'Oh aye,' murmured Hannah and Fred simultaneously.

'I was coming up, to see if you wanted anything doing, and Maggie said she'd come with me, just for the run, didn't you?' John nodded to Maggie.

'That's it.'

'Oh aye,' chorused Hannah and Fred again.

It was a relief to get out of the house when John went to split logs and Maggie quickly offered to help.

'See what I mean?' he said. 'They're just curious about you. I'll shut them up if we have to,' said John. 'We won't stay long, and next time'll be easier.'

Tea was waiting when the log boxes were full and more logs stacked against the wall by the back door. Before they went in, John whispered, 'Look at the rugs, on the floor. Fred makes them himself, out of rags.'

Before she could do so, Maggie found herself under scrutiny again. She'd unwound the shawl from her head and Fred looked at her with undisguised interest.

'By God,' he said, 'that's an 'ead of 'air, what a colour, look at that, Hannah. When ye get it cut, lass, give it to me. It'll mek a grand rug.'

Maggie's eyes had adjusted to the light and she looked at the floor. Rugs littered the stone flags, six or seven across the room, each one different, with geometric shapes and blocks of colour.

'Fred makes hookie rugs,' said Hannah with obvious pleasure. 'Uses rags that folk give 'im. Makes up the shapes and that. We sell a few. That Miss Plane, she sells 'em for us, to 'er posh London friends. D'ye know Miss Plane?'

'No, she doesn't,' said John quickly. 'We've not been to Newton yet.'

'So she doesn't know Jessie?' said Hannah, looking at him with her one good eye.

'No,' said John quickly. He looked hard at Hannah and shook his head, warning her off. 'I met Maggie and 'er dad at the rugby in Kells, just a few weeks ago.'

'Where does your dad work, Maggie?' said Fred, picking up the need to change the subject. 'Was 'e in the war?'

'E's in a wheelchair,' said Maggie, 'Roof fall in pit.'

'That's a shame, pet,' said Hannah.

'We manage,' said Maggie.

'Are you working?' Hannah asked.

John interrupted again. 'Maggie 'as a little girl,' he said.

'Judith,' said Maggie, 'seven next birthday.'

'Growing up wi'out a dad,' said Fred.

'Growing up wi' a dad's hard sometimes,' said Hannah.

'Pick a rug,' said Fred suddenly, 'for the kiddie. Any one you like.'

Maggie looked at John.

'He means it,' said John. 'Pick a small one, we can carry it on t'bike. Go ahead.'

Maggie picked the smallest one she could see, a mix of blues and greens.

'That's very kind,' she began.

'Think nowt about it, lass,' said Fred. 'If you make our John 'appy, that's all we want.'

'We'll be off, then,' said John, seeing Maggie wilt under the weight of assumptions. 'Got to get Maggie back.'

He shook Fred's hand, kissed Hannah and steered Maggie out of the front door before they could embrace her, promising to come back before Christmas.

Outside he took her arm and they walked back to the bike, which he had leaned against the wall by the bridge.

'We don't 'ave to go yet,' she said, as he turned to wave to Hannah who was standing watching them.

"I could see where it was heading,' he said, pulling on his leather helmet. 'They'd have been asking about your love life next. Don't cover your hair right up, we're just going up the valley a bit further. We've got a couple of hours and there's something I want to do while the sun's still out. We'll be back in time, about seven, OK? It'll be dark before that but we can drive back in the dark, easy.'

John turned the bike to the left as they joined the road up the valley, and they drove for few minutes to the edge of a wood, at the bottom of a steep slope where the road climbed sharply. He stopped the bike where a stream ran below them through a gorge. He pointed up, first to a gap in the wall on the far side of the stream, and then higher, to the skyline where clouds were racing across. 'We're going up there, up Harter Fell,' he said. 'Quite rough in places, but what a view! We have to do it, before the light goes. I know you'll love it.'

Maggie was surprised by her willingness to follow his lead without argument. John seemed transformed from the shy man she had seen before. This was his place, and he was showing it to her, like Judith showing off a picture she'd drawn at school.

'Not done much walking,' she commented, 'just to work and back.' She stopped, realising what she'd said. 'Before I was wed,' she added, 'before Judith.'

'Where was that?' he asked, as she knew he would.

'At the Haig, in the canteen, doing teas an' all that, for t'bosses.'

'I would have noticed you if you were there now,' he said. 'Come on, we'll need to stride out.'

And stride out they did, up the clear path that led over from Eskdale into Dunnerdale. Before it reached the highest point, they branched off to the left, up the steep flank of the mountain, zigzagging to lessen the incline, then steep again as they neared the top.

As they stepped past the cairn, the view made her gasp. It stretched across the green valley below them and its lines of stone walls, and then up again to the central peaks of Cumberland. To their left the distant Irish Sea gleamed in the low golden light of late afternoon.

'Isn't it grand?' said John. 'Look across, you can see right up to where the river rises, and Bowfell up at the top of the valley.'

'Looks like a pyramid,' she said, 'with equal sides.'

'Aye, I love the way it sits alone. Crinkle Crags to one side, then on the other side the ridge goes on to Esk Hause, and Scafell and Scafell Pike. The highest mountains in England, right on our doorstep.'

'What's that down below?' she asked, pointing down to a clear rectangle marked on a flat patch of ground close to where the road wound up and over the pass.

'What does it look like?'

'Square, Straight lines, like someone planned it.'

'They did,' he said. 'It's Hardknott fort. The Romans built it to protect this pass. They had a fort at the coast and another one at Ambleside, and soldiers would go across here. Grim up here in winter.'

'Poor buggers,' said Maggie, 'so far from home, stuck up here. How d'you know about it?'

'Read it in a book at Hannah's. They read a lot those two, but I think her good eye is bothering her now. Did you notice?'

'Summat I did notice, when we were there,' said Maggie. 'You talk different with them, more local, not so posh.'

'Posh?' he laughed. 'Do I sound posh?'

'Aye, you do. I like it mind. But it comes and goes.'

John thought about this for a moment.

'You do the same,' he said. 'You talk different with me than you do at home.'

'Nay,' said Maggie.

'But you do,' he repeated. 'Maybe we all do it, change to fit where we are. I talk local when I'm with Hannah and Fred, and you talk posh when you're with me.' He smiled.

'I can talk posh if I want to,' she said. 'I don't want our Judith to get stuck, just 'cos of how she talks. I want more for her than that.'

'And for yourself?' John asked.

'Aye, me too,' she said. 'I could've gone on at school. Had to leave when me dad was injured. No choice then, we needed the money. But some day I could go back, not to school but somewhere, to do more learning.'

'Everything seems possible, sitting up here,' said John. 'That's what I love about climbing, getting up high. Makes you think about bigger things.'

'Do you want to talk local wi' me?' she asked.

'What do you want?'

'Give me a chance to practise talking like you. Don't tell anyone. Can't do it at home. I don't want Mam and Dad thinking,

70

you know, that I'm better than them somehow.' And what would the girls at work think, she wondered.

'It's not about being better,' he said. 'It's about choosing what you want, not being trapped. I talk like my mam and dad did, not posh, just Ulverston. And I can do that with you too, if you like.'

'Feels strange, like talking French or summat,' she said. 'It's our secret, you and me.'

Another secret; both of them thought for a moment about the tangle that lay between them and how it might unravel in the end. Maggie looked slowly around, taking in the browns and greys of bracken and rock, the blue and gold of sky and sea. It was like a map in an atlas, spread out far below. Her auburn hair caught the up draught and lifted in a cloud of curls above her head. She reached up with both hands to spread it flat against her head and coax it down. John saw what she was trying to do.

'Let me,' he said, holding the hair down on either side of her face while she flapped the shawl in the wind to straighten it and then wound it tight around her head. He eased his hands out from underneath the shawl and stood for a moment looking down at her.

Maggie stepped away from him and lowered her head. She was frightened now, more than before. The longer she went on not telling him about the screens, the worse it got. She had to do it, but not here, not now.

'This is a grand place, John,' she said. 'I could have lived my whole life so close and never seen it, never known.'

'It's what I love,' he said. 'The mountains, being up here, ever since I was a lad at school. We went climbing with one of the teachers, I must have been about fourteen, and I knew then. That's why I moved up here when Mam and Dad were both gone. I know I must seem sad to you, no family close, no friends. But I do have friends, out here, that I see when I have the chance. And that's all I need, all I've needed.'

He hesitated. He could smell rain on the wind, and far out to sea the horizon had disappeared, although further north the sun still shone, sinking slowly into dusk. He wanted to say more about how he was feeling, but he didn't dare.

'Come on,' he said. 'We'll go down the ridge towards the pass and down the road. That way we can walk more easily if it gets wet or dark.'

For the last half hour of their walk they strode out again, down the twisting road carved out over centuries by people and animals. Maggie felt the pinch of her shoes on the downward slope, and the sharpening wind had swung round, pricking their faces with tiny heralds of the rain to come. As they drove back down the valley and then up the coast road to Kells, she pressed her face into his coat.

CHAPTER 8

THE WINDOWS OF THE NEWTON SCHOOLHOUSE were dark when John stopped the bike outside two days later. He tried the door, but it was locked. There was nobody there. He was about to go home again, regretting the waste of fuel, when he remembered that Jessie often stayed at Applegarth when Agnes was in London. Two minutes later, he wheeled the bike down the steep drive and leaned it against the garage door. There was certainly someone in the house. If it were Agnes he would have to reconsider. He needed to see Jessie alone.

Before pushing the doorbell, he glanced into the lamplit sitting room and saw Jessie sitting in an easy chair by the fire, reading. Then he stood for a minute in the porch, listening for Agnes's voice. Silence. He pushed the bell and heard it sound inside. The front door opened. Jessie seemed surprised to see him.

'I remembered,' he said, 'about you staying here sometimes when Agnes is in London.'

'Yes, that's right,' she said. 'It's such a comfortable house. And Agnes likes to have someone here, keeping the place warm, you know. Come in, John. I didn't hear the bike.'

He stepped into the hall.

'Go through. I'm in the sitting room.'

He stood awkwardly. He'd thought about what he had to say

but knew that she wouldn't like it. Even after all these years, he was still afraid of her, of her energy and fierce defence of herself.

'Sit down,' she said, but he stayed standing, twisting the leather helmet in his hands. 'Is something the matter, John?'

'Not really, it's just that, I – I need to ask you something.'

'Ask me what?'

'Well, tell you really, about – I've met someone, a girl, well a woman actually …'

'Oh, that's grand,' said his mother, but her look and her voice betrayed the sudden anxiety that hit her. 'Is it serious?'

'Not yet, but I'd like it to be. The thing is, I want to tell her the truth.'

'About what?'

'About us. That you're my mother, not my aunt.'

Jessie stared at him. 'But why?' she said. 'What's the point? She can't have asked you about it, can she?'

He shook his head.

'Then why?'

'I want to be honest with her. It's important to me.'

'But what about me? If you tell her, she tells her family, and that's it. Might as well put it in the *Evening News*. Where does she live?'

'Whitehaven.'

Jessie sat back in the chair. 'Sit down, for heaven's sake,' she said, 'I can't keep looking up at you.'

He perched on the edge of a small chair by the window. Jessie got up suddenly and closed the curtains.

'Does this girl –'

'Maggie,' he said. 'She's called Maggie.'

'Does Maggie have to know about it, John, really?'

'No, but I have to tell her. I wanted to tell you first, so that you could –'

'Could what?' said his mother, hearing the walls of her privacy crashing down. 'If you do tell her, could you ask her to keep it to herself, at least for a while?'

'I could ask her. It's a very close family, she lives with her parents.'

'Just a girl then,' said Jessie.

He was stung. 'No, she's a grown woman,' he said. 'She lives with them because she's a widow with a child and it makes sense.'

'Oh dear,' said Jessie.

'What do you mean? What's wrong with that? She had the baby while her husband was in the army. He was killed.'

'So was Clive,' said Jessie.

'And you gave me away, Well, Maggie didn't abandon her child. I want her, Jessie, and I have to tell her the truth.'

Jessie shook her head.

'Don't shake your head.' John's voice was loud in the quiet room. 'And don't tell me it was my idea to hide the truth about us. I was young and upset and I wanted you not to send me away. But that was a long time ago. I'm grown now. I want my own life. I could have told her on Saturday, I wanted to but I waited. I'm telling you now to give you the chance to do something yourself, if you want to. I don't know whether she'll tell anyone else, even if I ask her not to. It's been long enough. I want to stop lying.'

He stood up. Jessie was looking into the fire. Her eyes were bright.

'Maybe it's time I gave up the job,' she said quietly, as if to herself. 'They don't want me there.'

'Who doesn't?'

'The other teacher, the one who was in the navy, and the vicar. He was in the war too. They talk about it, about me. I think Alan Crompton wants my job. He thinks I'm old-fashioned.'

'What's that got to do with it?'

75

'You've never understood all that, have you?' she said, looking up at him. 'I changed my name and lied about you all this time to protect myself from people like that, people who think someone like me can't do a job, can't have authority. If – when – this comes out, that'll give them the chance they want. They'll have me out of the school, and that means the house as well. That's what he really wants – Crompton. He wants the house.'

'But that's so old-fashioned,' said John. 'Things have changed. Women work now, if they want to.'

'Teaching's different, John, even now, and especially if those two are prepared to make a fuss. They could stir up the parents, enough of them anyway.'

'But you've been there for years,' John said. 'You could fight them.'

'I'm not sure I want to,' she said. 'I've been teaching for nearly thirty years. Maybe it's time I let someone else do it. I've still got enough energy to try something else. The money's not so important any more.'

'What about the schoolhouse?'

'Alan's right about the house, I suppose. It's too big for one person. He has two children. It makes sense for him to have it. And I have an alternative.'

'Here?'

'It's what Agnes has always wanted. When you came along, she wanted us all to live here, don't you remember? Like a happy family.'

John had forgotten that. 'Isn't that a bit … you know, strange.'

'Not really. Two spinsters, sharing a house as they get older. People would talk about it, but it wouldn't really matter.'

John pushed back towards what had brought him here.

'It's all falling apart, Jessie,' he said. 'Face it. We can't keep this up any longer.'

His mother was thinking, her hand to her mouth. 'When do you want to tell her?'

'Soon.'

'What's she like?'

'Maggie? She's wonderful. A bit like Hannah, but younger. And she's beautiful, and straightforward. She says what she means. I like that. She would expect me to be honest with her.'

'Does she have a job?'

'I don't think so. She's never mentioned it. Her mother does something at the pit, and her father is at home. He was injured, he's in a wheelchair.'

'How long have you known her?'

'Only a few weeks. Seems longer. My life might be going to change. I want it to change. Time is going by and I want to be happy.'

'You make it sound so simple,' said his mother.

He looked at her. 'What will you do?'

'Nothing much. I won't need to. If you tell this person –'

'Maggie,' he prompted.

'Yes, well, the word will gradually filter down the coast, like whooping cough, carried on the wind. Agnes already knows. I'll tell the Leadbetters myself. And Dr Dawson,' she added, thinking about how he might react. 'I don't know what will happen after that. Things will change.'

'Lying makes me tired,' said John.

'Me, too,' Jessie agreed. 'How long have I got, did you say?'

'I'm seeing Maggie on Friday, I want to tell her then.'

She looked up suddenly. 'Friday? That's impossible. I can't tell the Leadbetters now, with Lionel so ill. He's out of hospital and getting better, but – I need longer, John. Can't it wait till Christmas at least? Fresh start in the New Year?'

John hesitated. He hardly knew the Leadbetters, and didn't

care about them, but he knew they were important to Jessie. Could it wait? It had been only a few weeks. He might be wrong about Maggie.

'Alright,' he said finally. 'I'll wait a bit longer. I hope Lionel gets better.'

'Thank you, dear. I understand, I do really, but it's all such a rush. I have to think what to say. And I'd like to talk to Agnes.'

'When is she back?'

'They're letting her go early for Christmas. I don't really know how her job works. She doesn't talk about it. I think she said the middle of December. I could ring her and check.'

John had stopped listening. He was disappointed with himself. Jessie had got her way, again, or that's how it felt.

'I have to go,' he said.

'Thank you for coming.' She was smiling now. He left the house quickly and drove home too fast. He had come so close to getting what he wanted, and then he'd crumbled. Maggie wouldn't have done that, but she was stronger than him. He felt unworthy of her, and the thought haunted him until he fell asleep, late in the night.

* * *

Jessie heard the bike engine revving away up the drive and sat back in the chair. The fire was nearly out and she took the precious coal in her fingers, placing it carefully one piece at a time, to make it last a little longer. Then she lay back, her head thumping with pain. Suddenly she thought about Andrew. He wouldn't care about John; he'd known for years that she was a liar. Maybe that was why she kept thinking about going to Toronto. It wasn't just about a fresh start, away from having to count pieces of coal and slices of bread. She yearned to be able to drop her guard, to be in a place where the people around her neither knew nor cared about the past. Or maybe she wanted to be with Andrew because he wanted her. He saw in her what others seemed to miss. All her life she'd been respected for her brain, but she had a body too, and that's what he'd loved, with all his young passion. There had been that one bad night when he had hurt her, but the Andrew she had seen recently would not do that. The war had mellowed him. He would protect her in a new life, if she chose to take that risk.

Risk. Was changing your life such a risk when you didn't want the life you had, or it didn't want you? She could walk away, let the new men take over the school, and the village, and the church and everything else. Who would miss her, she wondered. She listed the people in her life, one at a time. She was part of their lives, but not the most important person for any one of them. Nobody really loved her. Apart from one: Jessie knew that Agnes loved her. She'd known it since John had come back into her life, but maybe even before that. That's why Agnes had been so upset about Andrew. She didn't want Agnes, not like that. But she could trust her: Agnes was the only one who knew it all.

For a little while Jessie lay quietly on the comfortable sofa in Agnes's house, listening to the faint crackle of the fire, thinking about her life. She had much to be happy about, but she knew she was not. Looking ahead brought no comfort. She could find the energy to fight back, or she could take the easy way out and leave, as Andrew had done, when the pull of the future and fear of the present had combined in an irresistible urge to be gone.

CHAPTER 9

'ARE YOU ALREET, PET?'

Maggie realised she'd been unusually quiet as she and her mother walked to work. Even when other people had joined them, heading for the early shift in the morning dark, Maggie hadn't joined in the conversation and had slipped to the back of the group. Now she and her mother were tucking their hair firmly into place under scarves and hats, preparing for the first rush of unsorted coal into the shed and the start of the toiling day.

'Aye, Mam, I'm fine,' she said. 'Just thinking, you know.'

'Is it that lad?'

'Hush, Mam. We're not talking about that, not 'ere. You know what they're like.'

The noise of the shed cut the conversation mercifully short. Maggie didn't want to talk, not to her mother, or the girls at work. She wasn't sure about anything except that she liked the man and didn't want to share anything yet with anyone. At first she'd thought he was clumsy and awkward, but seeing him with those people in Boot had changed that. He was so relaxed there. They were good people, honest, and they obviously thought highly of him. She could feel herself warming to him, perhaps because of his shyness, not despite it. He could be someone important. But that was the problem. She didn't want to fall again, like she'd fallen last time and got caught and trapped. She hadn't enjoyed marriage. She wanted someone to be close to, to lie with, to talk softly with. She didn't want to feel beholden, or obliged or responsible for anyone or anything except herself and Judith. She wasn't ready for anything else.

And now here was this man. He was a bit older than her, never been married – as far as they knew – and no kids. He had his own place, a good job. He liked her, she was sure about that, and he was kind and different, but what did he want? If he wanted to settle down, she'd done that and it hadn't worked. Maybe she didn't have it in her to be a good wife, and she shouldn't lead him on, or let him lead her. And anyway, he didn't know about this, about the screens, and when he did – if he did – that would be the end anyway. He could have any girl he wanted, so why would he want a screen lass? She should tell him, and that would solve it. He would disappear, move on to someone more suitable, and leave her alone.

* * *

'I need to tell 'im, Mam, about the screens. That'll settle it.' Maggie and her mother were standing by the range in the back room of the house in West Row. The clear cold of the morning had turned to drizzle before the end of their shift and they were both cold and wet by the time they reached home. Tea was required, even before they washed off the smell of the day.

'Are you sure 'e doesn't know already?'

'Aye. It's never come up – 'e probably thinks I'm at 'ome. looking after Dad and Judith. God knows what we'd live on, but 'e's got money. May not even think about it.'

'It's too early, Maggie. That'll be the end of it. Make 'im like you a bit more. We'll say nowt, I'll tell your dad to watch what 'e says. Give yourself a bit more time. You're a fine lass, catch for

81

any feller, and you've grieved for that Isaac Lowery long enough.'

Maggie turned to her mother. 'That's just it, Mam. I didn't grieve for Isaac, not after the first shock wore off. He tried, but 'e were useless, Mam. Never told you, but it couldn't've lasted, even if 'e'd come back in one piece. Look at Brenda, the Colman lass, what's 'er name now?'

'Hadwin?' said Violet.

'Aye, 'er. She's 'aving a rotten time since 'er Maurice came back. He hits 'er, everyone knows that, and the boys, poor wee sods. That would've been me, Mam, except that I'd've been off if Isaac raised a hand to our Judith. Beer and 'is mates, that's all Isaac really cared about. Honest, Mam. I never said 'owt, didn't want you to worry, but it was no good and I don't want to make that mistake again.'

Violet didn't respond to the information about Isaac, which came as no surprise. 'But this one's not like that, is 'e?' she asked.

Maggie shrugged her shoulders. 'Who knows? He seems like a good man. Those people we went to see in Boot, the ones 'e stopped with, bit funny like, but they rate 'im. And how do you really know, until it's too late and you're stuck with it?'

'Well if it's you 'e wants, pet, 'e won't wait forever, not at 'is age. How old is 'e? Thirty something and never married? Someone'll snap 'im up, you watch.' Violet hesitated, then added, 'Is 'e a Catholic?'

'No idea,' said Maggie. 'We've never talked about church. I only met 'im a few weeks ago. It's not church that bothers me, it's work. Secrets are bad when people matter. I can't keep lying. If 'e throws me over on account of the screens thing, I need to know now, not waste energy on 'im and then watch 'im walk away.'

With Judith home from school, tea was made and drunk, water heated, bodies washed. Maggie heard her mother in the front room, spelling out to her father the dire consequences of letting anything slip. Every whispered word was audible through the thin walls of the house. She knew what they wanted for her, but it wasn't necessarily what she wanted for herself.

When John arrived at the door on Friday night, prompt at six as promised, Maggie was there at the first knock. They'd already wheeled Frank into the kitchen to keep him out of the way and Violet made only the briefest of appearances. John suggested going down into town for fish and chips but that was definitely no good at all; far too many people knew her, and there were some who might recognise him too. He'd hadn't brought the bike, but she'd planned for that, and her alternative suggestion was ready. Fish and chips from the chippie round the corner, wrap them up well, bus to Sandwith and eat at his house. The pub was close if they wanted a drink. She was sure that no one there would know her. She would say what she had to say about being a screen lass, but wait till after they'd eaten. If the evening was ruined, at least she wouldn't be hungry.

The range oven in John's tidy kitchen was warm when they got in, and he stoked the fire to warm up the chips before they ate them out of the newspaper they were wrapped in, sitting at the tiny table, still wearing their coats. John licked his greasy fingers.

'Drink?' he said, standing up. He was looking forward to being seen in the pub with this lovely woman.

'In a bit, maybe. I want to tell you something first, then we'll see.' John looked at her, turning his head slightly with the unspoken question.

'Nothing bad, not really,' she said, 'and this is a good time.'

John sat down again. She looked serious.

'You've never asked me about where I work,' she said.

'Work? I thought you were at home, with your dad, and the bairn.'

'I was when Judith was a babby, but since she's been at school, well, I wanted to do something. We need the money.'

'So where do you work?' asked John, as she obviously wanted him to.

'On the screens,' she said. 'At the Haig, same as you.'

'In that shed, sorting the coal?'

'Aye, in there.'

'But I've been in there, when that dog …'

'Aye, I saw you that day, standing up there with Geordie, looking down at us.'

'But where were you?' said John. 'I didn't see you.'

'You saw a gang of women covered in clothes to keep out the dust, different shapes and sizes, but all much the same. Like nuns, just our faces showing. One of them was me.'

'Nuns! They don't swear like you lot.'

Maggie felt a flush creep up her neck. 'Well, that's where I work. I'm a screen lass. Look.' She pulled up her long sleeves and held out her battered hands to him. 'Look,' she said again. 'I didn't lie to you. You never asked.'

John looked at her face. He saw the pale skin, slightly freckled around the nose and cheekbones. He saw the glorious hair, held by a scarf but defying control. He saw her eyes, grey-green, watching him carefully by the light of oil lamp that hissed on its hook above the table.

'I didn't ask because it doesn't matter,' he said after a long pause. 'You needed a job, and you found one. But that job's so hard. Show me your hands again.'

She raised her hands, turning them over to show him the ingrained dirt and damage to skin and knuckles and nails. 'Judith rubs Vaseline into them for me, but they still hurt.'

'I couldn't believe that women could work like that,' he said, taking hold of her hands in both of his. 'And you're so strong, not just the work but the way you are, together. I think Geordie's frightened of you.'

She laughed. 'We know he is,' she said. 'Most people are. Are you?'

'Yes, I am,' he said. He was leaning forward now, still holding her hands in his, his elbows on the table. 'I've never felt strong like that, except sometimes when I'm out climbing. I wish I did. I envy you.'

'Envy? No one envies screen lasses. We're the lowest of the low. We know it, that's why we stick together.'

She wanted him to react. He was too polite to tell her to go away. He would take her home, and just not call again. If he saw her at work, he would pretend he didn't know her. But what would he say, now?

He said, 'Do you mind if we stay here a bit longer. We can't talk in the pub.'

'Fine,' she said, guessing that he'd already made up his mind and didn't want to be seen with her so close to his home.

John turned away and fiddled with the stove.

'Come in the front room. I'll light the fire. It's better in there.'

Her heart began to sink.

Maggie watched from a small armchair while John rolled up some newspaper, carried in some kindling, arranged it all in the grate and lit it, blowing to help the flames to thrive. Then he went back into the kitchen to wipe his hands before returning, all without saying a word.

'You've been honest with me, Maggie,' he said, finally, sitting down on the other side of the fireplace and looking down at his hands. She waited for more.

'Don't know what you thought I'd do or say, about what you do. I'm not from round here. The screen lass thing doesn't mean much to me actually. But I'm sorry about your poor hands.'

Still he didn't look up. But she was sure he had more to say, and she kept quiet, hardly breathing, hearing the snap and popping of the kindling as it caught.

He got up again, taking logs from a bucket to put onto the flames. She was confused. If he didn't care about the screen lass thing, what was he trying to say that just wouldn't come out.

'I have a secret too,' he said finally. He rubbed his hand over his face, leaving a smear of coal dust down one side of his nose. 'You know I was adopted when I was a baby.'

'Yes, you told me that,' she said.

'But I didn't tell you about my real mother.'

'I thought you wouldn't know anything about her. Isn't that how it works?'

'There was no proper adoption back then,' said John. 'No papers. no names. I only found out that I was adopted when my mother, the woman I thought was my mother, was ill, just before she died. She thought I was her husband, and she talked about getting me, just after I was born.'

'Getting you? Sounds like you were in a shop or something.'

'They got me from the home, where my real mother ... where she had me. It was in Carnforth.'

'She had you and then she gave you away? How could she do that?'

'She had no choice.'

Maggie shook her head. 'Did she tell you that, herself? You've talked to her?'

'Yes, we've talked. She said it was all arranged, and there was nothing she could do.'

'When did you find her? Where?'

'It was Christmas time, in 1937.'

'What happened? Tell me.'

John sat by the stuttering fire. He told her almost everything, about the names he'd found in their Ulverston house, about the photo in his Aunty Anne's loft, about how he tracked his mother down. He stopped, wondering if he could avoid saying any more. But Maggie hadn't heard enough.

'So where did you find her, after all that? Where is she now?'

'I found her in Newton, just south a bit from here, where the Esk runs into the sea. She's the schoolteacher there.

'What did you say to her?'

'Nothing much, I think she'd already guessed. I first met her, by accident, at Hannah and Fred's. She fainted on the floor when she saw me. Apparently I looked so much like my father. But she didn't let on. In the end I worked it out, and I went to see her.'

'What happened then?'

'It was difficult,' he said, still hoping that he wouldn't have to go any further.

'Difficult? She knew that you were her son, and that she'd found you again, after all that time. How could that be difficult?'

'I know,' he said, still wanting to protect Jessie, as he had done for so many years. 'I know it sounds strange, but she never expected to see me again, She'd changed her name, moved away, moved on. Neither of us really knew what to do. She would have lost her job, if people knew.'

'So what?' Maggie couldn't believe what John was so slowly revealing to her. She leaned forward, her face close to his. 'She loses a job, but she has you, a son. What's more important?'

John blinked, and Maggie continued, her voice stronger. 'When I had Judith, and Isaac was killed, my sister wanted to take her, but I would never have let her go, never. Your mother gave you away, to strangers.'

'Not complete strangers,' said John, trying to turn away the anger. 'The Pharaohs knew her mam,'

'She gave you away,' Maggie insisted. 'And when you found her she worried about her job?'

87

'We made a deal. I was to say she was my aunt, so people wouldn't know.'

'That was a dreadful thing to make you do, John,' she said. 'Why did you go along with it?'

He didn't want to tell her, but it was too late now. He was in too deep and there was no use pretending any more, not to this woman.

'Actually, it was my idea,' he said. 'If people saw us together they would guess we were related. And people knew bits about who I am, where I'd come from, so I thought ... I said that I could be her nephew, given away by her sister who went to New Zealand. It felt ...'

John's voice tailed away as Maggie got up from the small chair and stood facing the fire, her back to him.

'What kind of woman would do that?' she said. 'And why didn't you stand up for yourself? It's like she gave you away twice. And now – don't tell me it's still going on.'

John nodded miserably. 'I wanted to tell you the truth. I hate all the lying, but I talked to her and she asked me to wait.'

Maggie turned around. She was angry now.

'When did you talk to her?'

'Earlier on this week, when I knew I would see you tonight and I wanted to tell you. I promised I wouldn't, but then you told me something important and I – I wanted to do the same. I've lied for so long.'

Maggie stepped towards him, and he flinched away from her.

'Look at you, for God's sake,' she shouted at him. 'I was only going to throw the chip papers on the fire. What did you think I was going to do? Bully you, like she's done all these years? You've let her do this to you, John. You owe her nothing, nothing, and she's led you along like a dog on a string. It was *her* choice to have you, to give you away, to make you lie all these years. It doesn't matter whose idea it was. She's denied you, John. You're her son, and she's rejected you. And now I'm more angry about it than you are. Where's the sense in that?'

'Don't, please,' he said, standing up. 'I've finished lying. I've told you, and you're the most important person to me. I can't undo it all. I can't make her change. But it doesn't matter that much any more.'

'What matters,' she said, turning away from him, looking back into the fire, 'What matters is that I have to respect you, if – if you and I are going to be together, even for a while.'

'But I've told you,' said John desperately, 'when I promised I wouldn't. I have stood up for myself, because you're more important to me than any of that stuff. I was afraid then, that she would push me away altogether, deny it all. It wasn't easy for her, I understood that.'

'That's your trouble, John. You understand what everybody wants except yourself.' Maggie stood up straight and squared her strong shoulders. 'I want to meet your mother.'

'When?' John sounded alarmed.

'Soon. We've been walking out for a while. You've met my parents. I want to meet your mother.'

'I don't think –' John began.

'Good,' she said, 'don't think. You think too much as it is. If you won't take me, I'll go meself. She's called Jessie and she works at Newton School. I'll find her. And now I'm going home. I can walk on my own, or you can take me on the bike. Your choice.'

They didn't speak again that night. John drove Maggie home, and she cleaved to his back, her hands at his waist. Of course John didn't want her to meet his mother, but she already knew it was something she had to do.

CHAPTER 10

IT WAS ALMOST MIDNIGHT on Armistice Day. Jessie always found the day depressing: the hymns, the laying of a wreath at the war memorial outside the school, looking at all those names. John's father Clive had died in the Devonshire Dock: he had dropped like a stone from the high roof into the water, but she always thought of him as one of the casualties of war. His death had changed her life forever.

She had gone to bed early in her front bedroom at the school-house, to get the day over with for another year, and slept deeply, dreaming as she often did about wandering half dressed in a house full of people who were dancing, laughing at her behind their hands. Someone was banging on the door and she was trying to reach it, but they wouldn't let her through. Then she woke, and she realised that the banging was from downstairs. She heard a woman's voice shouting, 'Miss Whelan, Jessie.'

She looked at her watch. The voice came again. It was Nellie Kitchin. She opened the window and called down into the darkness, 'Is that you Nellie?'

'Oh, miss, thank God you're 'ere. Can you come and 'elp us, miss? It's our Lucy.'

'Stay there,' Jessie called. She shut the window, pulled her gown around herself and hurried to open the door. 'What is it?'

she asked, pulling the distraught woman into the hallway.

'It's our Lucy, miss, she's taken real bad. It must be the babby coming, miss, but she's not due for weeks. The doctor, miss, we need 'im, but it's too far.'

'Who's with her now?' Jessie was thinking quickly.

'Our Harry, but 'e's scared stiff, poor lad. I told 'im I wouldn't be long.'

'Go back, Nellie, do what you can to keep her warm. Get as much water heating as you can. Have you got coal?'

'Some, not much.'

Jessie ran upstairs and returned with her arms full of towels.

'Take these,' she said, thrusting them at Nellie. 'I'll go up to Applegarth and call the doctor, then I'll come to the house. I'll bring some coal.'

She dialled Dr Dawson's number, and the telephone rang for a long time before someone answered. It was a woman's voice.

'Is the doctor there?' Jessie asked, 'It's Miss Whelan from the schoolhouse in Newton. We need some help, urgently.'

'He's at the hospital in Whitehaven. This is Ann,' the sleepy voice replied. 'He should have been back hours ago.'

'Thank you,' said Jessie. She broke the connection and asked the operator to call the hospital. It took quite a while to find Dr Dawson. He was snatching a few hours sleep stretched out on a couch in the doctors' mess, but he recognised Jessie's voice immediately.

'Jessie? What it is? They said it was urgent.'

'It's one of Nellie Kitchin's daughters,' she said. 'Sounds as if she's in labour but Nellie says it's too early and it's not right. I've sent Nellie home and I'll go down there myself.'

'What time is it?'

'Just gone midnight.'

'I've got the car here. It'll take about half an hour at this time of

91

night. I know where it is. I'll meet you there.'

By the time Matthew Dawson arrived at the Kitchins' house it was clear to Jessie that the baby, two months premature if the dates were right, was on its way. Lucy was agitated, gripping her mother's hand as the pains came. The terrible cries brought back to Jessie memories that she had tried to bury. Nellie's small kitchen was full of steam and fiercely hot, but they had not been willing or able to move Lucy into the other room. Harry watched open-mouthed from the doorway. He was the first to hear the doctor's car.

All three women were past caring about modesty as the doctor examined Lucy, but Nellie was quick to push Harry into the other room and shut the door firmly against him.

'Give her something for the pain, Matthew,' said Jessie. 'She's been screaming for hours, she must be just exhausted.' And we are too, she thought to herself.

Mercifully the magic worked and soon Jessie and Nellie could hear and follow the doctor's instructions. When the baby finally appeared it was a boy, tiny, blue and quite dead.

Jessie put her arm round Nellie's shoulders, feeling the choking sobs. Lucy lay in the wreckage of the makeshift bed, her face turned to the wall.

'She's young and strong,' said Matthew Dawson. 'Can you make us all a drink, Mrs Kitchin? I'll stay a while to make sure there's nothing more untoward. And I'll take the child's body. Maybe you could find me a box, or a basket. I'll sit in the other room, give you a bit of space and Lucy some quiet.'

Jessie splashed her face in some of the warm water and tried to push her hair into some kind of order. She hadn't had time before she left the house to do anything but pull on some clothes. She went through to the other room where Matthew was already sitting in a battered chair, his eyes closed. He heard the door creak and watched her as she crossed the room.

'You were quite right to call me,' he said. 'She certainly needed more help than you could provide, or her mother. She should be alright, but I'll stay a while just to make sure.' He glanced at the door and lowered his voice, 'Do we know who the father is?'

'Lucy says she does,' said Jessie, 'but she won't tell anyone, not even her mother. Those children had a hard time growing up, learned to keep things to themselves. Even now they still do it, when they know their father will never hit them again.'

'Yes, I heard Bill Kitchin was quick with his fists, but I thought that was just Nellie.'

'She did try to protect them,' whispered Jessie. 'Do you remember poor Alice?'

'Indeed I do,' he said. 'That was a terrible business.'

Nellie brought in two cups of tea and disappeared again. They sat in silence. As the hot tea revived her a little, Jessie thought about telling him the truth about John before anyone else did, while she had the chance. He'd been very understanding when she'd needed his help, the night when John had found her in the snowdrift, all those years ago. She'd wondered then whether he'd guessed the truth, but he'd never mentioned it. During the war he'd been away, working in a hospital in London during the Blitz, then in Newcastle, clearing up after the bombs and the fires and fear they left behind them.

Jessie looked across at him. He seemed to be sleeping, but probably wasn't. It was a good face, she thought. She wasn't sure how old he was. Matthew's wife had died during the war, but Jessie wasn't sure what had happened. Maybe Agnes knew. Agnes carried secrets well, which was a blessing.

Matthew stirred in his chair.

"There's no need for you to stay,' he said. 'Can you walk back, or would you like me to take you?'

'I'll stay a little longer,' she said. 'A few hours less sleep won't do me any harm.'

They sat in silence for a few minutes, aware of each other.

'Not seen you for a while Jessie,' he said. 'How are things at the school, with Mr Crompton back?'

She looked at him carefully.

'Have you heard something?'

'No, but I guessed it could be tricky.'

'Between ourselves, Matthew, it's more than tricky, He's not used to working for a woman, and he clearly doesn't like it.'

'Ah,' said the doctor. 'Nothing worse than hurt male pride.'

'And of course he has an eye on the schoolhouse, with me rattling around on my own and him with a wife and two children. The house goes with the job and I have the job, for the time being at least.'

Matthew was interested now, and sat up a little straighter in the low chair.

'Have you thought any more about giving up?'

'Again between ourselves, Matthew, I have thought of it. But it's been so busy, since September. Maybe at Christmas I'll have more time to put things in perspective.'

He hesitated for a moment, as if making up his mind about something. 'Since that night at Applegarth, I've realised how much I look forward to seeing you, and it doesn't happen often enough.' He hesitated again. 'Could I ask you to have dinner with me sometime? We could get dressed up and take our minds off things for a while. Or maybe the cinema? I could come and pick you up, or we could meet in Whitehaven.'

'What a lovely idea,' she said, and she meant it. 'I don't think I've had a proper date since I was a girl, in Barrow, before the first war. Seems like the last century. Are you sure?'

'Certain. I'll check my shifts and send you a note.'

It was another hour before he felt able to leave Nellie and her daughter, and drive back up the valley to his home by the river. He dropped Jessie at the schoolhouse on his way past. Before she got out of the car, he leaned over and kissed her cheek.

'Thanks for your help tonight,' he said. 'Next time we see each other, it will be in happier circumstances. It's time we both had some fun.'

He drove home in the dense dark of the winter night. The cloud blocked any light from moon or stars, but at least the road was free from frost. He thought as he drove. It was four years since Joan's death, and he had thought of no other woman in all that time except this one. There'd always been something about Jessie, something below the surface of her cheerful competent self. Something had happened, when she'd hurt her ankle that Christmas, in 1937. There had been a secret in the house that day that no one would share, and he still had no idea what it could have been about.

Then the war had come with the chaos of bombs and casualties and he'd forgotten how drawn he was to Jessie. Joan had been there, warm and familiar, soaking up his love and care, caring for him in return. And then she'd been taken ill, something minor, innocuous. A few days in bed, she'd be fine. Why hadn't he noticed, why hadn't she said? By the time they got her to hospital it was too late. She died, still a young woman, and he blamed himself. Maybe the girls blamed him, too. And now, he could feel himself falling in love again, with this strong self-contained woman who gave so little away. He believed Joan would have understood, but he wasn't sure about his daughters. He still felt that he had let them down, that he had not acted quickly enough, that he had let their mother die. He would need to take care, not rush into anything.

* * *

A week went by with no word from Matthew Dawson. Jessie began to doubt that he'd meant what he said, and found herself very disappointed. She wondered how long John would wait before he told his new girlfriend about her. She would much prefer to tell Matthew herself, in her own way, than to let the gossip begin to circulate unchecked. A note did arrive, but it was from Caroline Leadbetter, reporting on Lionel's continued improvement, and how glad they were to be getting regular letters from Andrew. It was in the postscript that Jessie read,

So pleased to hear about you and Dr Dawson, dear. Such good people, both of you, and good news amidst all the gloom.

News travels fast, she thought.

Agnes read the letter too, when she returned from London a few days later.

'Well,' she said to Jessie. 'Have you heard from him?'

'Not yet,' said Jessie, 'but I think I will. He seemed quite serious about it. I hope so, anyway. Until that night at Nellie's I hadn't paid him much attention. But he is a really nice man.'

'I hope he is, dear,' said Agnes. 'You don't need someone leading you a dance, not after – not at our time of life.'

'Let's not talk about my taste in men, Agnes. Or our age, come to that. I'm going to get my hair done tomorrow.'

'The annual shearing,' said Agnes, smiling. 'Ready for the festive season.'

'Or my first date in decades,' said Jessie.

They both laughed. Agnes quickly moved on to talk about something safer, although the demolition of the old ordnance factory at Drigg was proving to be anything but safe for the men working on it.

'Turns out the site is riddled with unexploded nasty things,'

96

she said. 'So they're having to work very slowly.'

'What's going to happen when it's clear?' Jessie asked. 'I hope it's something that employs a lot of people.'

'Courtaulds, I heard,' said her friend, 'but there may be other plans.'

'What other plans?' said Jessie, looking up from the ironing. The room was full of the smell of starch and hot fabric.

'Oh just something they were talking about at work,' said Agnes, getting up. 'Nothing definite. We'll have to see. Tea, dear?'

Later they were walking back together, arm in arm, from a whist drive at the village hall when Agnes asked about the school.

'The thought of giving up keeps popping into my mind, so I must be thinking about it at some level,' said Jessie. 'Alan Crompton is controlling his discipline and exercise mania a little better, but I'm still concerned about him bullying some of those children in less obvious ways. He shouts at them so loudly sometimes you can hear him outside. I can write my worries down, but who would back me up if it came to a proper row with him? The vicar and he are clearly very friendly.'

'There are other jobs you could do,' said Agnes. 'And my house is your house, you know that. I've always thought how happy we could be here, together.'

'I know,' said Jessie. 'You're a great comfort. I would need to work, if I wasn't at the school, but at what I'm not sure. I could volunteer, but I'd prefer a proper job.'

'Well, I think you should prepare yourself for an alternative, in case the chance comes up.'

'How would I do that?'

'Shorthand,' said Agnes. 'You should learn shorthand. It's just like learning another language and I'm sure you could do it without difficulty. Best thing I ever did. It's a useful skill, like driving, and that's something else you should learn. Modern times, Jessie. We need modern skills. You've got years of useful contribution left in you, and all that experience too – far more than some of these younger women have to offer. You could teach yourself shorthand out of a book, and I could teach you to drive. How much notice would you need to give to school?'

'Whoa,' laughed Jessie. 'Slow down, Agnes. Life moves slowly up north you know, not like the big city. We country folk need time to think.'

* * *

Two days later, a note arrived from Dr Dawson, inviting Jessie to accompany him to the pictures on the coming Friday. At the end of school that day, as Jessie checked her new haircut in the mirror in her room and was pleased at what she saw, she noticed a woman standing by the school gate. When she left the building and walked down the yard towards the gate, the young woman was still there, looking at her.

'Miss Whelan?' Before Jessie had the chance to respond, the confident voice continued. 'My name is Margaret Lowery. I think we need to talk. It's about your son. John.'

Chapter 11

Jessie took a moment to register what she had heard, and who this person might be. She looked back towards the school. Alan Crompton was turning his bike around at the top of the yard and was about to walk down towards them.

'I would prefer not to talk here,' said Jessie quickly. 'My house is just around the corner if you'd like to follow me there.'

Maggie understood. She hesitated, debating whether to say something within the hearing of the man who was approaching them, presumably one of the other teachers. Jessie watched with twisting apprehension until Maggie looked away from the man and followed her towards the privacy of the schoolhouse. Jessie knew that Alan Crompton would have noticed, but she could deal with that later.

Jessie went up the steps to the back door, opened it, stepped inside and gestured for Margaret to follow. She thought about taking the woman straight into the front room, usually the preserve of guests, but then decided against it. She put down her basket and took off her coat. She did not sit down, nor did she invite Margaret to do so. Those few precious minutes had restored her mind and her breathing to the control that she needed.

'I'm sorry,' she said, 'I didn't catch your name, Miss …?'

'Mrs,' said Maggie immediately. 'Mrs Lowery.'

'Ah,' said Jessie, nodding her head slowly as the pennies began to drop. 'And you say you need to talk to me. What can we have to talk about, I wonder?'

'I told you, it's about your son, John. John Pharaoh.'

'I know John's name, and you'll notice that it is not the same as mine. Who told you that John is my son?'

'He did,' said Maggie. The two women were both standing, on opposite sides of the small table, like boxers eyeing each other before a fight that lacked a referee. 'He told me that you gave him away to a couple called Pharaoh who brought him up as their own.'

'And what, may I ask, has any of this story to do with you, Mrs Lowery?'

'Mr Pharaoh is a friend of mine,' said Maggie. 'We have been walking out for a while now, and he wanted to tell me about himself.'

'That's as maybe,' said Jessie, using the curiously formal slow conversation to gather her thoughts. 'But it doesn't explain what you and I could possibly have to talk about.'

'I was shocked by what he told me,' said Maggie. 'Not only did you give him away, to strangers, when he was just born, but then you rejected him when he found you again, all those years later.'

'They were not strangers, Mrs Lowery. I made a mistake as a young woman, and took the consequences of that. It was wartime, long before you were born. You cannot judge my actions.'

'They weren't family,' said Maggie. 'Family is different. They were strangers.'

'They gave John a good home, better than I could have done.' Jessie felt herself being drawn into a conversation she was not prepared to have with this woman, whoever she was. 'You are a stranger to me, Mrs Lowery, and I do not wish to discuss this matter with you.'

'I'm sure you don't,' said Maggie. 'Don't think you can frighten me, Miss Whelan, with your posh job and your schooling. Your son came to find you and you turned him away.'

'I wasn't sure …' Jessie began, wondering if there was any point in denying that John was her son, when this woman appeared to know all about it. As she hesitated, Maggie interrupted.

'You made 'im keep quiet about it.'

'I did no such thing,' Jessie could feel herself rising to the bait. 'I did not seek John out. He found me, and when he did, I wasn't sure what to do. It was his suggestion that we pass him – that we tell people that he is my nephew. I agreed and the arrangement has been satisfactory for both us, until now.'

'Satisfactory?' Maggie raised her voice. 'What kind of word is that, about family, about a lad you gave birth to, for God's sake?'

'There's no need to blaspheme,' said Jessie.

'Don't patronise me,' Maggie was shouting now. 'You've made the man lie, all these years, about who 'e is and where 'e came from. It hasn't been "satisfactory" for 'im, I can tell you. He hates it, 'e told me so. And I couldn't believe it. What kind of mother are you, to treat 'im like that?'

Jessie turned away, wishing that this woman would just go away and leave her alone. What would happen if she just told her to leave? She might go to the shop, anywhere, and just start talking. That couldn't happen. If the truth had to come out, it would be on her own terms, not some screaming redhead from God knows where. Maybe it was blackmail.

Jessie needed to put herself back in charge.

'Mrs Lowery, I suggest we calm down, and talk about this matter sensibly, if we truly need to talk about it all. I'm still at a loss to understand why you've come all this way to find me. You're not from here, or I would know you.'

'No I'm not. You may not even know that Mr Pharaoh lives in

Sandwith, and I live in Kells, with my family.' Maggie knew she was shouting but she didn't care.

'Please don't raise your voice in my house,' said Jessie. 'I think we should sit down in the front room and talk. Can I offer you a cup of tea?'

'No, thank you.' The instinct for politeness was strong, and Maggie could not avoid the customary response.

Jessie turned and led the way through to the small sitting room at the front of the schoolhouse, looking out towards the lane. She sat down in the middle of the sofa, leaving Maggie to perch awkwardly on the higher chair by the door, still wearing her heavy jacket. Jessie hoped that the woman would feel uncomfortable and leave quickly. The conversation was ridiculous, but she dare not antagonise her too much.

'You say that you and Mr Pharaoh, John, are "walking out"?'

'Yes we are. I've been a widow since 1942, for your information.'

'And why did John feel he had to tell you this story? Does he know that you are here?' Jessie wondered whether John had asked this firebrand to come to Newton, as some kind of punishment.

'John doesn't know. And he told me because he said he'd lied for long enough and he was tired of it. I could tell that he'd never stood up for 'imself as far as you were concerned and I was angry about that.'

'I still don't understand,' said Jessie. 'Whatever you may have heard is between John and myself. It doesn't concern anyone else, least of all someone,' she hesitated, 'someone like you.'

'What do you mean, someone like me? I'm a respectable woman, and I'm very fond of your son and he of me. He wants something from you, and you've denied him, so I'm here to say what he dare not. I don't want to marry a man who's pushed around by 'is mother like you're doing.'

'Marriage?' said Jessie. The idea surprised and horrified her. John married, to this woman with the flaming hair and the flaming temper? 'You and John are to be married? When?'

'Well, no,' said Maggie. 'But we might, and –'

'Mrs Lowery.' Now it was Jessie's turn to interrupt. She chose her words with care and blessed her quick mind and fluent mouth. 'Let me understand this correctly. You and my son are "walking out" whatever that means. He has told you that I am his mother, and a few other details, and he doesn't know that you are here. I know John, perhaps even better than you do. He would be mortified if he could hear and see you here with me. He respects me, and the decisions I have made, and he would never threaten and shout in this way. I think you should leave now. I will put this outburst down to your youth and some misguided urge to protect my son. I would advise to mention nothing of this to him, and I shall do the same.'

She stood up, and gestured towards the front door, hoping that the unwelcome visitor would give up and leave. Maggie looked defiant but said nothing.

'I assume you came down here on the bus, or was it the train?' Jessie continued in her best schoolteacher voice. 'In either case, they are frequent and you should not be too inconvenienced if I ask you to leave. We have nothing more to talk about.'

'I'm not done yet,' said Maggie, standing up and finding her posh voice again. She was a head taller than Jessie. 'I want to make it very clear to you, Miss Whelan, that I will support John through thick and thin about this. He wants to stand up for himself at long last, and I will stand beside him. He is a fine man, and he deserves better from you. He will decide when and how to tell people the truth about 'imself, and about you. He's past caring what that might do to you. You have made these choices, all along, to suit yourself, to protect your precious respectability. You're not the only one with pride. We have it too, my family and me. We will welcome John into our family, without strings, something you have never done. You're a selfish woman, Jessie Whelan, heartless. Maybe it's a good thing that John wasn't raised by you.'

For once, Jessie could find no response.

'I'll see myself out,' said Maggie. 'You needn't worry about me telling folk what I know. That's not up to me. But John will, and about time too. You ask 'im. He may not know I'm here but he'll agree with every word I've said. I'll leave you to your precious job and all that goes with it. The whole thing is built on sand and you know it. Good afternoon.'

Maggie let herself out of the front door of the schoolhouse and banged the door shut behind her. In the next cottage, just across the lane, a curtain twitched.

Jessie sat still for several minutes after her uninvited guest had gone. She was angry that her home had been invaded by this harridan. How dare she? Surely John would not agree with what she said. He was a polite, thoughtful young man. What could he be doing with this working-class widow with Viking hair? She felt unsteady as she went back into the kitchen to make some tea and noticed that her hands were trembling. The ritual of tea-making calmed her. It had been upsetting, but no real harm done. The woman had said she would not tell people, and she believed her. But what about John? Should she tell him what had happened, what had been said? No, she decided as her rational mind reasserted itself. John and this woman could not possibly be serious enough to marry, that was inconceivable. It would blow over, and John might never know. The best plan was to pretend that this nasty half hour had never happened. Jessie knew about pretence. She was good at it. She would brush her hair, change into her second-best dress and shoes, and accompany her doctor friend to the pictures, apparently without a care in the world.

On the bus back to Kells, Maggie felt exhilarated. She still wasn't sure why she had wanted so much to do what she had just done. But it had felt good, to stand in that woman's own house and say what she wanted to say. This was the woman who had twisted a good man round her little finger and she, Maggie, the screen lass who left school at thirteen, she'd found the right words and they had sounded fine. She recalled it all in her mind, realising as she did so that John and his mother didn't even look alike. It was funny about likeness, she thought, as the bus meandered north. We all have the same features, eyes, noses, and the same essential bits of our bodies, but the visible differences are still striking. Each of us is unique, she thought. And that's not just about how we look, it's about how we think and feel. John's mother, this contained unfeeling woman that she had just met, seemed as unlike John as was possible. He had been raised by other people, but was that what made the difference? Maggie wished she could have met John's father. She knew that he wished that, too.

One thing was very clear to her now: this tall man, with his soft hands was important to her. He liked her too, she could tell, but he seemed so shy. She needed to know what lay under that reserve. She would not tell him about today, not yet. She thought that Jessie wouldn't pursue it either, not after so many years of letting things lie. But she had no regrets about what she'd done. It felt good.

Chapter 12

It was still dark, but it was Christmas Day and Judith couldn't wait any longer. She could feel the weight of something on her feet. Then Maggie stirred next to her, holding her daughter close for a moment before she wriggled away.

'It's morning, Mam,' said the child. 'It's Christmas Day.'

Maggie looked at the little clock by the bed, then lit a candle that flickered and wavered in the cold air, before burrowing back into the bed.

'I don't think there's anything for you this year, pet.'

'There is, Mam,' said the child, pulling the lumpy stocking up towards her. 'Look!'

'Well I never,' said Maggie.

Judith was fiddling with the stocking. She pulled out an orange.

'It's an orange,' she said. 'I've seen them in books.'

'What else is in there?' said her mother.

'Some toffees.'

'Good,' said Maggie. 'Let's have one now.'

'And here's a little book, see,' said the child, 'with pictures of birds.'

'I wonder where that came from?'

'Uncle John bought it,' said Judith. Maggie smiled, pulled Judith to her and gave her a kiss.

* * *

Agnes had stuffed the turkey the night before, and she was weighing it again before putting it in the oven. If they wanted to listen to the King's speech at three, it would have to go in now. They would eat the main course, take a break while they listened to the radio, then have dessert afterwards. Perfect.

She helped herself to a sherry, just a small one. The house was quiet. Jessie was still asleep. Agnes remembered another Christmas, nine years before, when Jessie had been asleep upstairs. John had been here too, sure that Jessie was his mother and that she would love him. But it hadn't happened. Jessie had protected herself all these years, and now Agnes wasn't sure he would even come and see them this year. He had a friend, apparently, in Whitehaven. Jessie had told her no more than that. Maybe it was for the best. He was a grown man now, with his own life.

And Jessie? It was only a matter of time, Agnes was certain, before she gave up the school and the house and moved into Applegarth, where she belonged. It was what she, Agnes, had wanted and hoped for, for years, and now it was so close. By next Christmas it would be true: the two of them, living together here, enjoying each other's company every day, entertaining their friends, going on holiday, travelling together. Jessie had less money, but Agnes had plenty for both of them. She heard a creak on the floor of the bedroom above. Jessie was awake. Agnes put the bird into the oven, washed her hands, took off her apron, and made her friend a cup of special Christmas tea, with love.

* * *

Frank McSherry sat in his wheelchair in the front room of his house. They'd all been smoking since the first cups of tea three hours before, and cigarette smoke hung in the air. The front room was more crowded than usual. Violet's brother, Tom Pickthall, was visiting from his lonely digs in Bransty. The McSherry's son, Connor, and his family were at the in-laws this year, which was just as well; fitting them all in was getting harder as the children grew. Violet topped up the ale in Tom's glass, then her husband's, then John's. She and her daughter were drinking gin and lemon. Frank read out the names of fifteen men killed in the Harrington pit earlier in the month. 'Here's to 'em all,' he said. 'Could've been me, or you, Tom. Fifteen more, killed in t'bloody pits. Death traps, all of 'em, allus have been.'

'Why do you keep on working there, when it's so bad?' asked John.

'It's a job, lad,' said Tom Pickthall. 'Real money, man's work. Like going to war. You know it could kill you but it's what you 'ave to do. We all 'ave to die some'ow.'

'To 'em all,' said Frank, and they raised their glasses.

Tom drank his beer, wiped his mouth and put the glass down on the bare table.

'We're allus last up 'ere,' he said, to no one in particular. 'All them pits down south, and in Wales, nationalised already, and how long will it take 'em to get it done up 'ere?'

'And what difference when they do?' said Frank. 'Never change, these pits. Accidents'll keep 'appening, no matter who's in charge. My legs, those poor buggers in Harrington. Who's next? Could be any of us, any time.'

'For pity's sake,' said Violet. 'It's Christmas Day. Can't we talk about summat more cheerful than pits and work? Should've come to midnight mass with me and Maggie, our Tom. Father Pryce does a lovely service, teks your mind off such things.'

'He knows nowt about pits,' said Maggie. 'Can't talk about what you don't know.'

'He's a good priest,' said her mother. 'Better than some I could mention. Knows what to do.' She turned to her husband. 'Allus asks where you are, Frank,' she said.

'Tek more than 'im to get me out of the 'ouse at that time o' night,' said Frank.

''E said 'e might come to visit,' said Violet.

Frank groaned. 'You'll 'ave to stick around a bit longer, Tom. Protect me from that long streak o' –'

'Frank,' said Violet. 'That's enough.'

* * *

There were six people for Christmas lunch at Applegarth, seated comfortably round the oval table that shone with glass and silver cutlery, and the large silver gilt platters that Agnes's mother had given to her just before she died. Agnes was in charge of course, loving her role as hostess, with Jessie close beside her to help. Lionel had recovered from his stroke sufficiently to be there, although his wife had driven the new Bentley that was parked in the driveway like a royal coach. Matthew Dawson had left his car at the top of the drive, which his daughter Ann had been none too pleased about because of her new and rather delicate shoes.

Once the steaming soup was ladled into dishes and they could settle down to it, Agnes did her duty to bring the relative stranger into the conversation.

'We're so pleased you could be with us, Ann dear. You and I both spend much of our time in London, but it's so vast, isn't it? Much easier to meet people here rather than there.'

'They keep us busy at the Royal College,' said Ann, 'not much time for anything else really. And I come up to see Daddy when I have a few days clear. That's my life really, singing, working, all those essays and things. Busy, busy.'

'She's doing really well, too,' said her father. 'Aren't you, darling? Your mother would have been so proud.'

'Mummy had a fine voice,' said Ann, looking at Jessie. 'She was so talented.'

They murmured agreement. Lionel slurped his soup, and Caroline put down her spoon. 'So sorry everyone. Soup is quite a challenge, isn't it dear? Could we have a mug or a cup for Lionel, Agnes?'

In the flurry of apologies and trips to the kitchen, Jessie took the opportunity to have a good look at Ann. She was Matthew's younger daughter, training to be a singer at the Royal College of Music in London, that much she knew. Now she was wondering what her father had told her.

Matthew and Jessie had enjoyed their weekly trips to the pictures since that first time, the day of Jessie's unwelcome encounter with John's red-headed friend. Nothing more had been heard from her, as expected, but nothing from John either, which Jessie was more concerned about. Matthew had been a perfect gentleman; once or twice he had reached for her hand in the darkness of the cinema, and the kiss on the cheek at the end of the evening had become a little more prolonged, but nothing untoward. He was kind, patient, reliable and polite. Jessie admired him for those qualities. He's such a nice man, she thought.

Matthew wished he'd said more to Ann about Jessie, before today. He could feel his daughter's anxiety, and see Jessie watching, becoming more guarded. Maybe taking things so slowly had not been the best plan. Ann was not a child, and she had no right to dictate how he lived his life as a widower. But this was neither the time nor the place for dealing with any of it. They would get through this occasion, Jessie and he would continue to see each other, and enjoy each other's company, and Ann would have to come to terms with it. But not today.

'How's that nephew of yours?' Lionel's voice boomed across the room. The stroke had affected the precision of his speech, not the volume. Agnes looked up, to see how Jessie would respond.

'He's fine, thank you, Lionel. Still working hard at the Haig, running the wages office there by the sound of it, doing really well.'

'Married yet?' Lionel continued. 'Fine young filly at the table. Pity he's not here.'

Caroline coughed into her napkin. 'Now Lionel dear, that's enough,' she said. Jessie imagined he was being kicked under the table.

Ann looked down at her hands.

'Well, that boy's quite a catch,' Lionel went on, then winced and looked sharply at his wife. 'What's the matter with your legs?' he said.

Jessie lowered her head to hide a smile.

'John is a very agreeable young man,' said Caroline, trying hard to limit the damage, 'and I'm sure he'll find someone when he's ready.'

Ann looked up and spoke. 'I really don't understand why we expect everyone to be married, not these days. I'm perfectly happy on my own, and you are too, aren't you, Daddy, still grieving for Mother? Why would we want to rush into anything else?'

Matthew glanced at Ann. Jessie noticed that he looked uncomfortable. She also realised with mounting irritation that Ann's remarks were clearly aimed at her. First the Lowery woman and now this. Two young women, both apparently telling her what to do. And at the Christmas table, too. She could feel herself

111

blushing and hoped that the low light would hide it.

'I'm sure we all have our reasons for the choices we make,' she said, as carefully as she could. 'And those reasons may not be clear to anyone else, however close they are to us.'

Ann was not to be deterred. 'I'm just speaking for myself, of course, Jessie,' she went on in her refined small voice, 'and as the person who knows my father best.'

She looked around the table as if seeking agreement, but the other guests were not to be drawn.

Agnes noticed the flush on Jessie's neck. She looked at the watch on her wrist, and got to her feet.

'Matthew, if I bring the turkey in, will you carve?'

'Certainly,' he responded, hoping that Ann would stop before any more damage was done. There was indeed a necessary respite while the needs of the meal interrupted the skirmishing at the table. When Jessie went into the kitchen to help with the vegetables, Agnes closed the door and whispered,

"Has he asked you? Is that's what bothering Ann?'

'Who?' said Jessie. 'Who's asked me what?'

'You know very well, dear. Matthew, has he asked you to marry him?'

'No he has not,' said Jessie, 'and even if …'

The kitchen door opened. 'Can I help?' said Caroline, her face a picture of curiosity. Jessie picked up a dish of potatoes and left the room without a word.

Later, when Jessie and Agnes stood side by side at the sink, Agnes felt the need to break a frosty silence.

'Of course you're annoyed,' she said. 'Ann had no right to be so pointed about it, but she obviously doesn't want her father to marry again so soon.'

'Oh, really,' said Jessie. 'That young woman needs to mind her own business. I will not be dictated to. If Matthew asked me,

112

which he has not, I would make up my mind without any help from little Miss Narrow Mind, or anyone else.'

'Do you think he will ask you?' Agnes persisted.

'For heaven's sake, Agnes, let it drop, please.' Jessie threw down the tea towel she was holding and took off her apron. 'Matthew is a fine man, and has been a perfect gentleman on the few occasions when we have been out together. He has not swept me off my feet, if that's what you want to hear. I know you think I'm leading him on, but just at present, it would be nice to see a way out.'

'A way out of what?'

'Out of having no job, and nowhere to live, and being patronised by young women, and no bread, and coupons and not even having enough coal for the fire. A change would be good, and if I want to make a change, I will, no matter who may disapprove.' Jessie's voice was becoming shrill, and Agnes said nothing more.

* * *

It was late when Tom Pickthall and John walked back to Sandwith. The night was cold and clear and stars grew brighter as they walked south, away from the lights of the town. There was no space in the West Row house for Tom to sleep over, and John's offer of the spare room in his cottage had been rapidly accepted.

'You were married, weren't you, Tom?' John asked.

'Aye,' said Tom, 'I was that. She were a wonderful woman, my Honor. We were 'aving our first babby, Christmas time, 1925. She were just twenty-five 'erself, same age as century.'

'What happened?' said John.

'Summat went wrong. Midwife – well, not a proper one like, just a woman who 'elped out – she thought she knew what to do, but then we had to get the doctor, and 'e were out somewhere. By the time he got there, it were too late. Baby were dead and then Honor died, too. They couldn't save 'er. Worst night o' my life.

And every Christmas, I 'ave to remember it all over.'

John winced. 'And now I'm asking you about it. I'm very sorry, Tom. It must've been awful.'

'It 'appened in them days, lad, not like now. Doctors do more these days. Then they seemed think that some women just died in childbirth and nowt to be done. Our Vi says that if it were men who 'ave babies summat would've been done about it ages since.'

Probably true, John thought to himself. But he wanted to say more.

'Can I ask you something, Tom, about your wife?'

'I love to talk about her, lad, and don't get the chance. People think it might be too painful, so they never mention 'er.'

'Where did you meet her?'

'We were down the dance hall, the Roxy in Silloth, and she were there wi' a gang o' lasses. I liked the look of 'er, and one of 'er mates came up bold as brass and said that she liked look of me. Would never've 'appened before the war. Any road, we 'ad a dance like, and that were it.'

'How did you know you wanted to get married? How old were you?'

'Just twenty-three in the week we were wed. And she were twenty. We were nobbut kids, the pair on us. Lived wi' 'er folks for years before we got a place. Wanted kiddies right from the off, but nothing 'appened like. She 'ad a few, you know, slip-ups, but we never gave up trying. Well we weren't really trying at all, just enjoying each other, like. Then after all those years she managed to 'ang on to one, and it killed 'er. Broke me 'eart. Lost the kiddie, too, but I never knew 'im. It were my Honor I wanted. Never met anyone like 'er, before or since.'

John was listening carefully, thinking. 'D'you think there's just one person, out there, for each of us, Tom?'

'God knows, lad. I know if you find a woman you want, and

who wants you, and you're sure, you should get on wi' it. Life's short.'

They walked in silence for a while, their footsteps muffled by the muddy lanes as they dropped down towards the village and John's house.

'Is it our Maggie, the one for you?' said Tom. 'You look well together, the pair of you.'

'That's what I'm trying to work out, Tom. I think it is, but she's so, well, so much livelier than me. She'd get bored with me. And then you're stuck, stuck together. Don't think I'd ever get bored with her.'

Tom laughed. 'Not much chance o' that. It's that hair, makes 'er fiery, too.'

They reached the house. It was cold inside and they kept their heavy coats on and enjoyed the remains of a bottle of whisky before heading off to bed.

'I reckon you should just ask 'er, John,' said Tom, holding the empty glass in his hand as if to warm himself in its glow, 'If she don't want you, she'll say so. She's been wed before, knows 'er mind where that's concerned.'

'What was he like, her Isaac?'

'Shouldn't speak ill of the fallen, but 'e were a waste o' space, that man. Allus sad when a young man dies, don't get me wrong, but she were better off without 'im. He were nobbut a lad 'imself. Home on leave once, just for a few days and most of them 'e were pissed as a newt. Then 'e were off again and that were the last we saw of 'im.'

'Has Maggie had, you know, boyfriends since then?'

'Could've, fine looking lass like that, but I don't reckon she 'as. You know what they're like, them McSherrys, talking all the time. I would've 'eard – 'eard about you fast enough.'

'Me?' said John. 'What did you hear? When?'

115

'Months ago, after you were at th'ouse and that 'am fell through the ceiling. Our Violet was bothered about you not being a Catholic. She and Maggie 'ad a bit of a to-do about it. Frank reckoned right off that you fancied our Maggie and she could do a lot worse, that's what 'e said.'

John blushed. So much for discretion. 'He was right about me fancying her,' he said, laughing. 'I thought she was the most gorgeous thing I'd ever seen. Still do.'

'So what you waiting for, lad? You're a reet good catch, she'd be mad to turn you down. Good job, nice little 'ouse.'

'That's the problem. I want her to love me, not the job and the house.'

'Get o'er it, ' said Tom, putting the glass down and pushing himself with difficulty out of the low chair. 'You think too much.'

'That's what Maggie says.'

'And she's bright, too,' said Tom. 'Life's too short. Grab it while you can.'

'What about the Catholic thing? Does it matter?'

'Not to our Maggie. But Vi? Not so sure about that. She wants our Maggie to be 'appy, and that means 'aving a proper wedding, and the priest, all that. You might have to go and see Father whatsisname, but I can't see it being a problem. If Maggie wants you, she'll get you, church or no church. She's in no rush, I reckon, not after the last time. But don't wait too long, lad.'

Chapter 13

New Year's Day. The sky was clear, and light in the east just a gleam on the horizon, catching the white of snow and frost on the tops of the mountains The freezing air was perfectly still. In the barn behind John's house in Sandwith, beasts were awake and chewing, creating tiny wreaths of steam. John woke suddenly. He knew there was someone in the house: a faint sound, a draught. He sat up on his elbows. He had no recollection of going to bed. He was in his underwear and his head ached.

'Hello?' he called out, looking around for his clothes and boots. He felt trapped. The bedroom door was closed, and he could hear the stairs creaking. He pulled the blankets up to his neck with both hands and watched as the door opened slowly.

Maggie stood in the doorway, looking across at him. At the sight of her he blew out the breath he'd been holding and fell back onto the bed. 'I thought you were a burglar or summat,' he said, turning his head to look at her. She hadn't moved, still standing in the doorway, a long dark coat almost to her ankles and a bright green shawl pulled up over her head. She was smiling at him.

'Happy New Year,' she said.

John sat up again, clutching the blankets up to his chin. 'What time is it? How did you get in?'

'It's early. No one else in our 'ouse was going to be up for

117

hours, and it was so clear and calm. I was going to walk to St Bees Head, the way we walked that first time, and when I came past your 'ouse I wondered if you'd be up. I went to knock on t'door and it was open, so I came in.'

'The door was open?'

'Not wide open, but not locked.'

'Who left it open?' He was puzzled and his head was protesting.

'You look terrible,' she said. 'What did you do last night?'

He struggled to remember. 'I wanted a quiet evening. Can't manage all that New Year's Eve noise.' A shadow of memory flitted across his brain and he groaned. 'I must've dozed off downstairs before midnight. Then Albert from next door came in and said I had to do their first-foot and dragged me out. They gave me a piece of coal and I had to cross the threshold, and have a drink. Then someone else came and said I had to do it for them, across the green. It's supposed to be someone tall and dark apparently, or that's what they said. Those folk gave me a drink as well, and then some other people arrived with a bottle of whisky, and I can't remember much after that ... I must have woken up when you opened the door.'

'You were so drunk, they must have put you to bed. Look,' she said, pointing to the little chair by the window, 'there are your boots and your clothes, all piled up neatly.'

'Oh God,' said John, lying down again and turning his head away from her laughter. 'Someone must have undressed me. How humiliating. I'll have to move away.'

'It was New Year's Eve,' she said. She walked over, picked up his clothes and put them on the end of the bed. 'You got drunk, it doesn't matter. Just shows that your neighbours like you. Best thing you can do now is get your body out of that bed, put your clothes on, and come for a walk with me. That'll clear your head. I'll make tea. I brought you some stew from last night if you're hungry. I was going to leave it on the doorstep, like a present from the fairies. Don't be long.'

She left the room, pulling the door shut behind her. John rubbed his face and forced himself to sit up, swung his legs round and put both feet on the cold floor. He fumbled into his clothes, his heart racing, and pulled at his hair as he went down the stairs. Maggie was standing by the sink, her back to him, and then turned as he walked slowly towards her. She smiled at him, put out her hand and rubbed the stubble on his chin. It was too much. John pulled her towards him, leaning his face into her warm neck, feeling the softness of her hair, the warmth of her body as she clung to him. 'Maggie, Maggie,' he whispered. Suddenly he was overcome. He found her mouth and kissed her urgently, feeling her response. By the time he realised what was happening to his body it was too late and he could not hold back. He buried his face in the collar of her coat as the orgasm shook him.

'Hush, John, lovely boy, it's alright.' Maggie stroked his head and held him tightly as he leaned against her, pressing her up against the sink. They stood locked together for a while, as she stroked his hair. He raised his head a little and wiped tears from his eyes with his hand. She pushed him gently away and raised his face, kissing his damp skin.

'It's alright,' she said. 'It happens. You'd better go and find some clean clothes.'

'I'm so sorry,' he said. 'I never … Oh God. What a mess.'

'Go on,' she said. 'I'll still be here. No rush.'

'I'm sorry,' he said again, not looking at her as he stumbled back up the stairs.

When he came down again, she was sitting at the little table, steam rising from the mug in her hands. The kettle was hissing on the range.

'You want some tea?' she said. 'Sit down, I'll make it.'

119

John sat miserably on the little chair. He'd made a complete fool of himself last night, and now this. What must she think of him, a grown man doing that, like a boy who can't control himself? He was ashamed. She put the tea down on the table in front of him and watched him. He could not look at her.

He heard her say, 'Is it me you want, or is it just, you know …?'

'Oh God,' was all he could manage in response, turning his head further away from her.

'Talk to me,' she said. 'Tell me what you want.'

'I want you, more than I can stand. Look at me. Like a kid. I think about you all the time, dream about you, night after night. Seeing you standing there, and when you touched me, I …'

'Why didn't you say?' she said gently. 'I'm a grown woman, been married, remember. I'm not about to be shocked by 'owt you could tell me. Screen lasses know it all, hadn't you heard?'

'That's it,' he said. 'You kept quiet about that, for fear of what I would think about you. And then you told me. Then I thought … if I told you that I wanted you, you might think it was because I thought, you know …' He was hopelessly tangled and lost. No more words would come.

'You thought I'd be insulted? Oh John. All these weeks, you've never tried anything. I thought you liked me, but you must be saving yourself or summat. Maybe you are.'

'I don't know what I'm doing,' said John, turning to look into her face. 'I don't know about women. They've always been a mystery, saying one thing, meaning something else, laughing at me. All my life, since school, I've tried to work out what they wanted, and never guessed right. And I was afraid of losing you. I can't lose you, Maggie.'

'You've got me,' she said. 'You've had me since that first day when I saw you in the screen shed, the dog day. There was summat about you, even then. But I couldn't do 'owt about it. It was just luck you saw us at the rugby, I couldn't believe it. '

'Why didn't you say anything to me?'

"I wasn't sure what to say. I've been married, and it wasn't good. I've Judith to think of. I 'ave to be careful. And I wasn't sure how you felt, you've never even put your arm round me.'

'What are we going to do?'

'We'll keep it dark, whatever we do,' she said. 'We'll carry on walking out, not give folk the chance to gossip. And we'll be clever. You know how to lie, after all these years with your mam. We'll lie until we're ready to tell folk. We can be together here, if we're careful. We need time.'

John sipped his tea. More lies. He had to tell her something else.

'I've never done it,' he said suddenly. 'I've never had a woman.'

'Oh sweetheart,' she said. She stood up and took off her coat. 'Bring your tea,' she said. 'We're going upstairs.'

When he woke for the second time that day, the sun had reached its low zenith and was on its way down again. Everything felt different. She had helped him, patiently. She had let him into her, inside her warm body. He had felt the smooth skin at the base of her spine, held her full breasts in his hands. He couldn't believe it. He couldn't believe that married people did this, all the time, every day, whenever they felt like it. He wondered how he could ever look at her again. She had said nothing before she left. He lay still and thought about what to do.

It was dark when he was ready. He had drunk more tea, and a pint of water, and eaten the stew that she had brought. There was gingerbread left in the tin and he had eaten that too, in one big piece, scattering crumbs over the table and the floor. The kitchen was a mess, and he didn't even notice. The night was still and clear when he wheeled the bike out of the shed behind the house and set off north. He had to see her. He had to know what she would do, and say.

121

At the house in West Row there was so much noise that he had to knock on the front window before anyone heard him. It was Tom who let him in, and he called over his shoulder as he did so, 'It's our John.'

'Happy New Year!' shouted a chorus of voices from the front room. The house was blue with cigarette smoke that caught in John's throat and made his eyes prickle. Maggie took John's hand, squeezing it as she did so. 'No drink for you,' she said, 'not after last night.' She led him into the front room where Frank McSherry was holding court from his wheelchair. He shook John's hand.

'Reet good craic last night, our John,' said Frank. 'We missed you.'

'John was busy first-footing round Sandwith,' said Maggie. 'He's no idea who put 'im to bed.'

John heard the shouts that greeted this news, but he didn't care what they said. She was here, she was smiling and holding his hand. It would be all right.

'I can hear Mam shouting for me,' said Maggie, close to his ear. 'I won't be a minute.' She squeezed out of the room and into the kitchen.

'Shut the door,' said Violet. She turned towards her daughter, holding the back of a chair.

'Where did you get to today, creeping out before we were up? Our Judith was asking and I didn't know what to tell 'er.'

'I told you, Mam, I went for a walk.'

'Walk, did you, well I can guess where to. You've been with that man, 'aven't you? I can tell just by looking at 'im. Cat that got the cream, that look is. And you, too, look at you. You can fool the rest of them but you can't fool me, I'm your mam.'

'Yes I went to John's. I took 'im some stew, had a cuppa.'

'You 'ad more than a cuppa. What are you thinking of? You're nearly thirty, girl, wi' a bairn and working on t'screens. Might as well put a cross on your forehead like an "untouchable" – or whatever they did.'

'I knew it,' said Maggie. 'Just because John's not a good Catholic boy. Well I'm a grown woman and I'll make up me own mind, thank you, with no 'elp from you.'

'Grown woman who lives wi' er mam and dad.' Violet raised her voice, and then lowered it again quickly. 'It's a proper man you need, to give you a home and the bairn a father. He'll never marry you if you give it 'im for nowt. It'll get around, mark my words.'

Maggie copied the fierce whisper. 'If we want to marry, we will, and don't try to stop us. If the blessed Father Pryce doesn't like it you can both tek a running jump. I did the whole Catholic thing last time and landed up wi' that Isaac.'

'He were alright,' said her mother. 'Good family.'

'My arse,' said Maggie. 'You 'ad no idea what 'e were like and nor did I till it were too late. This one's different, and don't you dare try and mess it up.'

'We'll see. I'll 'ave to tell Father Pryce, Maggie, if you don't.'

'For God's sake, Mam, this is 1947 not 1847. I don't need your permission, nor any bloody priest.'

She closed the kitchen door with more than necessary force on her way back into the hall. John was standing by the half open front door, taking deep breaths of the cold night air to calm his itching lungs. Maggie took down their coats from the high pegs on the wall of the passage.

'Now we are going for a walk,' she said. 'Come on.'

CHAPTER 14

THE START OF SCHOOL IN JANUARY was always a flat time, and this year the gloom of midwinter settled on Jessie more quickly and more deeply than usual. She felt obliged to live mostly at the schoolhouse, aware of the resentment from Alan Crompton about her staying at Applegarth and the schoolhouse being left empty. Even Grace Crompton, Alan's wife, who had previously been obsequiously polite, cut her dead in the shop, quite deliberately and in full view of Newton's women who were queuing patiently for their ration of sausage.

When she saw Gideon Barker and Alan Crompton talking together at the school gate one dark morning, she guessed what it was about, and braced herself.

The vicar's voice grated on her as it always did. 'Mr Crompton and I would like to talk to you, if we may, Jessie – now – before the children arrive.'

Jessie looked mildly at the two men but said nothing. She led them into her room, turned to face them and remained standing. She did not want them to look down at her. Mr Barker adjusted the collar of his black overcoat. Mr Crompton stood behind the vicar, peeping at Jessie over his shoulder.

'How long have you been at this school, Jessie?' the vicar asked, although she knew that he already knew the answer.

'As I told you before,' she said. 'I came here from Liverpool in 1925, and then they asked me to become the headmistress'

'They?'

'The Board. They told me they couldn't get anyone else.'

'Ah,' said the vicar.

'Mr Crompton joined me here in 1934.'

'1935,' said Alan quickly. 'Just after I finished my training. Then I went to the navy when the war broke out.'

'To serve your country,' the vicar added, half turning towards him.

'Have you something to say to me, Mr Barker?' Jessie asked, trying to interrupt this tedious chronology.

He flushed. She knew he didn't like her, but she didn't care.

'Now that Mr Crompton has returned,' he said, 'we would like you to consider your position.' Jessie saw Alan Crompton's head nod in agreement.

'My position?' she said, pulling herself up, slightly taller than either of the men who confronted her.

'Yes,' Gideon Barker ploughed on. 'You are a single woman, living alone in the schoolhouse, while Mr Crompton here, with a wife and family, is obliged to rent a cottage down near the river.'

I knew it, thought Jessie.

'The house has always been available to the headteacher,' she said, 'since the school was first established.'

'And now things are different,' said the vicar. 'Times change, Jessie, and we must adapt. This is a new world, after the war. Men who have served their country deserve –'

'What?' said Jessie. 'What do they deserve, beyond our thanks?'

'Homes and jobs,' he said. 'Homes and jobs.' Alan Crompton's head bobbed again.

'Do you mean my home and my job, by any chance?' asked Jessie, without surprise.

'Well,' said the vicar, 'that's what we want to discuss.'

'Gentlemen,' said Jessie. 'The children will be arriving very soon. This is neither the time nor the place to discuss such matters, and I do not intend to do so. I take it you have alerted the Board to your concerns?'

'I have indeed,' said the vicar.

'I am prepared to talk to you further, Mr Barker,' said Jessie, 'but only to you, not to Mr Crompton. I hope that is understood.'

Alan Crompton began to speak, but the vicar turned and held his arm.

'I will represent Mr Crompton's views,' he said.

'I'm sure you will,' said Jessie.

Even so, when Mr Barker returned at the end of the school day later in the week, Alan Crompton seemed determined to remain in the room, and the vicar made no move to stick to their agreement. Jessie knew they had been planning what to say to her. She sat down this time, in the largest chair, leaving the two men to perch on the small chairs used by the children. Even before they had settled themselves she began to say what she had rehearsed.

'I have served this school well, I believe,' she said. 'There have been no complaints from parents. I would know if they were unhappy. The children of this village read and write as well as any of their peers in this area. The school inspectors have confirmed this and I'm sure you're aware of that too, Mr Barker.'

'The Board do not believe that you are doing a poor job, Jessie,' said Gideon Barker. Jessie hated the whining Yorkshire accent. 'But that's not what we're here to discuss. There's an issue of justice at stake here.'

'Justice?' she said, amazed at the man's pomposity. 'I would have thought that justice would support my remaining here.'

'We've come through a war,' the vicar went on. 'Men like Mr Crompton here risked their lives for this country and now find themselves with nowhere to live, nowhere fit for a growing family. People in London are having to take over empty houses just to put a roof over their heads.'

'But the schoolhouse isn't empty, Mr Barker, is it? I live there, by right, as the headmaster of the school did before me.'

'The headmaster had a family,' said the vicar, with unmistakeable emphasis. 'You live here alone.'

'If I were a single man, would you be saying this?' she asked.

Jessie noticed a look that passed between the two men.

'There are other problems in the school,' said Alan, shifting his weight on the uncomfortable chair. 'The older children need a firmer hand.'

'A man's hand, you mean,' she said, 'preferably on the back of their legs.'

'Mr Crompton has every right to chastise the children if he sees fit,' said the vicar, taking up his turn again. 'We stand in the place of the parents, and many parents believe their children need proper discipline.'

'Is that what your experience has taught you both?' she said. 'Did we fight this war for the right to beat our children?'

'The fact remains, Jessie, that it's time to make some changes. We hope that you will accept this fact and make your plans to move on.'

'And if I don't wish to "move on" as you put it?' said Jessie, realising that if they were determined to see her go, the Board would be unlikely to interfere.

'Then I will ask the Board to dismiss you. There are other schools where such decisions have already been made, since our fighting men have returned to work. I have no doubt that they will agree, however reluctantly.'

Jessie's urge to fight was strong, but suddenly she felt herself falter. Her secret past wasn't safe any more. Again she felt the flutter of uncertainty, the unravelling that had started with John and was now spreading into her work; but old habits of self-control served her well. She stood and looked at the vicar, hoping that this would make Alan Crompton feel like the interloper he was.

'I shall take as much time as I need to consider what you have said to me, Mr Barker. After so many years of service to the school I will not be rushed or bullied, and you will have to wait for my decision. If necessary, I shall write to the Board myself, and I expect that you, and your colleague, will keep this conversation to yourselves in the meantime. Please close the door on your way out.'

Gideon Barker stood for a moment, saying nothing, before he turned abruptly and left the room, with Alan Crompton right behind him. When Jessie heard the school door close, she breathed out slowly and sat down. Her knees were shaking slightly and she felt sick. She sat on the hard chair quite motionless for several minutes before gathering her things and seeking the solace of the schoolhouse.

As so many times before, the routines of her own home calmed her. She had loved this house from the very first, revelling in the privacy and independence it provided. The house was quite small, but bigger than her childhood home in Barrow, with two rooms downstairs, two bedrooms above, piped water in the kitchen and a toilet in the yard. The small garden to the side was enough to grow some food of her own, to eke out the rations of the past few years. The garden was hers, the house was hers, the job was hers, and she had defended them with fierce determination. Once before, during the lean years of the 1930s she had felt threatened, as women teachers were being sacked up and down the coast to give the jobs to men with families. Lionel Leadbetter had stood up for her then, but he was gone. During the war her job had felt safer, but now the men were back. Two of them had just told her that she should give way to them, and they would probably get what they wanted.

Jessie drank the cup of tea she always had at the end of her working day and thought about the possibility of leaving. Later this year she would be fifty years old; she had been working to support herself since her mother had thrown her out when she was barely more than a girl. She was a good teacher, she knew that, but was that all there was, for the rest of her working life? It would be easy, and rewarding in its way, but the thought suddenly appalled her.

The new government was making change but what might a new regime look like, if it ever happened? Sometimes it felt as if the rest of England were another country, where things happened that never reached this isolated place. She could not just sit and wait for things to change. Leaving the school could be an opportunity, but leaving the house would be a wrench. Applegarth was always there, and had been her second home for several years, more so since Agnes had been spending so much time in London. She had her own bedroom there, big enough for an armchair by the fire and her own radio and her books. But it was still Agnes's house.

Even so, when Jessie weighed her options she knew what would happen, whether she wanted it not. Without the protection of the vicar, she would not be able to keep her job and her house. If both were to be forfeit, she should surrender them with as much dignity as possible and make it look like a positive decision on her part. Even before Agnes's usual weekend phone call from London, Jessie had made up her mind.

'I'll make them wait,' she told her friend. 'They'll have to find another teacher, but that will mean some other man can get a job whether they're suitable or not. If that's what they want for the village, it's out of my hands. If I go at Easter, that gives everyone plenty of time.'

'Whatever you decide, dear,' said Agnes. 'There's room at Applegarth for you to have all your things around you.'

Even over the crackly line from London, Jessie could hear the delight in Agnes's voice.

'Have you told John?' Agnes ventured to ask.

'No I haven't, not yet. He's busy I know, and I don't hear much from him.'

'Such a pity we didn't see him at Christmas,' said Agnes, and Jessie heard a question in her voice. Jessie had said nothing to Agnes about her encounter with Mrs Lowery from Kells.

There was a long pause. Jessie wondered if they'd been cut off, and then Agnes continued. 'Does this mean that you'll be able to tell people about ... about John?'

The old lie about John had not even crossed Jessie's mind.

'One thing at a time, I think,' was all she replied, and Agnes knew she could say no more.

* * *

'Jessie wants to meet me,' John read aloud. He had picked up the letter from inside the front door and opened it before he snuggled back into the makeshift bed on the floor of his kitchen, which was warmer than his room upstairs.

'What about?' said Maggie, feeling suddenly sick about her encounter with Jessie. She must have been mad to go down there without telling him.

'She doesn't say, just says she's coming up to Whitehaven shopping on Saturday and will I meet her in the market café at two. That's all.'

He pulled her towards him, absorbing the heat from her body.

'Maybe it's about the school,' he said. 'I don't think she gets on

130

well with the teacher, the one who was in the navy. If she leaves, it wouldn't matter who knows about her and me.'

'Would you tell people?'

'Most of the people who matter know about it already. I'm glad I told you when I did.'

'She didn't want you to, though,' said Maggie.

'But I told you anyway,' he said, 'so it doesn't matter.'

'When will I meet her?' Maggie was glad he couldn't see her face.

'Whenever you want to,' he said. 'Don't bother about it now.' Jessie was fading from his mind, along with everything else.

'I've got a lot of catching up to do,' he said, shifting his body onto hers.

* * *

John was still thinking about Maggie's body as he waited for Jessie at the appointed time. The market café was as busy as ever on Saturday afternoon, although most of the shops had closed at noon. He ordered a cup of tea, just to occupy the table while he waited. When she arrived, they ordered more tea and scones.

'It's been a while, John,' she said, checking who was sitting close to them. 'How are you managing in this cold?'

'The house is freezing, like everyone's,' he said, 'and I'm sleeping in the kitchen by the range. Work's difficult with more men off than normal, but not as bad as it is down south, by the sound of it. Seems strange that they've got all that snow and we haven't got any, not yet at least. Is the schoolhouse warm enough?'

'That's what I want to tell you about,' she said, pouring tea from a brown teapot. 'I won't be living there much longer.'

'What's happened?'

'I've told the Board I'm leaving at Easter. That means I'll lose the schoolhouse, and I'm moving into Applegarth with Agnes.'

'Goodness,' said John. 'That's a bit sudden, isn't it, after all this time?' His mind was already working on the implications.

Jessie lowered her voice. 'The vicar couldn't wait to get me out,' she said. 'He never said a word about all I've done for the place. He even said I should get out straight away. He has the empathy of a block of wood.' She knocked lightly on the little table where they sat, leaning forward like conspirators.

John said nothing for a few moments, as he spread something that wasn't butter and something else that resembled jam on his scone and ate it slowly.

'Will you tell people now about – you know …?'

'I suppose I might,' she said, looking at him, trying to determine what he knew. 'What about your friend? Did you tell her?'

John looked away.

'Yes, I did,' he said. 'I had to be honest with her. Secrets do damage. She hasn't told anyone, it's no one's business but ours.'

'Yes,' said Jessie. Clearly he didn't know what the woman had done.

'Is it serious, with this friend of yours? What do her family think?'

'We're not going to discuss that here,' said John.

They finished their tea. Jessie was walking down to catch the bus back to Newton and John walked with her, carrying some of her bags. They were a little early, and John was about to leave, when she said suddenly, 'She came to see me, you know.'

John stared at his mother. 'Who did?'

'Your friend, Mrs Lowery.'

'When?'

'Just after Armistice Day.'

'In November?'

'Yes, she came to the school.'

'Are you sure it was her?'

132

'Oh, yes, I'm sure,' said Jessie. 'She was very clear about that, Mrs Lowery, from Kells.'

'What did she say?'

'She told me that she knew about it, about you. And that I had treated you shamefully, that was the gist of it.'

John couldn't speak. Two months. Right through Christmas, and New Year, and the hours in each other's arms, she'd not said anything about it.

'Why?' he asked. Jessie shrugged. 'No,' he said, 'I mean, why are you telling me now?'

'It's clear that you didn't know, and I think you should. Secrets do damage, you said it yourself.'

John turned away, angry, disgusted, humiliated. He didn't wait for the approaching bus to arrive. Jessie watched him walk quickly up the street, regretting what she had said, and knowing it could not be undone.

John didn't notice the Newton bus pass him before he walked up the hill by the harbour. The winter day was clear and blue, and bitterly cold. The sea glittered beyond the outer harbour wall. Behind him the western fells sparkled white but for once he didn't look or care. He didn't care what Maggie had said to his mother, when or how. What he cared about was that she hadn't told him. She knew how sick he was of deception and how it had corroded his life. He had trusted her. Now he knew it had been too good, too easy with Maggie. Life wasn't like that. You don't just meet someone, fall in love, take them to bed and live happy ever after. He'd been a fool.

Maggie was in the garden with Violet as he turned the corner into West Row. The grime of the Saturday shift had been washed off and the two women were looking at the frozen ground and the blackened remains of the sprouts.

Maggie saw him coming. He didn't hear what passed between

them, but Violet went into the house after the briefest of acknowledgements.

'I thought you were going into town,' Maggie said, instantly aware that something was badly wrong.

'We need to talk,' he said, taking her arm.

She pulled free, glanced at the window of the house, and they walked down the street onto a frost-hardened path that led towards the quarry.

'She told me,' he said, turning to face her when they were out of sight of the houses. 'She said you went to see her.'

Maggie knew it was no use denying it.

'I wanted to see her myself, to make her realise the damage she's done.'

'You should have told me. I could have taken you to see her.'

'But you wouldn't, would you?' Maggie hesitated. She could see how angry he was. She could fight back, or crumble and tell him how much she regretted what she'd done.

'You did whatever she wanted,' she countered, 'right from the start, as far as I can see. I don't have to kowtow to her. She gave her baby away. I kept mine. That was her choice, and she had to know the damage she's done.'

'That's not for you to say. It's my business, not yours.'

'But you never did say, did you?' Maggie was warming to her own defence. 'You never stood up for yourself.'

'So you did it for me?'

'Aye, I did. And it felt good.'

'Not to me, it doesn't.' John was trying not to shout. 'It makes me feel like a kid, and you the big sister who fights my battles. That's not good, not for me. And all this time, for weeks, Maggie, you've lied to me.'

'I've not lied, I've just not told you the truth.'

He put his hands to his head.

134

'How could you?' he said, his words freezing in the air between them. 'All this time, when we've been so … so close. You've kept this to yourself, like a blanket between us. Secrets do damage, that's what I said to Jessie and she flung it back at me. You've put secrets between us.'

'And what about you?' she said, trying to stop herself saying more, but failing. 'I need a man who can stand up for 'imself, who's not afraid of 'is bloody mother. Go away and think on that John Pharaoh, and don't come 'ere again until you 'ave.'

She stood in front of him, defiant, miserable.

For the second time that day, John walked away, his mind in turmoil, his future crashing to the hard ground.

Chapter 15

THE COLD CONTINUED. For three weeks John did nothing except work, find enough food to make and eat his evening meal, keep his house tidy, read his climbing books and sleep. Maggie had given him an ultimatum, and he didn't know what to do. Part of him wanted to say whatever she wanted, just to get her back. But he'd done that once before, with Jessie, and Maggie condemned him for it.

The choices tumbled around in his brain. He'd been alone before, for most of his life, and the routines were familiar and comforting in a way. When the long winter ended he would go back to his climbing and his mates, free from concern for anyone else. Doing nothing seemed the best way out. He and Maggie worked different shift times and could have gone for weeks without overlapping on the way into the pit, or in the yard. The screen lasses didn't mix much with others, and being in the office set John apart.

It was just bad luck that he caught sight of her one afternoon as he was crossing the yard and glimpsed the familiar shape, even more muffled than usual but unmistakeable all the same. He could picture what lay below the coat, apron, clogs, and shawl, and turned quickly away so that she wouldn't see him. What might she do? Point at him, laugh, call him a mummy's boy? If he gave in and went crawling back to her, that would make it worse. He had to show that he was stronger than she thought, even though her absence hurt him terribly.

The snow that had immobilised the south of England for weeks was slowly moving north. Wind was blowing bitter from the north and east, and snow would not be long, everyone knew that. As the wind increased in ferocity, John thought about the draughts in the West Row House, and pictured the new hookie rug, Fred's gift to Maggie, pushed up against the front door, wasting its beauty on the mundane task of keeping the house a little less cold.

Shopping for a new shovel on a Saturday morning early in March took John to St Bees rather than to Whitehaven, to avoid the risk of seeing any of the McSherrys. He went to the Crown for a pint before walking home, and there at the bar next to him was a man he'd not seen for a while.

Peter Sim was the innkeeper from the pub at Ganthwaite. In the days before the motorbike, John had ridden up the valley on Peter's wagon a few times and they had found themselves in agreement about the issues of the day.

'You used to stop wi' Hannah and Fred, didn't you?' asked Peter. 'Up at mill?'

'Aye,' said John. 'Go up there every now and then, just to see they're alreet.'

'Folk 'elp 'em out, when it gets bad like this,' said Peter. 'Someone in t'pub last week were saying Fred's been badly like.'

John put down his pint. 'What sort of badly?'

'Pains in 'is chest, or summat. Hannah wanted to get doctor but 'e wouldn't 'ear of it. Stubborn auld sod.'

John hadn't heard about it, but there were no phones up the valley, and neither of them was likely to write to him. They probably knew that word would get around, like it always did. Fred always said that if you sneezed up the valley everybody in the county knew you had a cold.

'So 'as the doctor been up?' asked John. 'Is it serious?'

'God knows,' said Peter. 'I haven't seen t'doctor's car.'

With an empty weekend stretching ahead of him, John decided to take the bike up the valley before the forecast snow finally came. He knew that Hannah and Fred had good neighbours, but he needed to be sure that they were all right.

He called at the shop in Boot and bought a battery for his torch. It would be dark by four o'clock and heavy cloud would block whatever light the moon might offer. He remembered the shock of impenetrable darkness that he'd first encountered when he left Ulverston, so dark that you could walk into a wall or stumble into a ditch without ever knowing it was there.

As he parked the bike as usual by the bridge below Mill Cottage, the millstream was still running; he could see and hear it below a top layer of ice. It was early afternoon, but low dark cloud blanketed the fell tops.

He knocked on the low front door and walked straight in.

'It's our John,' said Fred's voice out of the gloom. 'Na then, lad. We 'eard the bike, 'ad to be you.'

'On your own?' asked Hannah, straining her eyes to see if there was anyone with him. 'Where's that lass?'

Damn, thought John. Now they're going to start asking questions. He decided not to respond.

'I 'ear you're not so well, Fred,' he said, looking at his old friend who seemed to have aged since his last visit.

'Who told ye that?' asked Fred, shifting in his chair.

'I met Peter from the pub down in St Bees,' said John.

'E's a reet auld mitherer, that 'un,' said Fred. 'Folks talk too much round 'ere, nowt else to do.'

'You 'eard reet,' said Hannah to John, taking her chance while it was offered. 'This auld bugger's been bad for weeks, wheezing worse than ever. So he stays in th'ouse an' gets crabby.'

'Has the doctor been?' asked John, knowing the answer.

'Ain't seeing no doctor,' said Fred, with a sudden burst of energy. 'Waste o' space them doctors, and they cost. Nowt wrong wi' me a bit o' whisky won't cure. And some warm weather would 'elp.'

'It's only March, Fred,' said Hannah. 'Not goin' to get warm for weeks, and I'll have to stop 'ere, listening to you gasping and moaning.'

She turned to John. 'We'll be reet,' she said. 'I'll give 'im some of that nettle tea I used to give me dad.'

John looked at them both. 'Are you sure? Snow's coming, I can feel it.'

'Folk up 'ere dinna fret about a bit o' snow, lad,' said Fred. 'Best thing you could do to 'elp is chop some more logs for us, fetch some water in.'

'Shall I stay over? I can bed down on t'floor.'

'Nay, lad, unless you want to sleep wi' me,' said Fred. 'I've not been up them stairs in weeks.'

'I can't 'ear 'im wheezing when I'm up there,' said Hannah.

John recalled the old days, when Hannah and Fred couldn't keep their hands off each other. An image of Maggie hit him hard, her lovely face so near to his, her eyes closed.

It was as if Hannah had read his mind.

'Well,' she said. 'Where is she? Maggie, wasn't it?'

'Aye,' said Fred. 'Maggie from Kells, Frank McSherry's lass.'

'She's called Maggie Lowery,' said John. He knew he couldn't fend them off any longer. 'We had a falling out.'

'What about?' said Hannah.

John hesitated. 'She did something and didn't tell me.'

'She's a good lass, that 'un,' Fred added. 'You should 'ang on to 'er, lad. What made you fall out?'

John knew this would happen. He tried once more to avoid telling them.

'She did something I didn't want her to do. That's all.'

Hannah insisted. 'So why did you fall out over it?'

Fred looked up at them both from his hunched position in the low chair. The eyes were still bright in the drawn face.

'Come on, John lad,' he said quietly. 'We know you. That lass means a lot to you. We could see that. Whatever it was, get it out, don't just hide inside yoursen like you do. It must've been bad for you to just drop 'er.'

John looked away, towards the grey square of light and the brown ground outside. They could hear the rush of the beck at the bottom of the garden. Hannah started to speak, but Fred held up his hand, to stop her. They could see that John was thinking. When he spoke, he didn't look at them.

'I told Maggie about Jessie,' he said. 'About her being my mother, and how we'd lied about it.'

There was no response. They waited for more.

John sat down on an old chair that stood beside the front door.

'She was angry with me, about the lies. She said I'd not stood up for meself, and that she couldn't respect me for that … Then she went to see Jessie, at the school, without telling me.'

'What did she say?' Hannah asked, imagining how the two women might have dealt with each other.

'I don't know exactly, she didn't tell me. But I know she was angry with Jessie too, and she said so.'

'Good for 'er,' said Fred.

John turned around to face them. 'But she didn't tell me,' he said. 'I had to find about it from Jessie herself, in a café. I felt such a fool.'

'So that's it,' said Hannah. 'She made you look a fool.'

John hung his head. He knew how feeble it sounded, spoken out loud.

'And that's why you've fallen out?' asked Fred.

'Aye,' said John. 'We 'ad a row, and I've not seen 'er since then, two weeks or so. I don't want to forgive 'er but I don't want to lose 'er either.'

'Forgive?' said Hannah, 'What do you 'ave to forgive 'er for?'

'For not telling me. For getting involved without telling me.'

Hannah and Fred looked at each other.

'Shall I tell 'im, or you?' said Fred.

'You save your breath, love,' said Hannah. She walked slowly across the room and stood in front of John. He looked up at her.

'Now listen to me, our John,' she said. 'You're like a son to us, and we love you. You've helped your mam all these years by keeping it all quiet about you and 'er, but it were bound to come out sometime. And now it 'as. And the person you told cares enough about you to say summat. You were just a lad when you found your mam. Just a lad. Now you're a man wi' a life of your own, and that girl could be part of it. She's got spirit, that's why we like 'er. She said some things to your mam that might've needed saying, who knows? And she didn't tell you, and now you feel shown up. Is that it?'

John nodded.

'Get your 'ead straight, our John,' Fred joined in. 'Don't dribble on about forgiving 'er. What's to forgive? She's done nowt but stand up for you, in 'er own way.'

John stared at them both. They'd never spoken to him like this.

'What should I do?' he asked, looking from one to the other.

'Go and see 'er, for a start,' said Hannah. 'Forget about forgiveness. Do you love 'er?'

John nodded.

'Tell 'er that. That's enough. The rest'll sort itself.'

'But she lied to me!'

'Did you ask her, straight out?'

'Not until Jessie told me what happened.'

'So she didn't lie,' said Hannah, sitting down on the arm of Fred's chair. 'She just didn't tell you. We all keep quiet about things, all the time,' she went on. 'I 'ad to lie to me dad all the time about Fred. Didn't like it, but I'd no choice.'

Hannah leaned forward and put her hand over John's.

'Life's not that simple. Lies, truth, they're not so different sometimes, tha' knows. If we all told truth, all the time, it'd be a mess. Fred calls me beautiful, I call 'im a stupid bugger. Both lies. Don't mean any of it. It's what you do. Makes t'world go round. Reet, Fred?'

'She's reet, lad,' said Fred. He smiled. 'She's allus reet.'

'Lying again,' said his wife, smiling back at her sick husband in the chair.

'Don't let 'er slip away,' said Fred. 'Tha's waited for a lass a long time, and that's a fine lass. You'd be a fool to let that 'un go.'

John said nothing.

'There's lies and lies,' said Hannah. 'You and Jessie've lied all these years because she 'ad to and you went along wi' it 'cos she's your mam. No shame in that. Maggie'll know that too, deep down.' She squeezed John's hand.

'Does she want you?'

He thought about that.

'I think she does,' he said.

'Well don't 'ang around. Life's too short.'

142

'That's reet,' said Fred.

For the next hour or two John was busy outside, keeping the bitter cold at bay by chopping logs and carrying water into the house. As he worked, he went through what they had both said to him. Were they right about Maggie? He hoped so.

By the time the jobs were done and he was warming his hands round a mug of tea, he reckoned there were still a couple of hours of daylight left, long enough to get back ahead of the snow that he was sure would come.

'Think on, our John,' said Hannah as she watched him bundle himself up in as many layers as he could manage. 'Don't let that lass get away.'

He hugged them both, ducked through the low doorway and stood for a moment, looking at the sky, feeling the wind, thinking about driving back down the valley. Wind's behind me, he thought, and the road's dry. As he pulled the bike from its stand by the bridge tiny pinheads of ice blew past him.

Almost as soon as John turned the bike into the main road down the valley, the tiny flakes had begun to grow and thicken and he increased his speed, driving ahead of the wind, ahead of the curtain of snow racing down from the mountains behind him, inexorable, unseen. When the blizzard overtook and engulfed him, John soon realised he could not go much further. Seeing nothing but the walls on either side of him he had no idea where he was or how far he had come. White flakes swirled out of the dark sky, and soon the bike began to slide on the road. Horizontal wind screamed through his thin leather helmet and blew the snow into drifts.

John's stomach had begun to churn with anxiety when he recognised the driveway down to Applegarth on his right and he knew that he was within reach of Newton. Relieved and exhausted, he pushed the bike off the road, as far under the bushy

143

hedge as he could get it and set off to walk the last hundred yards down the slippery hill towards the schoolhouse.

All he wanted was shelter until the snow blew out. He hadn't seen Jessie since their miserable conversation in Whitehaven, when she seemed to taunt him with Maggie's behaviour, and had no wish to talk about it again, but there was nowhere else to go.

Chapter 16

JOHN SAW THE LIGHT in the front room change, growing fainter as the lamp was carried away from the window. Then he heard his mother's voice through the door.

'Who is it?' she called.

'It's John,' he called back, raising his voice above the whining of the wind. 'I'm stuck.'

The door was pulled open immediately and he stepped into the house in a whirl of snow. Jessie closed the door quickly behinds him and pushed him into the front room where a fire was burning brightly. John pulled off his sodden gloves and held painful fingers towards the heat.

'What is it?' said Jessie. 'What on earth made you go out on a night like this?'

'I went up to Boot earlier on, to see Hannah and Fred, and thought I could get back before the snow came. I got as far as Agnes's drive but I couldn't go any further, so I left the bike and walked down.'

'Get those boots off,' she said. 'And that wet coat. I've plenty of warm things if you're not fussy.'

Both of them were grateful for the distraction of necessary activity, getting warm, changing clothes, making and drinking tea. It was only when all that was done that awkwardness began to seep through the veneer. Talking about Hannah and Fred was safe, and they did so with enthusiasm for a while, before there was nothing else to say.

'I'll check what it's like outside,' said Jessie, 'see if I can get to the outhouse.' When she returned a few minutes later the embarrassment deepened with the news that the outhouse was inaccessible with drifting snow half way up the door.

'There's a commode in the back bedroom,' said Jessie.

John nodded, wishing he had set off earlier and was back in the privacy of his own little house, not stuck here with someone he really did not want to see.

He made himself useful bringing in more logs from the yard while Jessie made them some food. When the meal was over, both of them thought about the night ahead and tried to speak at once. 'You'll be staying over, of course,' said Jessie. 'I can light the fire in the back bedroom if you like.'

John shook his head: he did not want to be treated like a guest, to be beholden. 'I'll sleep down here,' he said. 'That's what I was going to say, before. No need to heat another room, and I'll pull the cushions onto the floor. That'll do fine. It'll have blown over by the morning, and then I can sort out what to do.' He looked at his mother. She doesn't want me here either, he said to himself. She's as uncomfortable as I am.

He was right. Jessie did not like surprises, and always needed time to prepare herself to see John, ever since their first encounter. In all those years, she had never spent more than a few hours with him, and now they could be marooned here together for much longer than that. What could they talk about? Their last conversation, only three weeks before, had been painful. Jessie had said more than she had intended, and John had been angry. Now, Jessie could not ask about Maggie and John would not discuss it. The only acceptable conversation would be about other things,

146

things that didn't really matter. Lying in her bed, Jessie went over a list of safe subjects in her mind: it was a short list. The best thing would be to avoid conversation as far as possible by keeping busy, and it was while making a mental list of necessary jobs around the house that Jessie finally fell asleep.

When she peered out of the window around eight o'clock the next morning she knew at once that there would be no early release from their confinement in the house. All night the wind and snow had continued and the landscape around the school-house was as bleak as the surface of the moon, save for the white outlines of trees. Drifts had reached the top of the wall around the school yard, but in the field opposite there were patches where the snow had been blown aside, leaving the frozen ground almost bare. Looking down the road towards the Farriers, Jessie could see no tracks, hoof or footprints. Nothing was stirring.

In the front room, John was picking up the blankets and cushions from the floor. As he turned towards her, Jessie noticed with a shock the white scarf he was wearing round his neck.

'Where did you get that?' she asked, remembering the last man she'd seen wearing it.

'I found it last night, under a cushion on the sofa,' John said. 'I think it's silk, like pilots used to wear in the war.' He stroked it with his hand. 'Where did you get it?'

Jessie hesitated. John had never known about Andrew, and he must never know. She had to think quickly, finding another plausible lie.

'It was a gift,' she said lightly. 'Caroline Leadbetter gave it to me, and she got it from her son.'

'Andy?' said John. 'I thought he was in Canada.'

'He is, now,' she went on, juggling truth and untruth in her mind. 'He was with the Canadian air force during the war, and when it was over he sent the scarf to his mother, as a keepsake.'

'And she gave it to you?'

'She was grateful,' Jessie lied on. 'I tried to help when Lionel was ill, when he had his stroke.'

'Well it's a splendid gift,' he said, raising the scarf to his face and sniffing it. 'Smells of something, soap maybe.'

'Yes,' said his mother, holding out her hand. 'I can find you another scarf ...'

'Oh, right,' he said, handing it back to her. 'Sorry.'

Jessie left the room. In the hall she buried her face in the silk scarf for a moment before putting it away, out of sight in the cupboard. She pulled another, longer scarf from a hook and took it back into the room with her.

'Here you are,' she said brightly, 'this should be better. Now, let's get the range fire going and warm ourselves up. Still snowing. You'd have trouble finding the bike, never mind riding it anywhere.'

'What about the trains?' he asked, wondering how long his unexpected stay would have to be.

'Hard to tell. Sometimes the coast gets less snow than here. Drifting will be the problem. If the snow eases a bit, we'll venture out, shall we, and see what's happening?'

Venturing out proved to be a problem. When they pulled the back door open, a wall of snow fell into the room and it took both of them several minutes to shovel it out again before the door could be shut. On one side of the house the snow had almost reached the window, while on the other there was much less. Together they planned the best way of getting out. First they wound some old cloth round John's trouser legs and boots to keep out the snow, and then Jessie held a chair while John stepped out of an open window on the side where the snow had largely blown away. He sank in almost up to his knees but managed to pull out one foot at a time and began to dig out a narrow path between the front door and the lane that ran down to the shop. One side of the lane was almost passable, while on the other side the snow was piled up against walls and doors.

The wind was merciless, pushing snow back as fast as John shovelled it away, and by the end of the morning he had given up, defeated by the force of the storm just as he had been the night before. Jessie had baked some bread while John was busy outside and the air smelled delicious. For lunch she made meagre sandwiches with the old bread and the last of the ham. They ate in apparently companionable silence, and Jessie was beginning to hope that the day might pass without incident when John leaned back in his chair and said, 'He always spoke very highly of you, you know.'

She looked up. 'Who did?'

'Andy Leadbetter. He'd had a bit too much to drink one night and started talking about what a fine woman you were. I was surprised, you know, with him being so much younger. He's only a few years older than me.'

Jessie got up from the table. Surely John didn't know about Andrew. He couldn't.

'What did he say?' she asked, keeping her voice as light as she could.

'Nothing much. I'd forgotten all about it until you mentioned about the scarf.'

'He drank too much, that young man,' said Jessie. 'I hope they sobered him up properly when he joined the air force.'

'He came home, didn't he?' said John, 'when Lionel had his stroke. Agnes mentioned it.'

Damn, thought Jessie. 'I think he did.' She lied so easily now. 'That must have been when he gave his mother the scarf.'

She glanced at the clock. 'Two o'clock already,' she said. 'And still the snow's coming down. It must stop soon, surely.'

'I could try and clear a path to the outhouse,' he suggested. 'If the wind drops, the snow might not blow back. It'll take a while. I'll go out of the window, same as before, and attack the drift from the other side.'

They both knew that this task was both unnecessary and probably fruitless, but they both agreed that it should be done. By the time the daylight was fading, John had cut a narrow path across the yard to the outhouse. He arms ached with the effort of shovelling, but when darkness finally forced him back into the house he was relieved to find that the atmosphere indoors seemed to reflect what was happening outside; it was less frigid and brittle than before.

While Jessie washed their evening meal plates in the sink, John fell asleep in the chair by the fire in the front room. For the first time in years she was able to look at him closely as he slept, unobserved by anyone else. How like Clive he looked, with his dark hair hanging over his face. Clive would have been proud of him, she felt sure. As it was, Jessie's feelings towards her son were always complicated, contaminated by fear and regret. Would that change, she wondered, once the secret was finally out? Could they start again perhaps, or was it too late? And what was there to keep them together, besides the blood link? He was a likeable enough young man, but nothing remarkable, she thought. Dependable, quite a catch for that young woman from Kells. It occurred to Jessie that John, her only child, was a disappointment to her.

John's eyes were closed, but he knew that Jessie was watching him. What does she see, he wondered. She doesn't know much about me, except that I threaten her respectability. He lay still, remembering how he had put together the puzzle of her identity and tracked her down. Would he do the same again, knowing what he knew now? Part of him wished he had never found her, or having done so, had just tiptoed away, out of her life. Now they had to deal with each other, and it felt like treading on eggshells. He opened his eyes just enough to see that she had turned away to tend the fire, and he feigned sudden wakefulness, stretching his long legs out in front of him.

'Feeling better?' she said. 'It was hard work for you today.'

'More tomorrow, if the weather improves.'

'It sounds as if the wind has dropped. And the snow seems to have eased off. The path to the outhouse is still clear.'

'If there's any chance of getting home,' he said, 'I really want to do that, even if it means leaving the bike where it is for now.'

'Of course,' she said. 'You'll need to get back to work … and to your friend.'

'No,' said John, suddenly confused. He sat up straight in the chair. 'I mean, yes, but … I don't want to talk about that.'

'Oh,' said Jessie.

He looked at her. Why did she say that, mention his 'friend' again in that same patronising way?

Jessie saw his expression change. 'Has something happened?'

'That's none of your business,' he said. 'I don't want to discuss it.' He felt his heart thump in his chest but looked away, trying to control his anger.

'I'll get some more logs,' said Jessie as she walked out of the room.

Suddenly John was furious, with himself as much as with her. Every instinct urged him to leave the house, but there was nowhere he could go. He stood up, stared into the fire and held his fist to his mouth, stifling what he wanted to say.

His mother came back in, carrying the basket of logs.

'I'm sorry,' he said. 'Nothing's happened, but it's personal.'

'Of course,' she said. 'You deal with the fire, I'll make us a drink.'

The moment passed. Nothing more was said. John looked on

151

Jessie's bookshelf, found a book on the history of Whitehaven and settled down to read while she sat with her sewing box and some mending. An observer could have believed, mistakenly, that they were both perfectly content. When Jessie said goodnight and went upstairs John made his bed and settled down, still thinking about how this tension between them might be resolved.

One thing he was very clear about: he had to make his peace with Maggie, and do whatever it took to keep her. He wanted to be with her, marry her, have children with her. What he wanted more than anything else was a family, and the proud, difficult woman upstairs was part of that family, whether either of them wanted it or not. Jessie Whelan would be his children's grandmother.

Before he slept, John resolved that he would take the first opportunity in the coming day to push through all the hurt and open himself up to Jessie in the same way that he always did with Hannah and Fred. He had to trust that she would respect him for doing so, and be honest with him in return. There was no other way.

Chapter 17

It was the light that woke him, brightening the gap between the curtains on one side of the room, but it was only seven o'clock. March, of course, he reminded himself, ten weeks on from the shortest day. And it was quiet, too, without the continuous whine of the wind. He struggled out from his nest of cushions and blankets and pulled the curtain aside. A sharp diamond of sunlight bounced and glittered off the snowy fields, turning them pink and grey.

He blinked, and noticed a movement where the whitened road passed the house. The movement stopped. A fox, glowing gold in the early light, stood in the middle of the road, looking directly at him. Its ears were pricked, eyes dark, and the long tail drooped down towards the snow around its delicate feet. For several seconds, man and fox gazed calmly at each other before the creature turned and trotted away. It must be hungry, John thought, realising that he was himself.

There was no sound from upstairs. John pulled on his clothes and spent a while lighting the fire in the range. When the fire was ready he put the kettle on and waited while it heated and boiled, and made a pot of tea. Still no sign of movement from upstairs.

He had been rehearsing what he wanted to say to Jessie for an hour or more now, and the delay was frustrating him. Should he take a cup of tea up to her? No, that was a bad idea. He drank his tea and listened, then tiptoed to the bottom of the stairs to listen again. The sound of the bedroom door opening caught him by surprise. He wanted to be sitting calmly at the kitchen table when she came down, and then he was resolved to seize the moment and say his piece.

Jessie was still in her dressing gown and slippers, rubbing her eyes, her hair unbrushed and wild. John was taken aback; he had never seen his mother like this before. It was as if she had forgotten he was in the house. Without speaking, she poured herself a cup of tea from the pot on the table and turned back towards the stairs.

'Not feeling well,' she said. 'Help yourself to food.'

'Can we talk?' he asked.

She shook her head without turning round. 'Later,' she said, and was gone.

All John's resolve crumbled, and the prepared statement blurred in his mind. He was trapped in this woman's house, but excluded by her. It shouldn't matter, but it did, and the same anger that he had felt the night before welled up in him again. He ate some stale bread and cheese from the pantry, put on as many extra layers of clothes as he could find and let himself out of the back door, clearing the drifted snow to make a path across the yard.

The exercise warmed his body and calmed his mind. He was making a noise, and might be disturbing her, but he didn't care about that. If she was so unconcerned about him, he could play that game, too. The air was still and cold, but less biting without the wind. John saw the tracks of the fox heading boldly between the houses and round the corner, and decided to start digging a path down towards the shop. He guessed that others might be doing the same, now that the break in the weather had finally arrived. He heard the sound of a shovel before he heard the man's voice.

'Miss Whelan?' cried the voice. 'Is that you?'

'No, it's John,' he called back, 'John Pharaoh. I'm stopping at the schoolhouse. Can't get home.'

'Are you coming down this way, to t'shop?'

'Aye, are you coming up?'

The two men dug in silence for a while, moving slowly towards each other along the narrow lane. 'Feels like we're digging the railway across America or summat,' the other man cried. 'Won't be long now I reckon.'

Each man speeded up as the other came close, laughing as they vied with each other to shift the final shovelful and complete the shallow trench that lay between them. Finally they stood straight, pushed their shovels triumphantly into the snow to one side and shook hands with great ceremony, smiling broadly.

'Cecil Geer, from t'shop,' said the other digger. 'I've seen you around. Mr Pharaoh, ain't it? Isn't Jessie a relative o'yorn?'

'My aunt,' said John. 'I was coming back from Boot the other night when the blizzard came. Got as far as Applegarth, on the bike, and couldn't go any further. Jessie took me in. Otherwise I might've been banging on your door, Mr Geer.'

'And reet welcome you'd've been, lad. Strong pair of 'ands allus welcome at a time like this. Bad eh! Not sure I've ever sin worse. Come down to t'shop, now you're 'ere. Missus was doing a bit o' bacon. Just the smell was making me 'ungry and that was afore this lot.'

In single file Cecil led John down their trench to the shop and they worked together to clear the area round the door.

'Not much to sell,' said Cecil, 'but folk'll be down just for the craic after being stuck inside for two days. Anything you think Jessie might need, you could tek back for 'er?'

John thought for a moment. 'Flour for bread,' he said, 'and maybe a bit of cheese?'

Cecil Geer tapped his finger on the side of his nose. 'We'll 'ave a look. Never know what you might find, by accident like. But come away in for now, lad. We need a bit o' food after all that digging.' He pushed open the door of the shop and shouted, 'Betty! Put a bit more bacon on, love. We got company.'

John relished the conversation as much as the breakfast in the cluttered room behind the shop. After the claustrophobic anxiety of two days with Jessie, he revelled in the craic, about the snow and the shortages and how it had been in times past, and who was doing what, and where, to survive.

There were stories of farmers breaking through barn walls with a sledgehammer to reach the animals inside, and of how many animals had already died or would do so if not found and fed very soon. Rumours too, about how and when things might return to something like normalcy.

News had passed from farm to farm, north from Millom, that a gang from the camp was out clearing the main coast road, and heading towards Newton sometime that day. Not for the first time John found that his knowledge of the area was assumed, and he had to ask for information when the camp was mentioned.

'I thought all the prisoners of war had gone home already,'

'They 'ave,' said Cecil.

'Then who's at the camp?' John asked.

'Them other foreigners, tha knows,' said Betty. 'What do they call 'em, DPs.'

John still had no idea.

'D stands for summat, and P stands for people, or persons, summat like that. What's the D for, Betty?'

His wife thought deeply for a moment, trying to find the word. 'Disturbed!' she said finally, 'No, dis- something else. Displaced. Displaced Persons, that's it.'

'Foreigners who were over here when war broke out, and got stuck,' said Cecil. 'Rum bunch, by all accounts. Don't get on wi' Russkies, and now their countries have been taken o'er, after war like, they can't go back. Summat like that.'

'Aye, that's it,' said Betty in confirmation. 'The DPs live at the old camp where the prisoners were before, down Millom way, near the sea. They go to work on farms and such, so now everywhere's under snow they'll use 'em to dig roads out. They're young, most of 'em, not injured or 'owt. Big gang could make pretty good progress if they've got the right gear.'

'We did alreet this morning, John, I reckon,' said Cecil raising his mug to salute his fellow excavator. 'Sometime today they should reach us, that's the craic.'

'And they're digging the railway out as well,' said Betty. 'That's what Harold from t'station were saying when he were in earlier. He'd come across fields like, walking on top of walls sometimes 'e said. And 'e reckoned there'd be a train through afore the end of the day, from Millom up the coast. Not so bad north of 'ere, they say. Men need to get to work. No miners, no coal, and God knows we're short enough already.'

'I'm at the Haig, in Kells,' said John.

'Didn't 'ave you down as a pitman,' said Betty. 'You've got nice 'ands.'

'Office,' said John. 'No idea whether they're working, but I ought to try to get there if I can. Now that things are getting back to normal, Jessie can do without me.'

'Strong woman, that Miss Whelan,' said Betty approvingly. 'They say new vicar's trying to get 'er out of school. I know the men need jobs but kids need learning, too. She did a grand job with our two, so why chuck 'er out?'

John nodded in agreement, although what Betty was saying was all new to him. Why hadn't Jessie said anything to him about it, he wondered. They knew so little about each other. It was time to go back to the schoolhouse and face her again, if she'd deigned to get out of bed. He thanked Betty and Cecil for their hospitality and company, and Betty gave him some flour for Jessie.

'Any cheese?' said John, hopefully.

'Just for you, lad,' she said, holding up a wrapped package. 'Payment for services, you might say,' she added, winking at him. John put on his outer layers of clothing, stuffed the food into his pockets and walked slowly back up the lane. Sparrows were twittering in the hedge and drops of water on the branches sparkled as they hung and fell. Must be above freezing, he thought, but it'll take a while to thaw this lot. As he pushed open the back door of the schoolhouse it took a moment for his eyes to adjust from the fierce light outside to the gloom of the kitchen. Jessie was there, standing by the range, dressed and looking her normal self.

'There you are,' she said, looking genuinely pleased to see him.

'I helped Cecil dig out a path to the shop,' he said, 'and brought a few things back with me. They didn't ask for any money …'

'Splendid,' said Jessie, checking what he'd brought. 'I'll make some scones with the old milk.'

John told Jessie about the DPs gang clearing the road, and the possibility of a train. He wanted her to be in a good mood when he made his effort to talk to her properly. As he bent to take off his wet boots, she said, 'Sorry I was bit preoccupied this morning. I was tired but it wasn't just that.' She hesitated. 'I'm not used to having someone around, all the time,' she said, as she put the flour away in the pantry. 'Living on your own, you get used to it. Strange to have someone here, especially someone ...'

'Someone you don't know very well,' said John. 'We don't really know much about each other, do we? Betty was talking about the school, and what the new vicar is doing. I had no idea, you never said.'

'Oh that,' she said. 'It's all rather silly in a way. The vicar feels that the men who've been away fighting need the jobs, and that I shouldn't be occupying this house all on my own. He has a point, I suppose.'

'Well Betty's not happy about it. Says you did a grand job with her kids.'

Jessie smiled. 'Did she? She never said that to me at the time. And they were a handful – ' She stopped, turned her head and held up her hand. 'Did you hear anything?'

They both stood quite still, listening. Jessie walked through to the front room and looked out, holding her hand to shield her eyes from the light. John followed and did the same. A hundred yards or so down the road a cloud of smoke or steam was hanging in the air, and around it blurred shapes, moving. John opened the window just a fraction and they both heard it, the unmistakeable sound of an engine, echoing off the stone walls.

'What is it?' she said, screwing up her eyes.

'I think it's a tractor. I can see someone sitting on top, and there are other men around it. It must be the gang from the camp, lots of them.' He began to count the shapes around the tractor. 'More than a dozen, I reckon. They must have worked really hard to get this far up, unless ...' He watched a little longer. 'Yes, there's a snowplough on the tractor, pushing a way through, and the men are shovelling the rest.'

'Heavens,' said Jessie. 'I haven't got enough cups to give them all a drink. We'll have to do it in shifts! Put your boots back on,

John, and go and meet them. There must be someone in charge. Ask them to stop here for a hot drink. I'll get two kettles going.'

By the time John returned, the kitchen was full of steam and Jessie had gathered containers of all sorts, mugs, jugs, even a gravy boat, and two big pots of tea were brewing on the range.

'This is Mr Rawson, from the camp,' said John. 'Offer of drinks very gratefully accepted.'

'First we've 'ad all morning,' said Jack Rawson. 'G'day missus, and thanks. Folk round 'ere seem to think the men are enemy agents or summat.'

Jessie shook his hand. 'Well, you're very welcome here, Mr Rawson. How many men are with you?'

'Fourteen, and me,' he said.

'Not sure I can fit you all in at once,' she said, 'but we can do it in shifts.'

'Any way you say, missus. The men'll be reet glad of a break. I'll explain what's happening and we'll get 'em sorted.'

John went with him to where the men were leaning on their shovels, smoking and talking together in a language John had never heard before. Or maybe it was more than one language, he couldn't tell. Jack Rawson gave some instructions to one of the men, who translated for two others, who passed the message on to others in turn.

'Some Poles, some Russians, some from Hungary,' said Jack. 'Only one with any English. It's like Chinese whispers.'

It looked as if the men were dividing into two groups, and the first group moved towards the house.

'See?' said Jack. 'Reet, lads, you lot first. Round the back, boots off, cuppa tea, then the next lot.' In the small kitchen, Jessie had managed not only tea but some cake, too. John watched admiringly as she organised the group with the efficiency befitting a headmistress. He could see why the village held her in such esteem. It was as if the unexpected challenge had ignited her energy and charm, both of which were clearly appreciated by the men who crowded into the kitchen.

'If they can leave their boots by the door, out of the way, Mr Rawson, they can go through to the front room and we can make space for the other group. It'll be a squash, but we'll manage.'

Jack pantomimed the instructions and the men trooped through with their tea. John went with them and watched as they stood awkwardly, smiling but not daring to sit down.

Jack Rawson came to the door. 'This is a first for most of 'em,' he said. 'Look at 'em, pleased as punch to be invited into someone's home, made to feel welcome. They're not used to kindness. I 'ope I can winkle 'em out again!'

'We're very pleased to see them, Mr Rawson,' said John. 'We've been stuck here for a couple of days now. Gets a bit claustrophobic.'

'Like our 'ouse at Christmas,' said Jack. 'Family all crammed in, on top of each other. After two days with the wife's mother I wanted to hit 'er over the 'ead.'

In both the front room and the kitchen almost everyone was smoking and the air in house was heavy and acrid. John opened a window, but quickly had to retreat to the back door as his chest began to prickle. Jessie didn't seem to mind, still pouring tea and smiling, as if having a house full of strange men happened every day.

In the front room, one of the men seemed to be teaching the others a few words of English. When they all shuffled out to find their boots and head off on the next stage of their task, each man shook Jessie's hand and said 'Thank you,' with varying degrees of success.

'Bloody 'ell,' Jack Rawson whispered to John. 'Your mam's got 'em eating out of 'er 'and.'

John didn't correct Mr Rawson's assumption; the old pretence seemed suddenly irrelevant.

'How many of them can speak English?' Jessie asked as Jack Rawson rounded them up.

'Just the one, as far as I know,' he said, looking around. 'Peter?' he called, and a young man put his head round the back door. 'Come in 'ere a minute.'

'This is Peter, miss. He's from Hungary.'

'Poland,' said Piotr. 'I am Piotr Gorski, madam,' he said to Jessie. He took her hand and raised it to his lips with a small bow from the waist. 'We thank you madam, for your kindness. Very good. I have a little English, but the other men,' Piotr gestured to the group outside, 'no.'

Jack Rawson was clearly anxious to be off, but Jessie held his arm.

'They need to know English, surely, Mr Rawson?' she said.

''Appen they do, miss,' he said. 'But they don't need English to dig out the road to t'station, and that's what we 'ave to do now.'

John made a sudden decision. 'I'm coming with you,' he said. 'Hang on while I get my coat. If that train gets through today, I need to be on it.'

John's urge to get away overcame his plan for talking to his mother. Something about the company and the smoke and the more benign weather brought the thought of Maggie urgently to his mind. His dream of family depended on her, and the rest could wait.

Jessie watched from the window as the tractor driver climbed up into the cab and started the engine, inching the snowplough round to find the right direction and angle before the gang moved slowly away, the cloud of exhaled breath settling around them. A few minutes later, as they got into a rhythm of shovelling the snow, she heard them start to sing. The tune hung in the air like a hymn in a quiet church. She listened to the fading sound, then turned away to reclaim her home, relieved beyond words to be alone again.

Chapter 18

Rarely had the sight and sound of the train been more welcome. It snorted into Newton station and stopped at the platform in a hiss of steam that enveloped John and the others who had gathered during the day in anticipation of escape. The train was packed. Condensation was running down the inside of the windows, making it hard to see out. Only the hollow rumble of the wheels told them that they were on the viaduct across the Esk. John wiped the window with his sleeve and peered out. Everywhere was white, but the snow was less deep than before, as if the storm had exhausted itself by the time it had reached the west coast.

'It's like the war again,' said the train guard on the platform at Corcickle. 'Brings out the best in folk when things are really bad.'

Once out of the train, John's first goal was to get to the pit, and the road up to Kells was passable. When he got to the Haig, looking out over the improbably blue sea, John was told that the bosses had given in and closed everything down for two days. Not enough men to work the shifts, half the screen lasses weren't in and the rest had been sent home. He thought about going to West Row himself, but he wasn't ready to face Maggie, so he walked the rest of the way back to Sandwith, working round the drifts, finding the easiest route.

He was pleased to be back, and relieved that his little house seemed to have survived the weather without harm. He lit the fire, boiled water, and had a good wash before he changed his clothes. For the following two days John did nothing except keep himself warm, eat, sleep and listen to his radio. The news was surreal: seas frozen, power supplies dwindling, food rations shorter than ever. Compared to some other parts of the country, the west of Cumberland seemed to have been spared the worst, but it was grim. John slept downstairs where it was warmer by the range, and lay there wondering where he could go to start a different life, somewhere warm, away from the rationing and shortages and the vicious weather. Would he be alone? That he didn't know, but he couldn't bear the thought of never seeing Maggie again.

The last conversation with Hannah and Fred seemed like weeks ago, and it was a while before the details of it came back to him with painful clarity. They'd said a lot about lies and forgiveness, and told him to stop feeling sorry for himself and get Maggie back any way he could. Easy to say, he thought. She's probably told her mam about it by now, or stopped talking about me altogether. They'll have noticed something's wrong. They're as nosey as Hannah and Fred. He pictured himself going back to the West Row house, and all the whispering and pointing. What if Maggie refused to see him? He burned at the thought of such humiliation, and his head began to ache again.

Then he decided he would write Maggie a letter. That way he could say what he wanted and not be put off by what was going on. She might read it, or she might tear it up, but it was a better plan than just knocking on the door. He couldn't try to talk to her at work, not with all those lasses watching their every move. The decision about what he needed to do made him get up and have some food. He lit the fire with the last of the logs. It was still snowy outside but he might find some dry wood in the outhouse, or even a bit of coal. Finding a piece of paper to write on was more of a challenge, but he discovered one in the end, just one, in a drawer. He would have to use that piece for the real thing and compose the words in his head beforehand. Up and down the small room he walked, rehearsing what to say, as if Maggie were in the room with him, sitting quietly, not interrupting. The fumbling words fell into the silence, punctuated by the hiss and crackle of the tiny fire as it took hold. He tried to remember what Hannah had said. He couldn't talk about forgiving Maggie, because that would mean he thought she'd done something that had to be forgiven, and the only thing she'd done was embarrass him.

Suddenly John stopped as the thought struck him: it was his mother he felt really angry with, and himself. It was their lie, the two of them, not Maggie's. When he began pacing and talking again the words he needed came more easily. There was not much to say in the end. He cut the piece of paper in half, so he could try again if the first attempt came out wrong. His best pen was at work, and there was no ink in the house, so he found a stub of pencil and sharpened it with his keenest knife. He wrote, as carefully as he could:

Dear Maggie,
I hope you are well in all this cold. And all your family, too.

He hesitated. That sounded silly, but he couldn't just launch into the important bit. He licked the pencil and carried on.

Last time I saw you I was upset and said some things that made you angry. Now I think I was wrong to say those things. I have missed you so much. Please can we talk again? I'm at home and the bike is stuck in Newton. Can't tell you about that now. Will you see me if I come to your house?
Please, Maggie. I love you.
Yours faithfully,
John

166

It was a long time since he'd written a personal letter. 'Yours faithfully' didn't look right but he didn't want to do it all again. He read the whole thing through, decided it was the best he could manage and put it in the envelope that he'd found after a desperate search. Would the post be working? That question was answered when a letter arrived later, a note from Arthur Curran telling him to be in work the next day. John picked his way across the snow to the post box on the green, slipped in his letter addressed to Mrs M. Lowery at the house in West Row, and went home to wait.

The prospect of going back to work helped him fill the waiting hours, but his mind was churning and he slept badly.

* * *

A letter arrived. It was from her, he knew it. He looked at his name on the envelope and felt sick with anticipation. Inside Maggie had written in a round childish hand:

> *Mam and Dad are going to the rugby club on Friday night.*
> *You can come to the house then if you want. Not before 8*
> *o'clock, so Judith will be in bed.*
> *Margaret*

That was all. He looked for something more in the envelope but there was nothing. He read the few lines again and again, but could not decide what they meant.

The next two days were the longest of his life.

'What's up wi' you, lad?' said Arthur, when John dropped a pile of papers that scattered over the office floor. 'I reckon all that digging took it out of you. Or is it some lass keeping you awake?'

You'd be shocked if you knew which lass it was, John thought as he fumbled around under the desk, picking up the papers. Arthur had clear views about the screen lasses, and none of them were complimentary.

167

When Friday evening came John thought carefully about what he should say. He'd said he was sorry in his letter, but he couldn't recall the exact words he'd used. Why hadn't he kept a copy? And saying he was sorry might not be enough. Maggie was stubborn, he knew that, and he hadn't seen her for weeks. He put on his best corduroy trousers and polished his boots, and it was well gone eight when he approached Maggie's door. He pictured himself stepping into the narrow hall and taking her in his arms before she had time to say anything, to show her that he was decisive and strong and wanted her.

When the door opened the prepared smile froze on his face. Violet McSherry stood in the doorway. She was not smiling.

'I thought –' he stammered.

'Aye, well, you thought wrong,' she said. 'I knew summat was up. Didn't take long to get it out of 'er. Maggie's dad and I want a word with you, young man. Come in.'

John stepped nervously into the hall, and followed Violet's pointing arm into the front room. Frank was sitting in his wheelchair by the window.

'Where's Maggie?' asked John.

'Never you mind,' said Violet, pushing him into the room and closing the door behind her. 'She's where she should be, out of sight till we've got a few things straight.' John looked at Frank, who shrugged his shoulders almost imperceptibly.

'We don't want to hear about what's 'appened with you and our Maggie,' Violet began. She was standing as far away from John as she could manage in the tiny room, so that she didn't have to look up at him. 'Something has, I know that, and I don't mean about you two falling out. Before that. I could tell. It were written all over your face, and 'ers too.'

'What?' asked John, suddenly confused. He looked at Frank again, who winked at him.

'She's a fine lass, a respectable widow with a bairn and she deserves a good man and a proper wedding, if that's what it's going to be. What's your parish?'

'My what?' said John.

'What's the priest's name, where you live?'

'I don't have a priest,' he said.

'I knew it,' said Violet. 'You're not a Catholic are you? Do you go to church at all?'

'No,' said John.

'I told you,' Violet said to Frank. 'The lad's a heathen. Not a chance of a proper wedding.' She turned back to John, who tried without success to step back and had to stand with one foot on the fireplace. 'What were you planning to do,' she said, 'run away to Gretna or summat?'

'Get married?' said John. 'No, we haven't …'

Violet's face was triumphant. 'Living in sin, was that it? Not with my girl, you don't. Do you want to marry our Maggie?'

Behind his wife's back Frank was nodding furiously.

'Well,' John ventured.

'Well? Do you or don't you?'

'Yes, yes,' John stammered. 'We haven't talked …'

'Too busy to talk were you?'

Frank smiled into his hand.

'Well now, we'll see what Father Pryce has to say. If we're lucky, he might agree to take you on.'

'Take me on?'

'For instruction.'

John was none the wiser and his expression betrayed him.

'To be a Catholic!' roared Violet. 'You'll marry in a Catholic church or you won't see 'er again.'

'Shall I call Maggie?' said Frank, trying unsuccessfully to move his wheelchair into the space between his red-faced wife and the pale young man standing in front of her. Violet opened the door.

'Margaret!' she shouted. 'Come in 'ere.'

John heard footsteps coming down the stairs. Maggie edged into the crowded room. She looked across at her father, who smiled. Then she looked at John. He tried to smile but his face didn't respond.

'We've 'ad a chat,' said Violet.

'I 'eard,' said Maggie.

'If Father Pryce will take 'im on, we'll make a Catholic out of John and 'ave a proper wedding. Right?'

'Right,' said Maggie and John, together.

CHAPTER 19

'DO YOU HAVE TO GO?' said Jessie.

Agnes smiled. 'Will you miss me?'

It was Saturday morning and Agnes was putting a few things into a small bag while Jessie watched from the doorway. 'You look exhausted. Couldn't they do without you for a bit longer?'

Agnes looked up. The shadows under her eyes seemed darker than ever.

'It feels like we're still at war,' she said, stretching her back. 'Coal stocks are right down because of the trains being in chaos, and the docks have been frozen up so we haven't even been able to bring anything by sea. Such a mess. We haven't noticed the blackouts up here as we don't have electricity anyway, but it's been chaotic down south. I have to go back, now that the London trains are running again.' She smiled at Jessie. 'Can you stay here at Applegarth while I'm away? It's such a comfort to know there's someone here, and now you've given in your notice that horrid Mr Crompton will just have to wait for the schoolhouse.'

'His wife keeps cutting me dead whenever I see her,' said Jessie. 'She's been talking to the others too, I think. When I went into the shop the other day there was a silence, as if they'd been talking about me.' She turned to look out of the window at the silent snow-covered fields. The thaw had started but it was slow, and it

171

felt as if the winter would never end.

'She's still punishing you for living at the schoolhouse?' said Agnes. 'Is that's what's bothering you? You don't usually look so down when I have to leave and you get the place to yourself.' She smiled. 'Will you miss me, really?'

Jessie turned. 'No – I mean, well, of course I'll miss you, but it's not just that. I don't know. It must be about leaving the school. I feel as if I don't matter here any more. And I miss the Leadbetters more than I ever thought I would, even Lionel!'

Agnes closed up her bag and pulled it off the bed. 'Well there's precious little comfort from church these days. I can't think what possessed the diocese to send us that dreadful little man. Barker by name and Barker by nature, like a dog who can't shut up.'

There was time for a last cup of tea before the car came to take Agnes to the station. The two women sat together, as they had done so many times before.

'I suppose I'm feeling lonely,' said Jessie. 'With school not on my mind all the time, my life feels a bit, well, empty. You're away a lot, I'm not blaming you for that, I know how important the work is. And John's up the coast and busy at work, and … well, he has a life of his own now.'

'But he was here with you for two days, wasn't he? You must have talked about something.'

'Well, yes, but mostly about the weather, and digging through the snow. We didn't have much to say to each other.' She hesitated. 'He has a girlfriend.'

'He does? How exciting! Have you met her, where's she from?'

Jessie poured some more tea. 'No,' she said, 'I've not met her, and he didn't tell me much. It's natural I suppose, but I feel left out of his life these days.'

Agnes knew there was little she could say about John without straying too far into the painful past. 'So,' she said brightly.

'Sounds as if it's time to think about what's next for you, my dear. You need a project, something to do, meet more people. Can't have you mooching around here feeling sorry for yourself.'

So like Agnes, thought Jessie. Always wanting to sort my life out. What about that woman of John's? What would Agnes make of her? And how will I deal with it, she wondered. What if they marry, and have children? The idea upset her so much that she went to lie down as soon as Agnes had gone and the house was quiet again.

It was the following day, just after morning church and another joyless encounter with the vicar that Jessie heard the Applegarth front doorbell ring. When she opened the door a man was standing with his back to her. He was quite short, not much taller than Jessie herself. His shoulders were hunched against the cold and his hands pushed deep into the pockets of a long shabby coat. He turned towards her, only the lower part of his face visible under a broad-brimmed hat.

'Yes?' said Jessie.

The man took off his hat and smiled. In his hand he held some holly with bright red berries, wrapped in newspaper like a small bouquet that he held out towards her. Something about him was familiar. It was only when he spoke that Jessie remembered him.

'This for you,' he said.

'Oh, it's Mr …,' she began, but the name escaped her.

'Piotr Gorski,' he said, with a brief bow. 'I come in the snow. We dig.'

'Of course. Mr Gorski. You were with the men from the camp. But that was at the schoolhouse,' Jessie pointed in the direction of her home. 'How …?'

'I went to shop,' he said, 'and they said to come here.'

'How clever of you! Do come in.'

He thrust the newspaper bouquet into her hand and pointed

at his boots, wet and muddy from the thawing lanes. He bent to undo the laces and took off the boots. Jessie noticed a large hole in one of his socks. When he took off his long coat she could see the badly fitting suit and a wide blue tie. The clothes were clearly meant for someone else. They sat on either side of the fireplace after Jessie had arranged the stems of holly in a brass vase and placed it in the middle of the mantelpiece. The room was cold.

'I walk, from the camp,' he said. 'I bring you something, to thank you.'

'Thank me?' said Jessie. 'It was you and the others who need to be thanked.'

'You give us food. You are kind,' said Piotr.

Jessie remembered what the man in charge, Mr Rawson, had said about how the men were normally treated.

'Yes,' she replied. 'It was the least I could do.'

'Thank you,' he said again.

'You walked all this way,' she said, 'to say that?'

'Yes, and to bring,' he pointed at the holly.

'Stay here,' said Jessie.

Five minutes later she returned with a tray: coffee, cake, and two scones fresh from the baking she and Agnes had done the day before. Every drop and every crumb was gone in a remarkably short time.

'Thank you,' he said again. He looked around the room.

'Piano?' he said. 'I play for you.'

She looked at his hands as he wiggled his long pale fingers. Then she got up and led him through into the dining room at the back of the house where Agnes's mother's piano stood, polished weekly by Nellie, but unplayed by anyone since Lionel's stroke. Jessie opened the lid and pulled out the stool, trying to recall when it might have been tuned. Piotr blew on his hands, stretched his fingers and sat down looking at the keys.

174

For a short while he sat quite still. The room was very cold and Jessie wondered if he was having second thoughts, or needed some music. When he began to play she was first astonished and then overwhelmed. She found an armchair and sat down, leaning forward to watch as the long fingers moved over the keys. The notes fell into the cold air of the room, clear, harmonious, passionate. She felt tears form in her eyes and brushed them away. He seemed transformed, younger, more energetic than the forlorn figure standing in the porch only half an hour before. Dark hair that had looked so lank now gleamed in the light from the window. The young man's eyes were closed but his body was awake. Energy poured from him as Jessie watched and listened, entranced.

The music reached a climax, and ended with the gentlest of chords leaving the air vibrating. For a moment Piotr sat very still, his fingers still touching the keys, before his hands dropped into his lap and he looked down. Jessie wiped her eyes with a hand-kerchief. No response seemed adequate. She leaned forward and took hold of one of his hands. He turned towards her and bowed his head, then got up and put her hand to his lips as he'd done the first time they met. She in turn put first one of his hands and then the other to her lips.

'Thank you Piotr,' she said.

'I play more?' he offered, and she nodded, sitting down again to listen, wishing that Agnes could have been there to hear the finest sounds the old piano had ever produced.

Piotr turned towards her, rubbing his hands together.

'Many months,' he said, 'I have not played. And this,' he touched the keys, 'this is good. A good piano.'

'Where did you learn?' said Jessie. She had many questions but knew that Piotr would struggle with too much English all at once.

'In Warsaw, before the war, before ...' He raised his hands, to compensate for words that could not come. 'My father brother,' he began.

'Your uncle?'

'Yes, Uncle Wlodya, he had money, for the conservatoire, in Warsaw. He is good to me. Give me money and I get away, before the Germans come.'

'Your family?' Jessie asked.

He shrugged. 'I do not know, I hear nothing.'

'And your uncle?'

'Nothing. And now, the Russians. Worse than Germans.'

'You want to go back?'

'No. But nothing for me here.'

'Except your music,' said Jessie, trying to comfort him.

'Music no good without money, without job,' said Piotr.

They looked at each other. There was nothing more to say.

It was nearly an hour before they spoke again. Piotr looked at Jessie's books while she made a meal for them. He showed no sign of leaving, and she did not want him to. She was intrigued by his strangeness, a visitor from a world she knew nothing of. She ate little herself, giving him the bulk of the food.

'Where did you learn English?' she asked.

'Conservatoire,' he said. 'But English no good.'

'It's fine,' she said. Then a thought struck her. 'Would you like me to teach you more? Then maybe you could find a job, leave the camp.'

He put down his fork, and looked up.

'Teach?' he said. 'But no money.'

'Not for money, Piotr. I could teach you at weekends. I could come to the camp, on the bus, or you could come here.'

'At the camp. Teach everyone,' he said.

She thought for a moment, remembering what Agnes had said

176

about a project. 'Why not?'

Suddenly she felt a rush of her old self, the energetic, confident Jessie that seemed to have disappeared. These lost men needed her, and she could help them.

'Why you do this?' said Piotr. He had eaten well for the first time in months. 'Why you feed me, help with English?'

'Because I can,' said Jessie. 'I have time.'

'Husband, he dead?'

Jessie hesitated. 'No, yes, he died, but a long time ago. In the first war.'

'Ah,' said Piotr. 'You have child, no, children,' he added, remembering the word.

'No – yes,' she hadn't had time to prepare the lies. 'I have a nephew, my sister's child. He's like a son to me.'

'He here?' asked Piotr.

'No,' said Jessie, 'He works in a coal mine, in Whitehaven.'

'Then you alone,' he said, 'like me.'

She stared at him. 'Yes,' she said reluctantly. 'Alone.'

Chapter 20

'NOT GOING IN THERE, ARE YOU MISSUS?' said the woman on the bus to Jessie at the camp gate. 'Bloody scroungers in there. Send 'em all home, my man says.'

Jessie walked through the main gate, round a central patch of grass yellowed by thawing snow, and towards the nearest building, a low-lying brick hut with small chimneys poking through the sloping roof. There was no one about. Most of the men were working on farms or digging drainage ditches. Suddenly a remarkably well-dressed man appeared round the side of the building: a short man, with a slight limp, and a worried expression.

'Miss Whelan?'

Jessie held out her hand, guessing. 'Mr Andrews?'

'You found us, then. Not hard to spot I suppose. Most people know where the camp is, but they get mixed up about who's here now. We try to call it a hostel these days, but the name sticks. Let me show you round before we talk,' he said. 'Give you an idea of how things work. I'm a bit slow.' He tapped his leg. 'Old wound, from the last war, but it's not far.'

Jessie was surprised by the extent of the camp. The sleeping huts were less crowded than they had been during the war, but it was a drab place: concrete floors, bare walls save for the odd faded photograph, old iron beds.

'Hard to make it homely,' said her guide as they peered into yet another bleak space. 'But there's something that might surprise you.'

Mr Andrews guided her to one of the huts, which from the outside looked the same as all the others. He opened the door and stood back to let Jessie enter ahead of him. She gasped. Every wall and the entire low ceiling were covered with painted murals and inscriptions. At the far end was an altar, and sunlight streaming in from the south picked up the rich colours of the figures painted on the wall behind it. Above the altar, reaching to the apex of the ceiling, was a carved wooden cross. On the altar itself a smaller cross, heavy and ornate.

'Amazing, isn't it?' he said. 'Every time I come in here I see something new, a detail I've never noticed before. Father O'Toole had to explain some of the symbols.'

'Who painted it?' asked Jessie, looking at each wall in turn.

'One of the German prisoners. They were here before the Italians,' he said. 'Can't remember his name. He was an artist in Germany before the war apparently. He got most of it done before they sent him home, and another bloke finished it off. They used their mates as models for the faces. Someone made the altar cross too, out of scrap metal, really solid and heavy. I'd love more people to see this place, but locals wouldn't come and it's too far from London for anyone important to bother.'

'Do they still have services here?'

'Oh aye. Catholic ones, like. Father O'Toole comes out from Millom regular, and spends a lot of time here with the men. All of them, not just Catholics. He's an amazing man. What day is it? Tuesday, he should be here later. Always comes on Tuesdays to see the men when they come back from work. Has supper with us often. Can you stay?'

This was more than Jessie had bargained for. She tried to recall the times of the buses back to Newton, but before she could reply, music reached them through the open door of the chapel. She cocked her head to listen. 'Is that Piotr?' she asked.

'It is,' he said, 'but how …?'

'He came to visit me in Newton,' she said, smiling at his astonishment. 'My friend has a piano, and he played for me, wonderfully. That was the day I decided I could help the men with their English.'

'He's over there,' said Mr Andrews, 'in the main hall. The piano's pretty poor but he doesn't seem to mind.'

They had been standing at the door listening for a while before Piotr noticed them. He stopped playing, and when he turned towards the light Jessie could see that tears were running down his face. He wiped them away quickly with the sleeve of his jacket and got up.

'Miss Whelan,' he said, with a small bow.

'Hello again, Piotr,' she said, inclining her head towards him. 'More wonderful playing.'

'Miss Whelan is having a look around,' said Mr Andrews. 'We shall see you later.' As they walked away he spoke more quietly. 'Very emotional, some of the men. Slavs, you know. They cry a lot.'

By the time Jessie and the warden had finished their tour of the camp and discussed the details of her proposed English lessons for the men, it was after five o'clock. They heard a car engine as it rounded the grass circle and pulled up outside Mr Andrews' office. A moment later a large head appeared round the door, followed by a burly body dressed in black.

'Father O'Toole, come in, come in,' said Mr Andrews.

'Good afternoon, Philip,' said the priest. His Irish accent was immediately obvious. Round black spectacles gave his face a scholarly expression, at odds with the body of a rugby player.

'This is Miss Whelan, father,' said Philip, turning to Jessie, 'from Newton. She's going to be teaching the men English.'

'Thank heaven for you, Miss Whelan,' said the priest, taking Jessie's outstretched hand in his. 'That's exactly what they need. Just enough to let them speak to the people they work with, or to the girls they meet at the weekend. Language – it's the key, don't you think?' He had kept hold of her hand: she felt the warmth of his grip.

'They're not back yet, father,' said Philip, looking at his watch.

'I came early, to see Piotr. How is he today?'

'He played for us,' Jessie interrupted, drawn to the energy that surrounded Father O'Toole. 'It was astonishing, full of longing,' she went on. 'I've never heard playing like it.'

'It's a gift right enough,' said the priest. 'And he's a sad soul, desperate to go home but afraid that his life there has gone, poor man. I'll see him before the others get back. Easier to get close when there's no one else around.' He turned to Jessie. She noticed the green of his eyes behind the spectacles. 'You'll stay for supper with us, Miss Whelan. That's a good Irish name, so it is.'

'She's already agreed to stay,' said Philip. 'Good chance to meet the men. Gives them a chance to meet her, too.'

It had been a while since someone had asked about her name. Jessie reminded herself of the customary lies about her family and hoped she could keep the questions at bay.

At supper Jessie sat with the group of men she'd met at the schoolhouse when they had come to dig out the road. After their meal Philip Andrews stood up to explain to the hundred or so men sitting at long benches that their guest would be offering English lessons. He paused and a dozen voices around the room spoke simultaneously in different languages, as one man from each national group translated for the others.

Jessie tugged at Philip's sleeve. 'Tell them how much we appreciate their help with the snow,' she said. He raised his hand for silence, waited until the babble of voices faded, repeated what she had said, and the babble started again. Group by group the men smiled and nodded as they understood what had been said.

Father O'Toole caught her eye. 'Tower of Babel isn't it?' he said to her across the din. 'But it works.'

On the late bus back to Newton, Jessie's mind was full. There was a whole world out there that she'd known nothing about. All these years her life had been confined in the cocoon of the school and the village, and today she had encountered people from all over Europe, each of them with a talent and a story that was a mystery to her. It was only when she let herself into the porch at Applegarth that she realised that the lamps were lit, and there were voices in the front room.

'Is that you, dear?' called Agnes. 'We're in here.'

Jessie pushed open the door from the hall. Agnes was on her feet, smiling, and getting to his feet beside her was a man Jessie had never seen before.

'Jessie, dear, this is Edwin Bennett, from my office in London. Edwin, this is Jessie Whelan. She's been the schoolteacher here for many years, and now she's looking for a new challenge, aren't you, dear?'

More new people. Jessie took off her coat and hat, giving herself time to take it all in.

'Have you eaten?' asked Agnes.

'I had supper at the camp,' she said. 'I wrote to you about it, giving English lessons for the DPs, you remember?'

'Of course,' said Agnes. She turned to Edwin Bennett to explain about Jessie's encounter with the men from the camp and her plans for helping them. Mr Bennett listened attentively. He wore round spectacles and a suit with a waistcoat. His small hands were crossed in his lap, and his small feet in polished shoes hovered just above one of Fred's hookie rugs on the floor.

'That's a very laudable thing to do,' he said gravely to Jessie. 'These men are here through no fault of their own, but some people treat them as if they were prisoners of war.'

'I think I'm going to enjoy it,' said Jessie. 'The whole experience was so interesting.' She told them about the chapel, and Father O'Toole, whom Agnes had heard of but never spoken to.

'Tell Edwin about your other plans for life after school, Jessie.'

Before Jessie could respond, Agnes continued. 'She's learning shorthand,' she said proudly, as if Jessie were a much-loved child. 'From a book. Making such progress. Just shows what a well-trained mind can achieve.'

'Another splendid idea,' said Edwin, positively beaming his approval. 'Teaching's loss will be others' gain, that's for sure.'

Jessie was curious now. She'd heard Agnes speak of Mr Bennett before, but what was he doing here? And why was Agnes so keen to tell him about the shorthand?

'Agnes tells me you've lived here for many years,' said the little man, shifting in his chair to look directly at Jessie through his round lenses. 'You must know the community very well.'

'I suppose I do,' she said, 'especially having taught so many of the children. You get to know a great deal about the families, sometimes more than you want to.'

'Ah, yes, discretion,' he nodded. 'So important in a small community, don't you know.'

Jessie began to feel alarmed. What had Agnes told him about her? 'It's important for a teacher, wherever they are,' she said, trying to move the conversation away from the particular to the general, but Mr Bennett continued his theme.

'There are always good reasons,' he said, 'why some things need to be, well, not exposed to the public gaze.'

Agnes interrupted, seeing the puzzlement in Jessie's face.

'Edwin is working on a very sensitive project,' she said, glancing at him. He nodded, and she continued. 'It concerns, rather it may concern, this area, and I've explained to him how easily information, or even gossip, can get around. We don't seem to need many telephones, do we?' Edwin Bennett's face creased into a humourless smile. 'Anyway, he's going to be staying here a few days, and maybe coming back again in a month or two. I said that was fine, but I wasn't happy about leaving you completely out of the picture now that you will be living here, too.'

Jessie wondered what was coming next. She excused herself for a few minutes. When she came back into the room the two of them were talking earnestly, their heads close together.

Agnes gestured slightly towards the guest, who began to speak.

'You see, Miss Whelan,' he said, 'We at the Ministry of Supply have been charged with finding a site for a new, er, facility. The site has to meet various … criteria, and I'll be looking at the old ordnance factory just north of here.'

'I thought that was all finished now,' said Jessie.

'Well, yes it is,' he said, 'but the site is a good choice for this new project. It has to be in a isolated area, just like the ordnance factory had to be.'

'Oh,' said Jessie. She still had no idea what all this might have to do with her. She looked patiently at Edwin Bennett, but he was sitting back, as if there was nothing more to say.

'It all sounds pretty mysterious, I know, Jessie,' said Agnes. 'I'm sure Edwin wouldn't mind me telling you that if this project goes ahead, the Ministry will be looking for people to be part of it, people who know the area and who have absolute discretion.'

'Jobs for local people, you mean? Seems a good idea to me.'

'But only very special local people to start with, with the right sort of skills,' said Agnes, emphasising 'right sort' as she looked meaningfully at Jessie.

'Oh, you mean people like me?' said Jessie, surprised. 'But I have a project of my own now, at the camp.'

A small cloud of irritation passed over Edwin's round face.

'I cannot share the details at this time, Miss Whelan,' he said, 'but suffice to say that this matter is of national importance, concerning the defence of the realm.'

'I see,' said Jessie, although she didn't see, at all. That's the end of that, she thought to herself. And so it was.

Mr Bennett stayed for a few days. Every morning after breakfast he and Agnes drove away in her car, returning late in the afternoon. Nothing more was said, the three of them passed their evenings playing rummy, and at the end of the week Agnes and Mr Bennett returned to London.

After they had gone, Jessie found a note from Agnes on her dressing table.

Sorry to leave you in the dark, dear. Couldn't say much more really without getting into trouble myself.

I'll fill you in when I get back, not sure when that'll be. I'll call you when I know.

Look after yourself. I've left some more food coupons for Nellie in the kitchen drawer.

All my love

A

Chapter 21

ON HER WAY TO THE CAMP, Jessie read the first paragraph of the letter from Andrew that had just arrived. She held it on her lap, glancing round the bus to make sure that no one could see either the letter or her reaction to it. She knew that she shouldn't keep writing to him, but she kept on doing so. 'Stringing him along' her mother would have called it. She craved the surge of excitement when the Canadian stamp caught her eye. Now that he was far away again, the contact felt safe. She'd told him about leaving the schoolhouse, and was unprepared for his response.

The worst thing about the whole business, he wrote in the barely decipherable scrawl that his writing had become, *is that you're going to move in with that woman. You may not have seen the signs but I've always known what she's up to. Maybe it takes a man to recognise it. She wants you, Jessie, in her bed, not just in her house. I saw what she was up to years ago, and I wasn't the only one. No one can hate men as much as she does without a reason. She was jealous of you and me. Remember how she went at you when she found out about us? 'Disgusted' that's what she said, you told me yourself. It's taken a long time but now she's got you where she wants you. That job of hers in London won't last much longer and then she can come back to you, so the two of you*

can live happily ever after. Makes me sick to think about it.
Get out of there, Jessie. I can send you the money. You could
have a lovely summer passage over here, bit of sightseeing in
Montreal or New York, and whatever you want after that.
There's no one else here for me, never has been.

Jessie was shocked. She read it again. Andrew had never liked
Agnes, and Agnes's attitude towards him had made it worse,
but this? He sounded jealous, but of what? She and Agnes were
friends, no more. How could he think such a thing? Agnes would
be mortified. Jessie folded the letter up carefully and determined
to destroy it when she got home. For the time being, she tucked
it down deep into her bag and took extra care with the bag as she
got off the bus.

For the first few weeks of her assignment at the camp, she'd been
surprised at the different aptitudes for learning a new language
among her small group of students. About twenty men had started
off, but now the numbers had reduced to eight or nine, as one by
one they gave up, defeated and depressed by the complexities of
the English language. It didn't help that the language they heard
around them didn't seem to follow any patterns of grammar or
pronunciation that she could teach them. To start with, she tried
to teach them 'proper' English, but gradually changed direction
towards the essentials of making themselves understood and
recognising what was said to them. Piotr's existing grasp made
him more of a fellow-teacher than a student, and her admiration
for him had grown since that first encounter in the snow. Now
before every lesson she met with him to explain what she was
aiming to do, and to take his advice about how to present it. He
translated for her too, using Russian as well as Polish to connect
with the other men.

Piotr was waiting for her that day as she stepped down from
the bus. He offered to carry her bag but she did not let go of it.

'The men will be late today,' he said. 'Truck not working. Mr Andrews say to use his office, make tea and wait.'

It was warm in the little office.

'A very nice day,' he said. 'We walk to the beach. Good idea?'

It was indeed a good idea. They walked down the path from the camp, over the rise in the dunes and looked out over the wide stretch of pebbles and sand. Behind them Black Combe lay like a sleeping animal, and to the north the hint of hills, the westerly edge of the high fells. Late spring sun warmed their faces.

'You stayed in camp again today?' she said. He nodded, without explanation. Piotr's health had improved slowly since the end of winter, but there were still days when he was not well enough for the hard work on the farm. Philip Andrews had told her that one of the farmers had singled Piotr out for particularly callous treat-ment and it was often easier not to send him out there. The other men understood and didn't resent the time he spent in camp, so long as he played the piano for them.

Jessie and Piotr sat side by side at the foot of the dunes, looking out at the retreating tide. A flock of curlews swept low above their heads and turnstones skittered along the shore, where the channel winked at the edge of the sloping beach. The song of the curlews reached them on the warm southerly breeze.

'I walk out there,' he said, pointing out to sea. 'When the water is low I walk out. There are hills in the sand. Sometimes no see this place. Why is that?'

Jessie looked at the shape of the beach, and thought about it, picturing the map in her mind's eye. She pointed down the beach to the south. 'Just down there, the river reaches the sea. This is where the river and the sea mix together,' she made a circling motion with her hand, 'and the water makes deep channels.' Piotr listened and nodded. 'When the water – or tide – is very low, you can walk out there and into those channels, like you did.'

'I see,' he said.

'Do you think you might go home soon?' she asked.

There was no response and she looked across at him. His black hair had grown long, falling across his face, and he hadn't shaved for several days. He picked up a small stone and aimed it at a large piece of driftwood on the tide line. It missed. He threw another, and another, and then a handful of sand that caught the wind and blew away.

'No go home. No home,' he said.

'What about your family?' she asked, remembering what Father O'Toole had told her weeks before.

'No letter. Maybe dead,' he said.

There was nothing she could say. He was right. His family could have died with a million others. A longer silence. 'Could you stay here?' she asked.

'Here is not my home,' he said.

'Have you talked to Father O'Toole about it?' Jessie knew the respect the men had for the priest.

'Good man, but he cannot help. No one can help.'

She thought quickly. 'Maybe we could find you a job here. I have friends in London, they might –'

'No,' he said, shaking his head. 'We go back now.' He got up and turned towards the path. They walked back to the camp in silence.

* * *

The end of Jessie's many years at the school came in a rush and took her by surprise. The final days passed in a blur of farewells from the children and some of the parents, those who hadn't followed Mrs Crompton's lead in blaming Jessie for the housing crisis. Jessie knew that after twenty years she must accept the ceremonials of departure, but some of them were hard to take, especially when Gideon Barker was part of it. The mutual irritation must be obvious, thought Jessie, but she shook his hand anyway, just to get the whole business over with. She had been packing up her things at the schoolhouse for a number of weeks, giving some away, having others carried up the hill to Applegarth. Now she had just one more week before Easter to finish the job and hand over the keys.

Working weekends at the camp had made the final weeks at school more bearable. They gave her a purpose and focus outside the school, away from the village. It was a short bus ride south from Newton, but the camp might have been on another planet, and the men she worked with were as different from her Newton pupils as it was possible to be. In some ways they reminded her of the evacuee children who had crowded into school during the war, whose Geordie accents were almost as impenetrable as the Hungarian and Polish she heard around her in a corner of the big room. 'The evacuee children were a handful, no mistake,' she said, explaining this thought to Mr Andrews in his office one day. 'And their mothers were worse! Even so, I missed them when they left. It was a challenge, like this one.'

This was an opportunity for Mr Andrews to thank her, yet again, and he duly did so. I think he likes me, said Jessie to herself, and the thought pleased her. The teaching space quickly became a permanent fixture, with its circle of chairs and tables, the blackboard on an easel and the shelf of unused books that Jessie had brought from home. At the camp she could count on the respect she used to enjoy at the school.

There was another regular visitor to the camp on Saturday afternoons. As the weather improved, Father O'Toole arrived towards the end of Jessie's class, changed out of his cassock into an old shirt and enormous pair of grey shorts and organised the men into teams for a game of football on the sandy grass that passed for a recreation area beyond the huts. When the Saturday games first started he appointed himself the referee, but very soon he had cajoled someone else to take this role, allowing him to join in without restraint, crashing around the pitch like an overgrown schoolboy. Instead of catching the first bus back to Newton when her work was done, Jessie stayed on to watch, cheering and shouting encouragement with any other spectators, or just by herself.

When Father O'Toole stopped his car one evening to offer her a lift home, she accepted with pleasure.

'Hop in, Miss Whelan,' he said, leaning over to open the passenger door of the old black Austin. 'I'm away to a meeting in Whitehaven. I could drop you right at the schoolhouse door.'

'I'm not living there any more,' she said, 'not since the end of last term.'

'Should I congratulate you or commiserate?' said the priest, looking over at her as he pulled away.

'For a while I wasn't sure about that, father. But I'm trying to see it as the right thing to do. With decent housing so short it was hard to justify just one person at the schoolhouse, and one of the returned servicemen wanted my job and the house so badly, that I decided to take the opportunity.'

'That's remarkably generous, Miss Whelan,' he said.

'Jessie, please,' she said. 'Miss Whelan still sounds like the schoolmistress.'

The afternoon light gleamed off the sea and fields still flooded since the thaw.

'The farmers have had a terrible year,' she said. 'First the winter and the snow, then the floods. Half the sheep are gone, I hear. One of our neighbours couldn't recover. His son found him hanged in the barn. Terrible business.'

'The poor soul. We can only imagine what depths he must

have reached,' said the priest. 'And so hard for the family. So much guilt.'

They drove in silence for a while.

'You have somewhere to live, I trust,' he said, mindful of what Jessie had said about leaving the school. 'I have time to take you to your door, wherever that is.'

'Thank you, father,' said Jessie. 'I'm living at Applegarth now, Miss Plane's house, just up the hill from the school. She and I have been friends ever since I came here, and I've been looking after her lovely house while she's been working in London. Plenty of room for both of us. I'm very fortunate.'

'Of course, Miss Plane. Her father was the dean in Carlisle, was he not? So what is she doing in London?'

'It was war work, with the Ministry of Supply, and it's just carried on. Sometimes it feels as if the war has never ended, don't you think? And Agnes is still needed, so there she stays. The past few weeks and months have been dreadful, and worse in the south. At least when you don't have electricity you don't miss it when it fails.'

The priest laughed. 'You can't miss what you've never had, that's for sure,' he said.

Jessie was letting herself in at Applegarth when she heard the telephone ringing. Unexpected calls always worried her, and she picked up the receiver wondering who it could be. Most people knew that Agnes was away, but only a few that Jessie was now living there.

'Is that you Jessie?' said Caroline Leadbetter. 'I got your post-card saying that you had something to talk to me about, and rang just on the off chance. Agnes told me you were at the camp quite a lot. Is it all going well?'

Jessie was taken aback. She had written to Caroline weeks before, after her conversation with Agnes about John, and had regretted it ever since. As the weeks had passed she hoped that Caroline would forget what she'd said, but obviously not.

'I'm sorry it's taken so long to reach you, dear,' said Caroline. 'Lionel keeps me very busy these days. He would love to see you, and now you're a lady of leisure …'

'It hasn't really sunk in yet, about the job,' said Jessie. 'While I was working I had no idea how I would spend my time when it stopped, but the days slip by and I seem to be still on the go.'

'Do you still want to come up? You could stay overnight; it's too far to trek here and back in a day, and we'll have a lot of catching up to do.'

* * *

Catching up, thought Jessie as she sat on the train a few days later. She had still not decided how to tell Caroline about John. After all these years, it felt like a dreadful risk. But she knew it was time. She was sure that her friendship with the Leadbetters would survive the initial shock. Eventually she would have to tell Matthew – maybe this was a way to check his possible reaction, a rehearsal.

The Leadbetters' house in Cockermouth was as comfortable as Applegarth, with a view of hills and trees south towards Lorton and Loweswater. Caroline took Lionel his lunch on a tray and then sat with her friend at a sunny table. It would have been so easy to pass the afternoon in undemanding conversation, as they had done so many times before. But Jessie had made up her mind, and now had her script ready.

'There's something I need to talk to you about,' she said, hoping that Caroline would pay attention and listen.

'Oh, my dear,' said Caroline, squeezing Jessie's hand. 'I've been hoping it would all work out. Tell me all about it. Lionel will be so delighted.'

Jessie stared at her. What could Caroline be so excited about?

'We saw him only last week,' Caroline went on, 'looking pleased with himself, but he didn't say anything. When did he ask you?'

'Who?' said Jessie. 'Ask me what?'

'Now don't be coy, dear,' said Caroline, smiling. 'Matthew, of course. I guessed that something would happen soon, but when did he ask you?'

'Matthew hasn't asked me anything,' said Jessie. 'That's not what I wanted to tell you.'

'Oh dear, do forgive me, Jessie. Silly me. But he will you know, it's just a matter of time. He's smitten with you, we've all noticed it.'

Jessie hesitated, taking in the implications of her friend's assumptions. 'It's nothing to do with Matthew. He hasn't asked me to marry him, if that's what you mean.'

'Oh.' Caroline looked puzzled. 'So what do you want to tell me?' Jessie thought about abandoning her plan, but she was determined to do it and pushed on. She took a deep breath and looked down at her hands. Caroline's interested gaze was too much to deal with.

'It's about something that happened many years ago,' said Jessie. 'Long before I moved to Newton, when I was just a girl really.'

'Yes,' said Caroline.

'I – I was engaged to a wonderful young man and we – I made a mistake. I fell pregnant.'

Jessie looked at Caroline, whose smile seemed to have stuck.

'These things happen, I know,' said Caroline after a slight pause. 'So you were married before we knew you. What happened?'

'No, that's not it,' said Jessie, her prepared script unravelling. 'He died. My fiancé died in an accident.' She expected Caroline to say something, but there was silence. 'I had the baby, and people took it.'

'People took it?' Caroline looked incredulous.

'Friends of my mother. They wanted a child and couldn't have one, and they took mine. I gave him away.'

'Oh, my dear, how awful for you,' said Caroline, struggling to envisage how this could have happened, not to some wretched girl but to her well-educated friend, a schoolteacher.

Jessie ploughed on. 'They brought him up, but they never told him about me, not until the very end, when the boy was twenty or so. When his parents, his adopted parents, died, he set off to find me, and he did.'

'When was this?' said Caroline. She had poured tea for them both, but it sat cooling and untouched on the table. A blackbird sang in the blossoming cherry tree outside the open window.

'Ten years ago,' said Jessie. 'He found me. I guessed who he was before he knew himself. He looked so like his father.'

'So you have a son, Jessie.' Caroline thought for a moment. 'Does Agnes know about this?' Jessie nodded.

'Ah,' said Caroline, as if she understood, 'I knew there was something, but this ... well ...'

Well what, thought Jessie. She persevered. 'I have a son. When he found me, I knew that I could lose my job, and the house, so I asked him not to say anything. He suggested that I tell people he is my nephew, my sister's child.'

Caroline's eyes widened. 'Do you mean John? John Pharaoh is your son?'

Jessie nodded again. A flush of shame crept up her neck. 'Yes,' she whispered. 'John's my son. It's been a secret long enough. I wanted you to know.'

Caroline got up from the table and paced up and down, her hands clasped tightly in front of her.

'Oh, dear,' she said. 'I had no idea ... Who else knows about this?'

'A few people,' said Jessie miserably. It all sounded so tawdry. 'John has a friend, in Whitehaven. I think he's told her. And Agnes of course, she's known from the beginning.'

'Does Matthew Dawson know?'

'Of course not, no.'

'Well he mustn't know. And of course we can't say anything to Lionel, not now,' said Caroline, with unexpected firmness. Jessie looked up at her. 'He's not well – it could kill him.'

'Surely not?' said Jessie.

'Let me be the judge of that,' said Caroline, sharply. 'He must not know, not until he's feeling better. It's just the shock. Of course we cannot judge you, and I can understand what you … but it's best not mentioned.'

'I wanted to put it behind me,' said Jessie. 'After all these years.'

'Why bother?' Caroline seemed to be talking to herself. 'It's been a secret all this time. No one any the wiser. I don't know what to say, Jessie, I really don't.' She sat down again and stared out of the window. Jessie was shocked. She thought Caroline would be sympathetic, as Agnes had always been, not angry like this.

Jessie got to her feet. 'That's what I wanted to tell you, and I've done it now. I think I'd better go.'

'Yes, yes,' said Caroline. 'I need a little time … to take it all in.' She put a hand to her mouth. 'You're not going to tell Matthew are you, about this?'

'Well, yes,' said Jessie, 'I thought …'

'Don't say a word to him, Jessie. It could ruin everything. His girls – well they wouldn't stand for it.'

'I can't believe that,' said Jessie. 'It would be a matter for Matthew to discuss with me, not his daughters, surely.'

'As you wish,' said Caroline. 'My advice would be to say nothing more to anyone. Let sleeping dogs lie, I say. You can count on me.'

On the train back to Newton Jessie felt her confidence and

belief in the future drain away. She knew her friends might find it difficult to accept that she had lied to them for so long, but she had not expected Caroline's reaction. Her stay in Cockermouth had been strained and awkward and it was a relief to leave for an earlier train than she had planned. All that seemed to matter to Caroline was what Matthew Dawson might think, or his wretched daughters, about whom Jessie knew little and cared less.

Suddenly her plans for putting the past behind her, clearing away the lies and starting afresh, had been swept aside by Caroline Leadbetter's fear of lost respectability. Maybe Caroline would calm down. Maybe she wouldn't. Jessie saw a lonely future ahead of her, with only Agnes willing to be her friend. And what if Andrew was right about Agnes? Alone in the house, Jessie felt the walls of loneliness closing in around her, and for the first time in a long time she cried herself to sleep.

CHAPTER 22

LOW MORNING SUN BURST over the fell tops and pierced Jessie's curtained window. She woke suddenly from deep sleep. Something, a memory or a dream was hurting her, sharp and unseen like a splinter below the skin. She lay still for a moment, uncomfortably hot in her winter nightdress. Her little bedside clock said it was after eight but she struggled to remember the day or the date. In a world without work the structures of time had blurred.

It was two days since her miserable visit to the Leadbetters. She had planned to be away for two days but the early return had left a day clear of obligations and she had done nothing and seen no one. Today she needed to do something, to soak up her energy. She would go the camp, and talk to Philip Andrews about what she could offer now that she had more time. He at least would be pleased to see her. She dressed carefully, happy to have a reason to do so. There was no hurry. Having more time than she needed was a luxury that Jessie revelled in.

It was nearly lunchtime before she arrived at the camp, and there was no one around. She put her head round the door of the empty office, and was heading off towards the main hall when she noticed Philip Andrews coming across the yard.

'Good morning,' he called across to her. 'Didn't expect to see you today. Have I got my dates wrong?'

'No,' she smiled. 'I had some unexpected time and thought I'd just come down, in case you could spare me a little while to think about future arrangements. I hope I'm not getting in your way?'

Neither of them admitted how pleased they were at the unexpected prospect of cheerful conversation.

'Come across to the office,' he said. 'I'll make us both a drink.'

'I thought I might have another chat with Piotr today,' said Jessie a few minutes later, sipping a cup of coffee that Agnes would have been unhappy with. 'He seems rather a lost soul. I've been thinking about him.'

'Yes, he worries me, too,' said Philip. 'Coughing a lot, and not talking much to anyone. He's around somewhere. Not well enough to go out today. He may still be in the dormitory.'

But the dormitory was empty. In the canteen, a woman who was wiping tables said she hadn't seen him. They walked over to the chapel, slowly as Philip's leg injury seemed to be troubling him. Jessie opened the door. It too was empty, but she had a sense that someone had been there. The faintest tang of tobacco lingered in the still air.

She called, 'Piotr. Are you here?'

Her voice bounced around the painted walls. 'He's been here. Someone's been here,' she said to Philip who was standing behind her. They looked around, not knowing what they were looking for. Then she noticed that something was missing.

'The cross, the one on the altar, where is it?'

Philip limped towards the altar. 'The wooden one's still here,' he said, 'but not the metal one.' He looked around on the floor. 'Might have been taken away, to be cleaned.'

'Who would do that? Wouldn't you know that someone had taken it?'

'I would think so, but where else could it be?'

Another thought flashed into her mind.

'The piano. Have you heard it?'

'Not today, but –'

This time she didn't wait, running from the chapel and across to the largest hut where she taught her English lessons and the piano stood in its far corner. By the time she reached the piano Philip had reached the door, leaning on the doorway, his face stiff with pain.

'Sorry …' he began, but Jessie didn't hear him. She ran her hands over the piano lid, tracing faint lines in the thin layer of dust. Something caught her eye, a tiny triangle of white. She opened the lid. A folded piece of paper lay underneath. She snatched it up. The writing was small and hard to read in the low light. Standing by Philip in the doorway she held up the scrap of paper and read:

I have no hope. Forgive me please.

'Oh God,' she said. 'Look!' She thrust the paper at her companion and steadied herself against the door frame, her hand to her mouth.

'Call the police, Philip. Something's happened.'

She stumbled out of the hut and began to run.

'Where are you going?' he called after her.

Jessie ran across the yard, to where the path led down to the beach. Gravel gave way to sand. One of her shoes came off and she kicked them both away. The path led across to the dunes, stony in places and fringed by marram grass. She stumbled on a sharp stone and fell heavily, but picked herself up and ran on, taking off her heavy coat and letting it fall.

The final dune was steep and she scrambled up, using her hands before reaching the top where the beach lay wide in front of her. She leaned over to catch her breath. A skylark rose into the air, singing its liquid song. The tide was half way out, or coming in. She couldn't tell. At the edge of the water, a hundred yards away, she saw a dark figure in a long coat, pushing out into the tiny waves.

'Piotr!' she shouted, but her voice was cracked, and it faded on the breeze.

Down the dunes she stumbled, onto the beach where large round stones at the top gave way to smaller pebbles and then gravel, dipping into a wide channel at the bottom of the slope. Another fall, and her knee protested as she rushed on with numbed feet on the cold sand. She stopped just long enough to see the figure waist-high in the sea ahead of her.

She shouted again, 'Piotr! Stop!' Ridges of sand made running difficult but she didn't feel the pain, her eyes fixed on him. When he turned she stopped, gasping for breath. In his arms she saw the heavy altar cross, held tight to his chest. She could not see his face clearly, and he turned back again, striding on into the water.

The final stretch of sand was smooth and firm under her bruised feet. She ran into the shallows, through the creeping waves, up to her knees now, hitching up the heavy skirt that was sodden and clinging to her legs.

When she looked up again, he was gone. The water ahead of her was flat, broken only by a slight swell and the faintest impression that the surface had been breached. For a second his head rose again, and then disappeared. She watched, helpless. Tears streamed down her face.

'Piotr!' she screamed, again and again, but there was nothing but the cry of a gull and the skitter of oyster catchers flying low towards the south. Jessie's knees buckled under her and she fell. The water reached her shoulders but she sat motionless, gasping, beating with her hands on the surface. Behind her, Philip stood at the top of the rise, calling uselessly into the breeze.

Philip helped Jessie out of the sea and supported her along the endless path back to the camp, picking up her discarded coat and shoes as they went. By the time they reached the yard, a police car was pulling in. Jessie sat in the office, her clothes dripping onto the floor, while Philip talked to the police outside, and the two constables set off running down to the beach. They were not gone long. There was nothing to see, and nothing to find.

They left her alone, shivering by the stove in the office. Philip Andrews told the constables what he knew and answered their ponderous questions. The scrap of paper in Piotr's spidery hand was passed around, held up to the light as if some other secret or solution to the puzzle might be found, before it was folded and pushed deep into a navy serge pocket.

Forgive me please, read Constable Eric Nuttall. 'What's he done?'

'Topped 'imself,' said the other.

'Is that all?' said Eric.

'Piotr was a Catholic,' said Philip quietly. 'Suicide is a mortal sin.' They nodded, still hoping a crime might be revealed, before heading off to retrace the desperate search of the camp that Jessie and Philip had made not long before.

Alone, Jessie sat with head bowed, the sweet tea they had made for her unnoticed on the desk. She did not hear the car, or the footsteps outside. Father O'Toole's dark shape loomed in the doorway and she looked up.

'What happened?' he said, putting down his black bag and kneeling beside her.

'He's gone,' she whispered. 'He walked into the sea. I watched, I couldn't stop him.'

'Oh, my child,' said the priest. 'I came as soon as Philip called me. I should have –'

'We all should,' she said. 'When we found the note I knew, but I was too late.' She sobbed. 'He took the cross, from the altar in the chapel. He was holding it. He saw me but he didn't stop.'

'Where's the note?'

She nodded. 'The police have it. We found it in the piano. It said: *I have no hope. Forgive me.* No,' she hesitated. '*Forgive me please.* Just that.'

Jessie turned and buried her head in Father O'Toole's coat. He put his arm around her.

The constables learned all there was to learn and drove away to make their report and arrange the search. Mr Andrews needed the office for phone calls and reports. Father O'Toole helped Jessie across to the chapel and sat with her.

'I tried so hard,' she whispered. 'I tried to help him find some hope. I said we could find him a job here, but he didn't seem to care. I told him to talk to you. He said his family would all be gone, but he didn't know that, not for sure. So why? He was young. And his playing, so beautiful. Why did he do it?'

'We can't tell, Jessie,' he said, holding her hand. 'We can't even guess. He was a private soul and we could not reach him. Perhaps he was very sick. Maybe that affected him. Bless you for caring for him, for trying to help. You did all you could. Don't blame yourself.'

She was crying as if the tragedy had unleashed sadness held back for many years. He took her home in the old car. Nellie was there, and together they helped Jessie up the stairs. Nellie promised to stay a while. Father O'Toole found Agnes's London phone number and called it, leaving a vague message with a posh anonymous voice for Agnes to call him or her friend at Apple-garth as soon as she could. Then he drove away, leaving Jessie to sleep and Nellie to make some food for her when she woke.

It was two days before they found Piotr's body. It had been pulled out to sea by the ebbing tide and then drifted north and was beached further up the coast, exactly where the local policeman had expected. Piotr had tied the cross to his chest with a woollen scarf and in the pockets of the coat were large stones from the beach. A strand of bright green seaweed trailed across one pale cheek.

Chapter 23

THE HEARSE WOUND THROUGH late spring lanes whitened with cow parsley, to the Catholic church in Millom. Behind the hearse was a bus filled with men in their faded pre-war suits, and behind the bus two flatbed trucks, like tumbrils to the scaffold, with more of the men standing together on the back. Jessie rode with Philip in his car. It was six days since Piotr's death, six dawns when she woke with the birds and lay sad and regretful, remembering the music and his slow, beautiful, accented voice.

'He had such promise,' Jessie had said to Agnes on the telephone the morning after Piotr's death. 'His English was coming on so well, he could have found a job if he'd wanted to.'

'Perhaps he didn't want to,' said Agnes, sensing the desperation in her dear friend's voice.

'I wanted to help him, but I couldn't reach him. Father O'Toole has been wonderful. I know he's right, but still I feel we should have known.'

'Did you say Father O'Toole,' said Agnes, 'Is he the priest at the camp?'

'Yes,' said Jessie. 'I forgot. He says he knew your father, in Carlisle. Do you know him yourself?'

'Only by reputation,' said Agnes. She hesitated. 'He had some trouble, ages ago, in Silloth or somewhere up there, on the Solway coast. I think it was about a woman. My father mentioned it once. And there was a picture of him. A good-looking young man, as I recall. It was a long time ago.'

'I think he's wonderful,' said Jessie.

'Be careful,' said her friend.

* * *

'Piotr took his own life,' Jessie said to Philip as they followed the hearse into the town. 'Isn't that a mortal sin?'

'Makes no difference to Father O'Toole,' he said. 'He called it an unfortunate accident and there was never any doubt about a proper funeral. I'm not a Catholic, but the man's a hero. Are you a Catholic, Jessie?'

'Not much of anything really. I wish I was. It must help, at times like this.'

'Nothing helps. A needless death. I wonder, did we miss something? Was there any hint of it?'

'He was very sad,' she said slowly. 'Sad about his family. He couldn't see a way out, or a way forward. But I had no idea. Could we have done anything?'

Philip shook his head.

People in the street stopped and stared at the hearse and the trucks loaded with men in their shabby suits.

'Piotr said the locals hate them. Is that right?' she asked him, watching the expressionless faces turned towards them.

Philip looked at her. 'Some people hate what they don't understand, strangers, new ideas. That way they don't have to deal with them. Some people are kind. It varies. When the men go to local dances at the weekend, they tell me that in some places the girls will dance with them, and in other places nobody will. They end up dancing with each other.'

Six of the men, all from Poland, carried the coffin between them from the hearse to the porch where Father O'Toole was waiting with two altar boys. They filed into the empty church. Someone was playing the organ. Jessie recognised the music that Piotr had played for them himself on the piano at the camp. They sang the old hymns. One of the men read a poem in Polish and a group of them sang, the unfamiliar tune echoing around the church. Jessie tried to sing the hymn that followed but she could not. Her voice cracked and wavered and she gave up. Even before Father O'Toole began to speak, she had fumbled for a fresh handkerchief in her bag. Philip squeezed her hand.

'Let us remember Piotr,' said the strong Irish voice. 'For seventeen years, it was a good life, the youngest child and much loved. So talented, such wonderful music. And then the evil of war caught him and so many millions of young men around the world. He was as much the victim of war as anyone killed on a battlefield. He struggled, but the evil overcame him and swept him aside. He did not know, nor do we, where his family are, if they survive at all. They cannot mourn, so we will mourn for them, for this young man, taken to God so early, too early. We will remember him.'

Jessie bent her head and wept. Philip drove her home before leaving to drink and sing with the men back at the camp. It was only six o'clock, but Jessie drew her bedroom curtains and lay down.

The rest of the week dragged slowly by. Philip had cancelled classes for a few days and Jessie did not go to the camp. Agnes was in London with no plans to return. Caroline Leadbetter had not been in touch since Jessie's visit. There was no word from Matthew Dawson, and Jessie wondered if anything had been said.

The weather was better than it had been for months and she tried to walk every day, letting the spring sunshine cheer her. At the church in Newton the last of the precious daffodils still nodded by the river. Jessie sat in an old box pew there for a little while each day, letting her sadness flow, before putting on a braver face for public view. But the nights were long and difficult. Among Agnes's records she found some Chopin piano music and played it repeatedly, sitting motionless in her chair by the empty grate. She was there when John knocked on the window early on the Friday evening, making her start. She saw his familiar shape silhouetted against the brightness of the garden where it caught the long light from the west. She turned off the record player before she answered the door.

'I rang the bell,' he said, 'but you can't have heard it. The music was really loud.'

'Yes,' she said. 'Come in.'

They sat in the front room. 'Do you want something?' she said. She did not really want to be disturbed, and John's rare visits usually heralded something upsetting.

'I have some news,' he said, 'but you look very tired. Are you alright?'

'It's been a bad week,' she said. 'You know I've been working at the camp, the one near Millom, teaching English?'

'Oh yes,' he said, remembering. 'That chap who drowned, last week. Did you know him?'

She nodded. 'He was a wonderful young man,' she said. 'I knew him well. We talked all about his life in Poland before the war, how he got out, where he'd been. Such an interesting person.'

'Oh,' said John. 'I'm sorry. I've chosen a bad time –'

'He played the piano, here in this house,' said Jessie, as if John hadn't spoken at all. 'So beautifully. Such a talent.'

'I see,' said John.

'And now he's gone,' she said.

'Yes,' said John. He got up. 'I think I should go, you're obviously upset, and – well, I should go.'

'But you've only just got here,' she said. 'And you hardly ever come to see me. Do stay a little longer. I'm going to have a sherry. Would you like one?' John looked at his watch. If he left now he could get the six thirty bus back.

'No, thanks,' he said. 'It doesn't matter.' Not to you, he thought. Aloud, he added, 'You're obviously upset about that young man.'

Jessie was pouring herself a sherry. 'It feels like losing a son,' she said.

John felt his face flush and a sour taste in his mouth. He turned away. 'I don't think so,' he said.

She looked at him. 'You've never lost a child, how could you know?'

He turned to face her. 'No, I never have,' he said, 'but you have. You lost me. Bet you didn't shed any tears over that.'

Jessie's hand carrying the sherry glass stopped halfway up to her lips.

'That's a terrible thing to say. You know how it was. We talked.'

'We did not,' said John, his voice rising. 'We never talked, not even when we were stuck in this house together for two whole days. You probably talked more to that dead man than you've ever talked to me. Have you ever asked me about my life, before we met? Have you?'

She faltered. 'I didn't think …'

'No, you didn't,' he said. Words poured into his head and into his mouth, bitter words. 'You never did. For years, when I was younger than that "son" of yours, I dreamed of you, finding you, having a mother, feeling part of a family. I searched for you, and you knew who I was. That day at Mill Cottage, you knew when you saw me and fainted away, you knew it was me. And you said nothing.'

'I couldn't be sure,' she said, sitting down on the arm of a chair to steady herself.

'You didn't want to be sure. You didn't want me upsetting your settled life. I was a nuisance to you. I still am.'

'No. John, no! That's not true. You said ...'

'Yes, I gave you the lifeline and you took it like a drowning man, didn't you?' She flinched. 'Your nephew, your poor bloody nephew,' he sneered, 'abandoned by your wicked sister. How kind you were to the poor boy, out of the goodness of your heart. That's what your fancy friends would say. Good, kind Jessie. They have no idea, do they? You still haven't told anyone. You're afraid to. Ashamed.'

'I did. I have,' said Jessie, desperately trying to fend off the anger that was pouring over her. 'I told Caroline.' She hesitated, remembering. 'It was awful. She wouldn't let me tell Lionel, said it might kill him.'

'What did you expect her to say?'

'I wanted her to understand, it was a long time ago.' She slid down to sit in the chair, looking at the empty fireplace.

'So she disappointed you,' he said, mercilessly. 'So now you know how it feels, to be disappointed. Maybe you can understand what it felt like for me? I didn't want much from you, and I got nothing, nothing. And now that poor bastard comes along, pours his heart out, plays his beautiful bloody piano and kills himself and you're in pieces. Is that what it takes? Would you love me if I was dead?'

Jessie stared at him.

'I'm going,' he said. 'Just came to tell you that I'm getting married, but I'm sure you couldn't care less.'

He slammed the door on his way out and ran up the drive. As he reached the bottom of the hill by the school the bus was pulling away. He swore and slammed his fist into the wall. Blood welled red from his torn knuckles.

For a long time after the front door slammed Jessie could not move. She sat motionless in the chair, looking at the same spot, the same dusty grate. She could not believe what he had said. And

210

his anger, his shouting. After a while she lay back in the chair and closed her eyes, but she could still see his flushed face so close to hers, feel the spittle on her cheek.

It was getting dark in the quiet room when she pulled herself up and climbed the stairs. She hadn't eaten since lunchtime. The glass of sherry stood neglected on the mantelpiece where she had left it. Upstairs she took off her clothes and got into bed in her underwear. When she woke the room was full of morning light, but she pulled the curtains across and lay down again. Sometime in the afternoon the telephone rang but she did not get up. She woke with a start when the telephone rang again, but she didn't want to speak to anyone and listened to its hateful jangling echoing through the house. Would it never stop? She wanted to pull the wires out and burn it.

When she woke again, she had no idea what time or even what day it was. The clock by the bed said six fifteen, but was that morning or evening? She crept downstairs to relieve herself, pulling an old coat round her before she stepped outside. Sunlight was hitting the west-facing door of the outhouse. It was evening. The bread in the pantry was old and stale, but she was hungry enough not to care. The food stuck in her mouth. She found it hard to swallow and threw the rest away. The fire was out. She drank some water. The floor was cold under her feet, and she went back to bed where it was warm and safe, discarding the coat in the hall. She picked up the receiver off the phone as she passed and let it drop, useless, to the floor. Then she slept again, dreaming of a baby crying somewhere in a large house but she couldn't find it. People were staring at her. Then she was outside, on a beach, and it was grey and cold. Guns were thudding in the distance, big guns.

The thudding stopped and there was a voice, in the house. She sat up suddenly, her heart pounding. Maybe that was what she had heard, her own heart. But there was the voice again, nearer. She pulled the bedclothes up to her throat and waited, holding her breath.

'Miss Whelan,' said the voice. 'Are you there?' It was a deep voice, with a familiar accent. A door creaked downstairs.

'Are you upstairs?' said the voice.

She tried to speak, but no sound came out, and she coughed.

'I'm here,' she whispered. 'Who is it?'

'I'm coming up,' the stairs creaked. 'Don't be alarmed. It's Father O'Toole.'

Jessie began to panic. Her mouth was dry. There was a faint tapping on the door.

'Don't come in,' she croaked.

'That's alright. I'll go down and light the fire. Can you walk?'

'Yes,' she said. 'I'll come … I'll come down.'

Jessie poured some water onto her hands and rubbed her face. In the small mirror she saw someone who looked like her, but the hair was flattened at the sides and the face haggard. It was the face of an old woman. Where was the brush? Jessie pulled at her hair with her fingers. The blue dressing gown hung on the back of the door, and she pulled it on, tying the belt tightly around her waist, making sure that her legs were covered.

A black coat hung on the back of the chair in the kitchen and a man was squatting in front of the range, blowing in to the fireplace. She stood at the door and watched him. As the sparks began to catch he drew back, and closed the door against the blue smoke that sidled into the room. She coughed and he turned around.

'There you are,' said the priest. 'We've been concerned about you. Sit you down and I'll make some tea.'

'In the canister, on that shelf,' said Jessie. Her voice sounded oddly far away. 'There's some milk, but …'

'We'll do without. A hot drink is the main thing.'

He looked into various pots on the shelf until he found some sugar.

'Sugar,' he cried. 'What a treat. We'll both have some.'

Jessie sat like a child, watching as the priest busied himself with the rituals of making tea. The smell of it tickled in her nose and her mouth felt sour. She wanted to drink and took a sip from the steaming cup that he placed on the table in front of her.

'Careful,' he said. 'Too hot.'

For a while they sat in silence, on either side of the oak table. She looked at the cup, watching the steam curl up, while he looked at her.

'You've been unwell?' he asked.

'Yes,' she whispered. 'I've been in bed for …' She didn't know. 'What time is it? What day is it?'

'We were concerned about you,' he said. 'There was no word, and you didn't come for the classes. Philip, Mr Andrews, tried to telephone you, but no one answered. He tried again but the operator said there was no connection. So I thought I would come and see how you were.'

'I'm alright, really. Just very tired. I've been sleeping.'

She sipped the cooling tea while he looked carefully at her.

'Is something troubling you?' he said.

Jessie looked down at the table. She could feel tears running down her face. She put down the cup and wiped her eyes with the cuff of her dressing gown. She did not look at the priest's kind face. She shook her head.

'Would you like to tell me about it?' he said.

'My son came to see me.'

The priest had turned away, as if hearing a confession, but he looked back at Jessie, surprised. 'You have a son?'

She saw his expression. She knew she had to start further back, and took a deep breath.

'When I was nineteen, I was pregnant. My fiancé was killed, at Vickers. He didn't know about the baby.'

Father O'Toole looked towards the window, at the small white flowers in the hedge outside.

Jessie didn't wait for a response. 'My mother and my aunt, they said I couldn't keep the baby. They wanted me to … to get rid of it, but I couldn't. So I had it, a boy. I didn't give him a name. Some people my mother knew came and took him away. I tried to forget. It was wartime. I got a job. When the war ended I went back to teacher training. I lied about my name. I was called Jessie Thompson. Clive Whelan was my fiancé, so I took his name instead. But I had no right to it. I should be Jessie Thompson.'

She sat with her head bowed, remembering things she had never spoken of before. All the strength she needed to maintain the lies had gone, drained out of her. There was nothing left but the truth.

'I gave the baby away, father. But when he grew up he found out that his parents were not really his parents, and he came looking for me.'

'And he found you?' asked the priest, so quietly that she hardly heard him.

'I saw him,' she said, 'by accident. He looked so like his father. I knew it was him, but I didn't say anything. I hoped he would go away. I wanted him to disappear again. But he kept looking until he knew it was me, that I was his mother.' She hesitated.

'What did you do?' he said.

Jessie covered her face with her hands and felt the tears. 'I didn't want him, father. I was afraid of what people would say. It was 1937. I would have lost my job, and the house.' She sobbed. He turned and handed her a large handkerchief, and she wiped her face and blew her nose.

'I told John we couldn't tell anyone. Some people knew already, but they would keep the secret. I made him pretend to be my nephew, not my son, in case anyone saw a likeness. Everything else was true, about his adopted family, his search.' She faltered. 'I gave him away again, father, do you see? I denied him. He expected me to be pleased, but I was afraid of him. I'm still afraid of him.'

'You said he came to see you.'

'After Piotr's funeral. John just turned up, to tell me something. I hadn't seen him for weeks. All I could think about was Piotr. I was very upset. I told John it felt like losing a son.'

'Oh dear,' said Father O'Toole.

'He just turned on me, suddenly. He was so angry. He's such mild person, a nice person, I was shocked.'

'Can you remember what he said?'

She shook her head but suddenly John's bitter words burned her memory. 'He said he would have to die before I could love him.'

The priest stood up and walked over to the window before he spoke again.

'What did John want to tell you?'

'That he was getting married. He said I wouldn't care.'

'Do you care?' he asked.

She thought for a moment. 'I've been trying to forget about him. He haunts me.'

'He's your son,' said the priest.

She sobbed again.

'I never wanted him. It was his father I wanted and he died. One day we were going to be married and I was happy, and then he was dead. I couldn't mourn for him properly, couldn't go to the funeral. By the time I found out, it was all over. And then that awful place in Carnforth.'

'You were there, of course,' he said, as if to himself. 'It was an awful place.'

'When it was over, and John was born, I just wanted to forget it all. And I did. Until he came back. And now he hates me. I hate myself.'

'God doesn't hate you, Jessie,' he said gently. 'Do you believe that?'

She shook her head.

'I'll make some more tea,' he said. 'And we'll sit outside for a while.'

They sat side by side on the bench in the far corner of the garden. It was surprisingly warm. Jessie sipped her tea, wondering what he must think of her.

'Remember all the good you have done, all these years,' he said. 'Have I?'

'At the school, for how many years?'

'Twenty-two,' she said.

'Hundreds of children have been in your care, Jessie, learning from you, becoming the people they are. You have made mistakes, but not with your teaching. Remember that.'

'Other people's children,' she said, 'but not my own.'

'It's not too late,' he said. 'He is going to be married, you say. There may be children, God willing. Your grandchildren. Think about that.'

She did, remembering the woman's red hair and the pride.

'I'm not sure his friend, the one he will marry, likes me.'

'You've met her then.'

'She came to see me,' said Jessie. She looked up. 'It was diffi-cult, father. She blamed me for not accepting John as my son. I was angry, too. I sent her away.'

'Then you have some bridges to build, Jessie. And you must build them, however hard it will be. If I were your confessor, that's what I would tell you. No Hail Marys for you, that would be too easy.'

'What should I do?' she asked.

'You must decide. Do it for yourself, to find the peace you need. All those lies, for so many years, no wonder you're exhausted.'

'Should I tell other people, about John being my son?'

'You must decide that, too. If they love you, they will understand.'

'And if they reject me?'

'That's the risk you have to take.'

She thought for a moment.

'There's one more thing, father,' she said. 'There is someone else, a man who says he wants to marry me. He doesn't know … about all this.'

'Will it make a difference to him, do you think?'

'I don't know. I will have to tell him, I know, but … first I must talk to John. I owe him that.'

'I think you do,' said Father O'Toole.

Jessie said no more. The secrets were tumbling out of her, and there was still one she didn't choose to let go of. Andrew was in her past, and would stay there. She knew she would never see him again.

Chapter 24

John sat uncomfortably in the Catholic chapel in Kells, waiting. It was cold, and he had no idea what would happen or what was expected of him. All he knew was that if he wanted to marry Maggie it would have to be in a Catholic church, which meant he had to be a Catholic. Violet had arranged for him to see Father Pryce at five o'clock this evening, and here he was, waiting.

The outside door creaked open and a thin man in a black suit came in. He had an oval face and sharp nose, bearing small, round rimless glasses. He wore a large black hat, which he removed, revealing a pink smooth forehead. He looked very young. John guessed he might be about the same age as himself.

'Mr Pharaoh?' said the young man. 'I'm Father Pryce, parish priest here at St Mary's. Mrs McSherry tells me that you wish to marry her daughter Margaret but that you are not of our Church.'

'Yes, vicar, I mean no, I'm not a Catholic.'

'You will call me father, not vicar,' said the priest. 'Vicar is for the Protestants.'

'Sorry, father,' said John.

'You are a Protestant, I take it?' John noticed his accent, from Liverpool he thought.

'I think so,' said John. 'My mother, my adopted mother, was a Methodist.'

'A Methodist? I see. And you were adopted. Have you been baptised?'

'I suppose so,' said John. 'I must have been, mustn't I?'

'And confirmed? Did you take communion at your church? Where was it?'

'In Ulverston, father. I seem to remember something, when I was about twelve, would that be it?'

'Whatever it was, Mr Pharaoh, it does not appear to have had a profound effect.'

'Well, no,' said John. He was wondering how to answer these questions. If being a Methodist was important, would that mean it would be harder to be a Catholic? Or would it be easier to start from scratch, as it were. He had no idea. He'd already decided however, that he did not like Father Pryce and that Father Pryce did not like him.

'What do I have to do, father?' he asked. 'I want to marry Margaret, and I know she wants you to marry us, here at St Mary's. So what do I have to do?'

'You are asking to become a Roman Catholic, Mr Pharaoh, not joining a club. I will instruct you in the principles of our faith, and you will learn them. It will not be easy. It is not meant to be easy. You will search your soul and confess your sins. When you are ready, you will be received into our faith.'

'Will it take long?' John persisted.

'Yes,' said the priest, looking at John with something approaching disdain.

* * *

'I can't do it, Maggie,' said John. 'It's no good. He wants me to say I believe it all and I can't. I don't believe any of it. I don't even believe in God, haven't since I was a kid.'

'What does Father Pryce want you to say?'

'That I believe in all the Catholic stuff, you know what it's about. You grew up with it. I grew up Methodist and stopped going to church after Enid died. That was a relief, it meant I could go climbing on Sundays not mess around in some gloomy place singing and saying things that made no sense to me.'

'And you don't believe in God?'

'No, I don't.'

Maggie said nothing. They were sitting together on the beach at Fleswick Bay. Before them the sea stretched pale and gleaming in early evening light. Sometimes from there the outline of the Isle of Man was clear against the horizon but now there was nothing to delineate sea from sky; they merged into a shining bowl that enveloped the lovers, and their discussion of the infinite.

'Look at this,' she said after a few minutes' silence. 'Who made all this?'

'Was it made? Does it have to be made? Could it not just happen?'

He turned to her, and she raised her face towards him. He kissed her.

'Does it matter all that much?' he said.

'Not to me, but it will to Father Pryce. And to my mother. If we're not married in church, according to my mam we're not married at all. We'd be living in sin, and if we have children they'd be bastards.'

'Like me, you mean?' he said, smiling.

220

'I'm serious, John. Father Pryce won't marry us if you say you don't believe, and that's what Mam's fretting about. To her it's a mortal sin. And she won't change. I know her. She's stubborn. Drives me dad crazy, but that's the way she is. Father Pryce has her wound round his finger, and not just her, either. It makes me sick to see them all fawning over him, but they do, and he loves it. So much for humility or whatever it is they're supposed to have.'

They took off their shoes and stepped awkwardly down the hard pebbles to the edge of the tide. John rolled up the legs of his trousers, Maggie pulled her skirt up short and they ran in and out of the incoming waves like children. When the sun began to dip and cool they walked slowly back to the lighthouse, watched the wheeling birds for a while and then turned towards the farm and home. There was no one around. 'Down here' said John, taking Maggie's hand and pulling her along a path at the edge of a field of green barley towards a stand of oak trees.

In a corner of the quiet field, under oak branches drooping and heavy with leaf, they made love. They didn't hesitate or speak, following each other in the dance of sex until they lay back, side by side, looking up into the branches. A bird was looking down at them, bigger than a thrush, with a banded chest. The bird cocked its head; they could see its bright round eye.

'It's a cuckoo,' said John. 'It's watching us.' They lay quite still. After a timeless, breathless pause, the cuckoo spread its wings and flew away. They heard its two note call, very close and loud as the bird alighted on its song post. Then it moved away again and the call was muted, like a clock behind a closed door.

For a while afterwards they rested, John asleep, Maggie lying beside him, looking up at the deepening blue of the sky. 'They'll be home from Silloth soon,' she said, as John stirred. 'I hope Judith hasn't caught too much sun. Her skin's like mine.'

'Beautiful,' he murmured, turning to kiss her one more time.

They got dressed and brushed themselves down. He held her shoulders. 'I know how important the Catholic thing is and that you're worried about your mam. I'll talk to her about it. There has to be a way to do this without lying to everyone. I've spent the last ten years lying about myself, because I wasn't able to stand up to my mother. And what did you think of that?'

Maggie hung her head.

'You said you couldn't love someone who didn't stand up for himself. Well, this is me standing up for myself. I'm not lying about something as big as this, Maggie. I can't. Why don't you talk to your dad – or I could? See what he says. Maybe someone could talk to Father Pryce.'

'Not a chance of that,' said Maggie. 'I've told you, what he says goes in this parish. Even Dad's scared of him. Before the accident he'd be out the back door like a rat up a drainpipe whenever Father Pryce came calling. The only person we can talk to is our mam.'

'You or me?'

'Oh God,' said Maggie. 'Let me talk to Dad first and see. Don't say anything yet. When do you have to go again, to the church?'

'Next week,' he said. 'I nearly told him there and then that I wouldn't be back.' He hesitated. 'What's the worst that could happen, if I can't go through with all this stuff?'

'He won't marry us in church, and we go down the registry office and do it there. We're married, but not as far as the church is concerned.'

'Could you live with that, for us?' he asked.

She turned to him.

'I know what I want,' she said. 'I've been here before, and what I feel now for you is nothing like what I felt for Isaac. I married him because we'd been going out and he wanted to bed me and that was the only way it was going to happen. So he asked me to wed, and I fancied having my own place and a bairn or two, and he had a job and he was clean, so I said I would. I thought I loved him but I didn't, I know that now. I love Judith, but this is different. I'm not that fussed about marrying anyone again, but there's not only us to think of. If we have kids, that's when it matters.'

'Do you want kids?' he said. 'With me?'

'All in good time,' she said. 'Let's sort this mess out first. What about your mam? What will she say?'

'She's no place to say anything at all,' he said. 'Doing what's right for her, no one else, that's been her rule ever since I came along. I'm not even sure I want her at our wedding, however it turns out.'

'Was that my fault, when I went to see her?'

'Nay, lass, what bothered me was that you didn't tell me yourself. Made me a look a fool.'

'She didn't back down,' said Maggie. 'You'd have laughed if you'd heard us. All very proper, no swearing. Has she ever said anything about it to you?'

'Not much.'

'I said some hard things to her, and she came right back. Snide though, that's what I didn't like. Hinting at things, trying to put me in my place.'

John laughed. 'Putting you in your place! We could have sold tickets for that. Who'd've thought, two women scrapping over me. I was proud of you, deep down, you know. It made me realise how afraid of her I'd got over the years. Now it's your turn to worry about your mother.' He paused. 'You know I was so angry with Jessie the other day that I just stormed out, but we didn't settle anything. Maybe I should go back and do it properly this time.'

Maggie looked hard at him, gripping his arm. 'You wouldn't, would you?'

'See,' said John. 'That's how I felt. No, I won't go charging in, but someone needs to. I've spent half my life pretending and I'm not going to start my life with you that way. We deserve better than that.' He got his feet and pulled her up. 'Come on, it's cooling down.'

When John walked back to Sandwith alone later in the evening, it was still light enough to hide the stars, and the orange disc of the rising moon made him stop in his tracks and watch as it moved. A blackbird sang close by as if it were the middle of the day. The conversation with Maggie lingered in his mind. We don't choose our mothers, he thought. Jessie didn't bring me up, and doesn't even know me well. There is no special bond. We are who we are and very different from each other. So why it does it matter to me when she grieves for another young man, someone more exotic than me, more talented?

* * *

It was Sunday afternoon. Matthew had driven from Cockermouth to see Jessie, worried by a note from her in which she mentioned that she hadn't been well. The note told him very little, and he wanted to see for himself. He didn't write or call ahead, taking the chance that she would be there. She was taken aback to see his car turning into the drive while she was reading the paper in the sunlit sitting room. She was pleased to see him, but anxious too. Telling him about John was important and necessary, she knew that, but she wasn't ready to do so.

When she opened the front door he stepped straight in and put both arms around her, holding her tight before stepping back to take a good look at her.

'You look wonderful,' he said. 'You've caught some sun and it suits you.'

She smiled. 'I spent quite a few days in bed, a couple of weeks

224

ago,' she said. 'Maybe I needed the rest. And the past few days I've been mostly in the garden.' She closed the door and looked up at him. 'I'm enjoying the garden here more than I expected to,' she said, remembering their earlier conversation about her life after teaching. 'I'll show you later.'

She ushered him into the sitting room, clearing away the newspaper so that they could both sit on the large sofa.

'So what was it?' he asked, 'What sent you to bed?'

'It's a long story,' she said. 'Let me make us both some coffee. Agnes brings it from London and it's really good. Come in the kitchen while I'm doing it. It's so good to see you.'

Jessie talked as she made their coffee. 'You remember that tragedy at the camp? It was in all the papers,' she said. 'The man who died was one of the ones I've been teaching English to. He was a wonderful person, and I was very fond of him. I knew he was sad, and if I'd realised what he intended a bit earlier, I might have saved him. Guilt. It eats away at you.'

'If he was determined, there was probably no way to stop him,' said Matthew. 'What did he do?'

'He wrapped a heavy cross to his body, put stones in his pockets, and walked into the sea. I watched him drown. It was awful, Matthew.'

'How dreadful. Poor you,' he said, putting his arm round her. 'No wonder you were upset by that.'

She leaned against him. That wasn't all she had to tell him, but it was all she could manage.

As they drank their coffee, he was quiet. Then he said, 'Do you remember I told you about Joan dying? There was so much guilt there, too. I'm a doctor, I should have seen how ill she was. But I was so wrapped up in the work at the hospital, with other people, most of them injured. I just took it for granted that my normally healthy wife, with no visible symptoms beyond a sort of 'flu, just needed a few days' rest. And she never complained, but I should have known. She could have been saved, but by the time I got her into hospital it was too late. By that time her heart had been too strained and it just gave up. She died in my arms, and the girls were there, too. We've never really talked about it, not in all the years since. It's as if they can't let her go – Ann especially.'

'Is that why she worries about me?' said Jessie.

'Does she?'

Jessie smiled. 'Can't you see it?'

'She's my daughter,' he said. 'She looks so like her mother. It's hard to deal with your adult children as if they were your friends.'

Jessie realised how true that was. Why did she say such crass things to John sometimes, things that she wouldn't say to anyone else?

'Enough,' he said. 'Show me the garden. Let's see what you've been up to.'

* * *

It was in the garden that John found them, standing close together among the runner beans, as Matthew took Jessie in his arms and kissed her.

John had noticed the car as he wheeled his bike down the steep drive at Applegarth. He knew it didn't belong to Agnes, so whose was it? There was no response to his knock on the door, but he could hear voices from somewhere close and followed the sound round the side of the house to the back garden. It took a moment to spot Jessie among the high trellises of sweet peas and runner beans, and a moment more to realise that she was not alone. A man was with her. Neither of them saw him, and as he watched the man kissed his mother.

John froze, wondering what to do. He could feel a blush seeping up his face. Then he stepped slowly backwards, around the corner of the house and out of sight. He retraced his steps to the front porch, hammered once again on the door and this time called out.

'Hello,' he called, 'anyone at home?'

He waited. Jessie appeared round the side of the house, brushing back her hair, straightening the collar of her blouse. She looked surprised to see him. They both stayed where they were, separated by a few yards, and by mutual incomprehension.

'John! I didn't know you were coming today.'

'I was passing,' he said, speaking the first lie of the afternoon.

'I'm in the garden,' she explained. 'Come round. I have another visitor, he's been helping me.'

They reached the spot from which John had retreated in confusion. This time the man in the garden was looking in their direction. He looked flushed and was smiling, holding a bunch of sweetpeas in his hand like an elderly bridesmaid.

'It's John, Matthew,' said Jessie. 'John, you remember my friend Matthew Dawson, the doctor. We've been picking sweet-peas.' She blushed. 'And talking,' she added.

'Yes,' said John. 'Hello, Dr Dawson.'

'We're finished out here, just heading in for a drink. Will you join us?' said Jessie.

Questions unasked and unanswered fluttered round their heads like moths as the three of them sat in Agnes's cool kitchen, drinking elderflower water from the pantry. The sweetpeas lay in the sun on a chair by the door, their soft fragrance creeping in and around them. Jessie was the first to let her curiosity break the awkward silence.

'Was it me you were looking for, or Agnes?' she said.

'You,' said John.

'Would you like me to leave?' said Matthew, scraping his chair on the flagged floor as he tried to stand up.

'No,' said Jessie and John simultaneously.

'So, what is it?' said Jessie. She remembered the bitterness of their last meeting. Surely John would not speak to her like that in front of someone else.

'As I said, I was passing, and wondered, you know, how you are. Last time I saw you, you weren't … very well. The young man from the camp, who –'

''Yes,' said Jessie. 'I'm feeling better now, as you can see.'

'Yes,' said John. He sipped his cordial, wondering what was going on with Dr Dawson and his mother. 'I told you,' he said, addressing himself to Jessie, 'that I'm getting married.'

'I remember,' said Jessie, as the bitterness of their previous encounter washed over her again. 'Have you set a date?'

'Not yet. There may be a problem with the church.'

'What's wrong with the church?'

'Well, it's with the priest, Father Pryce. My fiancée is a Catholic, and Father Pryce won't marry us unless I believe in God, and I don't.'

'Oh dear,' said Matthew.

'I've been going for instruction, as they call it. He looks like a young bloke, the priest, but he treats me as if I'm a child. There's no discussion or anything, he just lays down the law, like the headmaster when I was at school.'

John saw his mother smile.

'What can you do?' said Matthew.

'Maggie's mother is a stubborn woman. She's the one who says we have to do it in church or we're not properly married, and if we have children …'

'I see,' said Matthew. 'That's a tricky one.'

Jessie got up. 'You two have a think about it, and I'll put those sweetpeas in some water before they wilt.'

John was annoyed. It was Jessie he'd come to talk to, not

someone he hardly knew, and the two men sat in silence when Jessie left the table. Suddenly John recalled with absolute clarity when and where he had first met Dr Dawson. It was in this house, the day that he had come to confront his mother for the first time, nearly ten years before. Jessie had cried, and shown him a photograph of his father. And then she told him that they could not be together as mother and son, and his dream of belonging had crumbled away. His mind raced. Ten years was long enough. He had to speak.

'I remember the first time I saw you, Dr Dawson,' said John. 'Ten years ago, when I first came to this house. You were here that day.' Jessie stood at the pantry door, holding the vase and the bright flowers.

'John,' she said, raising her hand. Water trickled from the vase onto the floor.

'We had found Jessie by the road, Agnes and I, and brought her here. She had hurt her ankle. Agnes sent for you, and you came.'

Matthew Dawson nodded slowly. 'Joan came with me,' he said. Jessie didn't move.

'After you left, I talked to Jessie,' said John. 'I told her that I am her son.'

The vase dropped to the floor. Water and glass and delicate petals splashed and scattered over their feet. Jessie cried out and fell to her knees, scrabbling at the stems with her fingers. Matthew bent and held her hands. 'The glass,' he said. 'Be careful.'

John looked down at them both. He took a deep breath, and stepped back as Matthew pulled Jessie to her feet. She put her hand to her mouth, and blood smeared against her lips.

Chapter 25

'WHY DIDN'T YOU TELL ME?'

Jessie and Matthew were alone again. John had left without another word and his angry presence still hung in the room.

Jessie blew her nose and wiped her eyes. 'I wanted to. After Piotr died, when I was so upset, I wanted to tell you the truth then, but Caroline had said –'

'Caroline Leadbetter?'

'Yes she said on no account should I tell you, that you might not want to see me again.'

'She had no right … and she was wrong about me. I don't judge people. I've seen too much, over the years.'

Jessie wiped her eyes again. 'I'm sorry this happened, like this. What shall we do?'

'About us, you mean?' Matthew Dawson kissed Jessie's hand. 'Everything I said to you an hour ago in the garden remains the same,' he said quietly. 'We've both been lonely long enough. But it's a big step and there's no rush, is there? I'm going to stay in London with Ann next week, and that's the best time to talk to her. We're planning to see Emily, too, on our way back. We can talk about it, all of us.'

Jessie wondered what Matthew would say to his daughters, and they to him.

'You understand, don't you, dear?' he said, squeezing her hand. 'So can we keep all this to ourselves, for now?'

'Of course,' she replied.

'We will be together, soon, but I want to do things properly.'

'I understand, truly I do,' she said.

Before he drove away, they stood together inside the front door, and kissed again. For the first time Jessie felt the urgency in his touch, the kiss of a lover, not just a friend.

So much was on her mind that she could not share. She thought of the one person she could confide in about Matthew and John and her own turmoil, someone who would never tell.

The following Tuesday, she made the familiar journey to the camp, for the first time since Piotr's funeral, to talk to Philip about re-starting the men's English class. The bright light of summer as well as her own sunnier mood warmed the drab buildings. Philip Andrews was pleased to see her, and so was Father O'Toole when he arrived for his usual weekly visit. At the end of the afternoon, Jessie and the priest sat together in the decorated chapel. Through open windows they heard the gulls wheeling between the camp and the beach, and the sound of a football game after the men arrived back from their work.

'I've tried to put the past behind me, as you suggested, father. I've thought about the choices I made all those years ago, and since then too.' Jessie looked up at him, like a schoolgirl too anxious to please. 'I'm trying to be more honest with people.'

Father O'Toole nodded.

'And how is John?'

Jessie hesitated. 'We struggle,' she said. 'He's a grown man now, and doesn't want to pretend any more. Thinking about his own marriage has made him more determined to tell the truth. I just didn't expect …'

'What happened?'

'John came to see me,' she said. 'My friend, Matthew Dawson was there, and out of the blue John told him that he is my son. It was so sudden. I thought I would faint.'

'And did you?'

'No, I didn't. I just dropped something.'

'So the truth is out, and the sky did not fall in.' He looked at her. 'Your friend, Mr Dawson, is he important to you?'

'He's Dr Dawson, from Cockermouth. I've known him for many years. His wife died during the war and we've – we're very close.' She hesitated. 'He has grown-up children. He must talk to them, before we make our plans.'

'I see,' said the priest. 'Are you happy, Jessie?'

'He's a good man, father, so kind, generous. I always thought of him as a friend, and now … maybe more.'

'I'm glad for you.'

They sat together in silence for a few minutes. Jessie was grateful for his undemanding presence. A thought crossed her mind.

'There's some thing else, father,' she said. 'It's about John. He's not a believer, but the woman he wants to marry, is a Catholic. She lives in Kells.'

Father O'Toole nodded. He knew all the priests up and down the west coast.

'Mrs Lowery's family want John to become a Catholic, or else they can't be married in church.'

'Mrs Lowery?'

'Oh, she's not divorced, she's a widow. I believe her husband died in the war.'

'Is your son a good man, Jessie? Honest, and kind?'

'I believe so father. But the priest in Kells seems to have taken against him, or so John says. He doesn't know what to do. I can't remember the priest's name.'

'I know him,' said Father O'Toole, picturing the joyless young man who seemed to revel in the adoration of his congregation. 'And have you met Mrs Lowery and her family?'

Jessie thought for a moment. 'Not the family, no, but she came to see me,' she said. 'We talked about John. She was very –' Jessie struggled to find the right word, 'very committed to John, very loyal.'

'Is she a good Catholic? And does she love him, truly?'

'I cannot vouch for her as a Catholic, but she does love him, I'm sure of that.'

Father O'Toole pressed his fingers together and thought for a moment.

'Becoming a Catholic is a very serious matter, Jessie. I'm sure your son understands this.' Jessie nodded. 'The priest who instructs you is like your teacher. No doubt there are pupils that you have trouble reaching, and it's like that sometimes with a priest. If John sincerely wants to convert, and feels that he cannot take instruction from Father Pryce, then I might be allowed to help him. I will talk to Father Pryce, of course. We both want to bring another soul to God, and to see John and his fiancée married in the eyes of the Church. Let me see what I can do.'

Light from the open door of the painted chapel picked out the colours on the walls. Jessie's face was dark by contrast, but the eyes she turned towards the priest were bright. There was no sound except the sighing of the wind around the parched field and the peeling huts of the camp.

'This is a difficult time for you, Jessie,' he said, looking at her. 'God can help you, too, if you will accept him.'

'I've been a churchgoer for many years, as many of us are. But I've managed without much faith for most of my life, father,' she said, after a long pause. 'I've had to rely on myself alone, and I've done so. I wish I'd done some things differently, but there were reasons. Now I want to make my peace with John, with my son.'

'Are you sorry, Jessie, for what happened?'

'I'm not sorry that I had him. When he found me, I was older. I …' Her voice faded.

'You need to talk to him, tell him what's in your heart.'

'I'll try, father.'

In the days that followed, Jessie's resolve weakened. She would talk to John, soon, but not yet. In the meantime she wrote him a letter, and knew that it wasn't enough.

Dear John,

I have been thinking so hard about what I did and said all those years ago. You know that I was confused and afraid when you found me, afraid of what people would say. That's how my mother was when I was having you. I remember how much she hurt me then, and I have hurt you, too. We cannot put the clock back. All those years when you were growing up I never knew you, nor you me. We are like strangers, despite the blood we share.

There is a priest who has helped me to see all this. I met him at the camp, and he gave the poor man who died there a decent funeral. I told Father O'Toole about your wish to marry a Catholic and he is willing to talk to you about it. You can find him at the Catholic church in Millom.

I don't know how these things work. Maybe he can help you.

There are other things happening in my life, too, but they can wait. For now, you must know that I am sorry for all that has happened between us. I understand if you cannot forgive me for the wrong I have done you.

Your mother,

Jessie

* * *

'He's done what?' Violet looked at her daughter. 'What d'you mean, John's going somewhere else?

Maggie glanced at her father for support, but Frank looked away. Both front and back doors of the West Row house were open to catch the breeze, but still the small front room was oppressively hot.

'John's going to another priest, Mam. He was afraid that Father Pryce would never … so he's found someone else.'

'Who, for 'eaven's sake?' cried Violet, for whom Father Pryce represented both God and the Virgin Mary.

'His name is Father O'Toole, from Millom.'

'Millom? That's miles away. Is 'e a proper priest?'

'He's older than Father Pryce. More patient, John says. They're getting on well.'

'Are you telling me the truth, girl?'

Maggie's face flushed. Frank looked anxiously at his daughter and his wife and wished he could get away. He knew what was coming.

'I'm not a girl, Mam,' said Maggie, regretting her offer to tell Violet what was going on.

The knock on the front door surprised all of them.

'Ehyup,' said Tom Pickthall. He had pushed the door, found it blocked by Frank's wheelchair, and stuck his head round, realising in an instant that hard words were about to be said.

'Tom!' shouted Frank. 'Thank God.' He shifted his wheelchair to let his brother-in-law into the room. 'Just in time, lad. We might need a referee.'

'I could 'ear your voice, Vi, as soon as I turned t'corner. Me an' 'alf the street. What's all t'shouting about, lass?'

'It's that John,' said Violet.

235

'Mam,' protested Maggie, but her mother raised a warning finger. 'I'm telling our Tom, Maggie, not you.' She turned to Tom. 'Listen to this. John went to see Father Pryce, about being a Catholic so him and Maggie can get wed properly.'

'Aye,' said Tom.

'But John doesn't like Father Pryce, so he's gone off to another priest, in Millom! What d'ye make of that?'

'I don't like Father Pryce either,' said Tom. 'Ardly out of college or wherever they come from, thinks he knows it all, looks at me as if I've crawled out from under summat.'

'And me, too,' said Frank.

'So John's gone to someone else, good for 'im,' said Tom.

'See?' said Maggie, triumphant.

Violet, looked accusingly at Tom and pushed past him out of the room. They heard the back door slam, and there was silence while they assured themselves that Violet had actually left the house.

'Shall I go after 'er, Dad?' said Maggie.

'Nay lass, leave 'er be. She'll calm down. Well said, our Tom. That Father Pryce gets reet up my nose.'

'And John's, too,' said Maggie. 'Father O'Toole's different, John says.'

'Ave you met him?' asked her father.

'Not yet, but I will before he marries us.'

'Bloody 'ell,' said Frank, 'Your mam'll go off the deep end over that.'

But by the time Violet returned, Frank, Tom and Maggie had it all worked out.

* * *

'Bloody brilliant,' said John. He and Tom were sitting outside the pub in Sandwith two days later, after a long day working on the

236

house. Maggie had wanted to help John bring piped water into his home, but Violet had put her foot down and wouldn't budge. 'Until you two are wed, you'll not set foot in 'is 'ouse again. God knows what people think when they see you there all hours. Bad enough you're running off to get wed like a pair of criminals. Let our Tom stop there and help John. You and Judith are stopping 'ere till after the wedding.'

'It's very good of you, Tom,' he said, 'to help out like this, and to persuade Violet to go along with it.'

Tom took a long pull on his pint and wiped his mouth with the back of his hand.

'I told you about my Honor, didn't I?'

'Your wife, yes, you did.'

'Those years wi'er were the happiest of my life, John. I know we all 'ave a good laugh about 'er indoors, and being 'en-pecked an' all that, but for me being married to Honor were a wonderful thing. Not just sex, lad. That were part of it, but it weren't just that. She brought out the best in me, and she said I did in 'er. People don't talk, do they, about the important things, well men don't any road. Down pit, in t'pub, we don't talk, not really. But me and Honor, we talked about anything, everything. And laughed, too. They were grand times.'

'And you never found anyone else?' said John.

'Not for what I 'ad wi'er. Sex, could've got that. Did once or twice, like.' Tom winked. 'But no one to wed.'

'Is that why you want Maggie and me to be married, so we can be as happy as you were with Honor?'

Tom laughed. 'There's summat else, too,' he said. 'When Maggie got wed first time to that Isaac, I were all set up to 'ave the back bedroom in West Row, until the poor bastard were killed and Maggie moved back in. I've been stuck in that shithole of a boarding 'ouse in Bransty all these years since. When Maggie and

Judith move out to live 'ere wi' you, I can 'ave that room at long last. So look after 'er and don't die on us, lad.'

'Longer walk for you down to William Pit from Kells,' said John.

'That's t'other thing, John,' said Tom. 'Come end of August, I'm shifting up to th'Haig. Allus wanted to do it, and there's a space in me auld marra's gang up there, so I'm off. Been at William twenty year and it's enough. Summat about that pit I've never trusted.'

Tom Pickthall raised his pint pot to John. 'So 'ere's to you and our Maggie, lad. I 'ope you're as 'appy wi'er as I were wi' mine, and that back room at our Vi's will do me fine. Hear that? Poetry!'

Chapter 26

'You won't be the first bride to go to her wedding on the train,' said Violet to her daughter. 'It's the price you pay for sneaking off, like a couple of criminals.'

'Mam, for heaven's sake. Father O'Toole has agreed to marry us, properly like you wanted, and why should we drag 'im all the way up here, or expect everyone 'ere to drag themselves down to Millom when there's no fuel and no money. So long as we're married, and in a church, that's all that matters to us. I thought you'd be pleased about it. Uncle Tom's coming wi' me because you wouldn't let me go down on t'bike wi' John. Anyone'd think you didn't want us to be wed at all.'

Violet sniffed. 'I'm sure John Pharaoh is a fine man, apart from being a heathen. You can't keep your 'ands off each other, so you'll 'ave to marry, and he's got 'is own 'ouse and a proper job, and 'e can look after you and the bairn properly. That's better than nowt.'

'So why can't Judith come to the wedding, Mam?'

'Our Judith's staying 'ere with me, and that's an end to it,' Violet insisted. 'Bad enough you two sneaking off, without dragging an innocent bairn along. And what kind of a priest is this Father O'Toole, going behind Father Pryce's back? Are you sure 'e's a proper priest, not something left over from t'war? No wonder 'e's

239

'anging around that foreigners' camp. God knows what kind of Catholics they are down there.'

Maggie gave up. They'd been round and round it, and her mother would keep on fretting until it was all over, signed and settled. Maggie had braced herself and persuaded Father Pryce to bless the two of them at St Mary's after the wedding, to convince her mother that everything was above board. It had been an awkward encounter.

'Where will you be living?' Father Pryce had asked.

'Mr Pharaoh's house is in Sandwith, father,' she replied.

'That's a fair way to come for Mass,' he said, and she was happy to tell him that St Bees was closer. With any luck she would never have to see him again.

* * *

The sun was well up but it was still early when John drove his bike down to Millom to be married on a Saturday in August. The hottest summer anyone could remember seemed to go on and on, and dust swirled from his wheels as he drove.

In the public toilets in the park he took off his jacket and trousers and shook as much dust as he could out of them before getting dressed again and brushing himself down. He rubbed his best shoes with grass and tied his best tie carefully before pushing open the heavy door of the church and stepping inside. The draught launched more dust into the still air, where it hung like tiny crystals in the sunlight streaming through the window above the altar.

Father O'Toole emerged, pulling his cassock straight as he did so.

'Is that you, John?' he called, squinting into the gloom at the far end of the nave.

'I'm here, father. I think I'm supposed to be early. Maggie's coming down on the train with Mr Pickthall.' He checked his watch. 'All being well, she'll be here in ten minutes or so.'

'Mr Pickthall is …?

'Maggie's mother's brother. Maggie's dad is in a wheelchair and her mam has made quite a fuss about us being married here, so Uncle Tom's representing the family, like, and giving Maggie away.'

'Splendid,' said the priest. 'We've just time for a tot. I've a bottle in the vestry for special occasions. Will you join me? Calm the nerves.'

'Whisky and I don't get along very well, father, thank you.'

'Come away in, anyway, and sit with me while we wait. I've a couple of witnesses coming, but they'll be here at the last minute.'

'I can't thank you enough for this, father,' said John, as they sat, knee to knee in the tiny vestry. 'It means so much to Maggie and her family. Her mother's not too happy about it, as I said.'

'I'm a great believer in the New Testament, John, and in bending a few rules, as Jesus did himself. Some of my brethren take a different view.'

'Will it cause trouble for you, father?'

'Nothing I haven't heard before, John, believe me. And who's to say what the future holds? You could turn to God yourself one day, when the spirit reaches you.'

John smiled. 'You're investing in me, father.'

'You could say so. You're a good man, and worth the risk. I would say. And Maggie, she's a fine Catholic woman, and you should be very proud.'

They heard the west door opening. John got to his feet and saw her, standing against the light from the open door, fixing a small blue hat on top of her russet hair. She was wearing a navy jacket and a full skirt, and shoes with a little heel. Despite the heat, she had on her best white gloves, to hide the darkened scars. Tom stood behind her, almost unrecognisable in a suit that had fitted him better once than it did now.

'Hello, you two,' John called out. 'Tom, come and meet Father O'Toole.'

As the two men shook hands John and Maggie looked at each other. His heart turned with love.

* * *

'Maggie and John,' said Father O'Toole, 'I now pronounce you man and wife. May you always be as happy as you are today.'

Maggie kissed everyone and the men shook hands again. Tom and John embraced as rugby players might after a sensational try. Father O'Toole was smiling. John took his hand in both his own. 'I can't thank you enough,' he said.

The priest leaned forward to speak to him quietly. 'Will you do something for me, John?'

'Anything.'

'Be kind to your mother.'

As they blinked into the bright morning, Maggie turned to her husband.

'If we go back on the train, what about the bike?'

'You and John are on t'bike,' said Tom. 'I'll be catching train.'

'But that means we'll be back at West Row in half an hour. We don't have to be at St Mary's until two o'clock.'

John smiled. 'We're going to Sandwith, Mrs Pharaoh. One or two things we need to do before it's time to face Father Pryce. See you later, Tom, and thanks again.'

Tom and the priest stood side by side, watching as Maggie climbed up behind her husband, and the bike puttered off down the quiet street.

John parked the bike in the tiny back yard of the Sandwith

house and then returned to the front door to carry Maggie over the threshold. They waved to the watching neighbours, and closed the front door firmly before scampering upstairs.

* * *

Compared to the wedding itself, the blessing of John and Maggie's marriage in St Mary's later in the day was a rowdy affair. Most of the noise emanated from a group of lasses from the Haig screen shed who had enjoyed a lunchtime drink at the Eagle and Flag on the High Road. It took several appeals from a mortified Violet and hard stares from Father Pryce before they agreed to vacate the front rows of the church and settle down more quietly further back, until hymn singing was called for, to which they made a particularly raucous contribution.

Father Pryce performed his duties with as much good grace as he could muster. His blessing on the couple was a little perfunctory, and Violet hoped that no one but she had noticed. It was all over soon enough, and the whole company led by the bride and groom spilled out on the High Street, acknowledged the applause of passers by, and walked down the hill and round the corner into West Row.

Tables and chairs had been dragged out of houses along the street and all the ration points that were available had been used up to provide food for the meal. Speeches were short and scurrilous, and when they were done, and the wedding cake cut, some of the party drifted away towards the Eagle, leaving twenty or so close family and friends clustered near the McSherry's front door. The summer sun was dropping towards the horizon, glinting gold off tiny ruffles on the sea stirred by a rising breeze and ebbing tide. Chairs were pulled round so that their occupants could watch the vision of light and colour being unveiled before them, like cinema goers watching the show.

'Look at this,' said Frank. 'This is where we live. All this beauty, but out there, under the sea, there's poor buggers bent double in them bloody seams, risking their lives digging out bloody coal.'

Violet scowled at her husband. He turned to Tom. 'How much longer will ye give it, Tom?'

'Year or two,' said Tom. 'Every time them sirens start up, I think that could be me, or any of me mates. If someone offered me summat up top tomorrow I'd bite their 'and off. I've 'ad enough.' He turned to John and Maggie and raised his glass. 'You're a lucky bugger, our John,' he said. 'Not just 'cos of that wife o' yours. You're lucky 'cos you can earn your pay without going down there in the filth and the sweat.'

'That's not luck, that's schooling,' said Maggie. 'That's why our Judith will stay at school as long as they'll let her, be a teacher like John's mam.'

'Where is your mam?' asked Frank. 'When are we going to meet 'er?'

John squeezed Maggie's hand. 'I asked her, but she said she wasn't ready to meet everybody.' He hesitated, aware that the explanation was feeble. 'She had a bad do in the spring, after that man at the camp drowned. She tried to stop him, I heard. Whole business left her pretty wretched. Just have to give it time.' He paused, embarrassed, willing Frank to ask no more about it.

'And what about those friends of yours from Boot?' said Frank. 'Didn't you say they were coming?'

'I thought they were, with Miss Plane. They said they'd be here this evening sometime.'

As if on cue, they heard the car engine before they saw it nosing round the corner at the end of the street. Agnes was driving, and pulled up before the long line of tables blocked her way. John and Maggie ran together down towards the car as Hannah and Fred emerged slowly from the back.

244

Hannah's good eye squinted into the low sunlight, and Fred took a while to ease his wooden leg into the right position to heave himself upright. John led Hannah, and Maggie supported Fred. Agnes, smiling, confident, and carrying a bag full of presents, brought up the rear of the group as they made their way slowly along the gleaming cobbles.

Introductions were made and the three new arrivals were quickly seated, talking of mutual acquaintance and realising without surprise how many people they knew in common. It transpired that one of Frank McSherry's cousins farmed not far from Boot and would have known Hannah's father when the mill was still at the centre of the local economy.

Agnes knew of Father Pryce, which pleased Violet very much, but the conversation about John and Maggie's defection to a church in Millom was too sensitive to be discussed. Fortunately, Agnes tried to reassure Violet, just a little, that Father O'Toole was well known and much loved down the coast, and a fine representative of the Catholic priesthood, but Violet's only response was to sniff her continued disapproval. Paul Conley and his son Paddy from two doors down emerged from their house with a fiddle and accordion.

'Thank God,' said Frank. 'Now we can stop talking about priests. Play us a tune, you two, to serenade the sunset.'

They played with such enthusiasm that Violet was persuaded to dance with her new son-in-law and the rest of the party clapped their approval. Before the flattened disc of the sun slid towards the grey horizon, Maggie fetched her father's precious bottle of port from under the stairs and very small measures went far enough for them all to toast the bride and groom.

In the afterglow, cotton wool clouds in the east caught the pink that spread slowly across the sky above their heads. They sipped from their crimson glasses in a final toast to the happy couple, before John and Maggie left to celebrate their marriage in John's bed in Sandwith and Agnes drove her guests back to the rare comfort of Applegarth for the night.

Jessie was still up when they got back, sitting alone in the fading light of the sitting room, where she had been all evening. She felt more than usually alone, longing for company but fearful of it. Privacy had become a terrible habit; she'd been convinced that it was essential for her survival, but now that conviction was crumbling. The truth about her past might hurt but it would not threaten everything. A man who loved her would stand by her, protect her, accept and understand what she had done and why she had done it. And her son was happy now, too happy to be angry with her, and that was all she wanted.

'We had a lovely time,' said Agnes as she ushered Hannah and Fred slowly into the room full of light and softness. Hannah perched on the edge of an armchair, feeling the fabric and stitching of the cushion beside her. Fred stared at the painting above the fireplace, and then at one of his own rugs, which was not on the floor under their feet, but on the wall, stretched and hung like a work of art. Agnes followed his gaze and smiled.

'Too beautiful to stand on, Fred,' she said. 'I wanted to see your work more clearly, to let its colours glow and brighten the room.'

'Aye,' said Fred. 'That's a good 'un, reet enough.'

'You've met Maggie, haven't you, dear?' said Agnes to Jessie who had watched and listened but said nothing as the news of the wedding party was relayed to her.

'Oh, yes,' she said, taking a moment to choose her words with care. 'Maggie and I had a chat a while ago, before they arranged to be married. I was struck by her straightforwardness, her energy.'

'It's the flaming hair,' said Fred.

'Did you see her daughter?' Jessie asked, suddenly curious.

'Too late when we got there,' said Fred. 'Bairn was in bed.

Name of Judith. Bright wee thing, they say. Maggie's very keen on schooling, her mam says.'

'She'll be a grand wife for our John,' said Hannah. 'He deserves a reet special lass, and that she is.'

Regret and sadness surged through Jessie yet again. When Agnes returned from showing Hannah and Fred up to their room, Jessie was crying. Agnes sat beside her, and Jessie lowered her head onto her friend's willing shoulder as the room darkened into violet and the short, star-filled night began.

CHAPTER 27

THE BLUEBRAE GUEST HOUSE IN GARLIESTON across the Solway on
the coast of Galloway was the most luxurious house that Maggie
Pharaoh had ever been in. John had used some of his savings
to pay for their honeymoon there, and chose it because it had
a bedroom with a view of Cumberland hills, and a private bathroom, just for them.

The landlady called it 'the honeymoon suite' and opened
the door with a flourish when they arrived, the day after their
wedding. Maggie was the first to enter, as John struggled up the
stairs with their bags.

'Oh,' she said. 'Oh, John, look!'

Maggie examined every detail of the room. She bounced on
the bed, felt the heavy smoothness of the curtains, and opened
and closed every drawer, but most of all she wanted to stay in the
bathroom.

'There's a bath here,' she called to John, 'with two taps!' He heard the taps being turned on, and after a moment Maggie called to him again. 'There's hot water coming out, John. If I put the plug in I could have a hot bath, anytime I want!'

'Yes you can,' he said, laughing. 'But there are some other things we could do to pass the time. Practice makes perfect, don't forget.'

It was the happiest week of their lives, and the warmth of August seeped into their bones. Perhaps it was the heat, or swimming in the sea every day, that caused the grime of the screens to lift out of Maggie's skin: she glowed. Both of them basked in the ease of life without their mothers.

'When I was stuck there in the snow with her,' said John on the Friday morning as they walked on the beach before breakfast, 'she was so wrapped in herself it was like I didn't exist. We had nothing to say to each other. But then, when the men from the camp arrived, she turned into this cheerful, kindly person, making them welcome, smiling. Sometimes I think I don't know her at all.'

'Is it any better now?' asked Maggie, taking his hand.

'Yes,' he said, 'but we're not close.'

'You two have to start all over again with each other. It'll take a long time.'

They walked further, the early sun warm on their faces, looking across to the Cumberland hills.

'I bet we could see West Row from here,' said Maggie, 'If we had a big enough telescope. All my life I've looked across here and wondered what it would be like.'

'That's why I chose this place,' said John.

She stooped suddenly and stood quite still, rubbing her forehead.

'Are you alright?' he said, looking into her face.

She paused before she said, 'Do you ever get a feeling that

something might be going to happen? It's a sort of twist in your stomach, or a buzz in your head.'

'A premonition?'

'Is that the word? I was thinking about Judith, just now, and suddenly felt it. Do you believe in things like that?'

'Not really,' said John. 'I reckon most things like that are based on something, something real.'

'So what could it be?' she said. 'Judith's fine with Mam and Dad, and it can't be school as they're not back yet. Something's happened, I know it, or it's going to happen. How would they find us, if there was something wrong?'

John thought about it. 'A telegram, I suppose. They know where we are.'

She looked up at him, her hair framing her face as the breeze caught it. 'I know it's stupid, but I can't help it, love. I can feel it, something bad, here.' She pressed her hands against her stomach.

'Come on,' he said, taking her hand. 'We'll have our breakfast and pay the bill and we'll go.'

'Now? Today?'

'Only a day ahead of ourselves. Even if there's nothing wrong, I don't want you worrying. If we get an extra day at home, there'll be plenty to do there before I go back to work. After that you can rest and get to know the place.' John bent his knees to take Maggie in his arms, stroking her strong back and her hair. 'Nothing's more important to me than you and Judith,' he said. 'If you want to go, we'll go. I'll drive really slowly, and we'll sleep in our own bed tonight.'

'Can I have another bath before we set off?' she said.

In the early evening, John turned the motorbike down the long hill into Whitehaven. He had expected busy roads at that time on a Friday but it was surprisingly quiet. Along the street as they passed, front doors were open and women stood in huddles on their doorsteps, their faces lit by the sun. The air was heavy and still. John braked gently to a halt at the corner of a street where a group of women and children were standing.

'Has something happened?' he asked.

'The William,' a woman said, pointing down the hill. 'Sirens went off ten minutes since.'

'An accident?' asked Maggie. 'How bad?'

'Bad,' said the woman. 'Men 'ave gone down to see.'

'Uncle Tom!' said Maggie, clutching John's arm. 'Which shift?'

If the woman answered, John didn't hear. He revved the bike down the hill until he could go no further. The way ahead was blocked by a van standing in the middle of the road. Bells were ringing and men running down towards the pit gate. John drove back up to the high road, south and then to the back road up to Kells. It was nearly seven when they got to West Row. Here, too, all the front doors were open, with people standing quietly in groups. Maggie jumped off the bike and rushed into the house. John found his wife a moment later, sitting on the bed in the front room with Judith in her arms, rocking back and forth. Frank was watching from his wheelchair by the window.

'It's Tom,' said Frank. 'He was on back-shift. Staggered shift men came up about half five. We 'eard nowt till after six, then all hell broke loose down there. Must be a big 'un. Ambulances, rescue teams, all the big shots, they all started pouring in. Nowt's been said but everyone knows. Our Violet's gone down, left Judith 'ere wi' me. God knows how many there must be down there by now. Can you go and find 'er, John? Find out what's 'appened. I can't do 'owt, stuck 'ere like a cripple wi' all the women.'

'Maggie, love,' said John. 'You stay here with your dad and Judith. I'll go to the Haig, they should know what's going on, then I'll go down and get your mam.'

'What about Tom?'

'There's nowt we can do that's not being done already, love. Don't let Judith see you too upset. I'll be back as soon as I can.'

John went down to the Haig, and into the office.

'It's a bad 'un,' said Arthur Curran. 'We're 'anging on to see what they might need. Chaos down there by sound of it. Hundreds of folk milling about already.'

'My mother-in-law's down there. Her brother was on back-shift, Tom Pickthall.'

'Aye' said Arthur. 'How was th'oneymoon?'

'Over,' said John.

He parked the bike on the south side of the harbour and walked round towards the William pithead. Arthur was right, it was chaos. Hundreds of women stood on either side of the road, watching the stream of lorries that inched past them, as rescue teams arrived from other pits around the town. John recognised the team from the Haig, grim-faced, waiting for orders.

He pushed his way towards them. 'What's up lads, what've you 'eard?'

'Explosion, gas. You can smell it from 'ere. First gang didn't get far in afore they 'ad to come back. Canaries collapsed. Roof's down. Can't get in without breathing gear. There were a dozen or so blokes on this side of whatever 'appened. They're coming up, sounds as if they're OK, but after that, nowt.'

'How many missing?' said John.

'Hundred, more. Looks bad.'

'Christ,' said John. 'A hundred.'

'More,' said the man, as the group shuffled off towards the shaft.

Suddenly a surge of men filled the yard. Volunteers for the search had been called for and two hundred men had pushed through the crowd, past the open gates. 'Shut bloody gates,' one of the managers was shouting. 'No more!' It would take hours to reach the spot where survivors might be found, if there were any. Slipping out of the yard as the gates opened again for more lorries and ambulances coming through, John began to scour the faces in the crowd, looking for Violet.

It was a beautifully warm and sunny evening. Dust from weeks of dry weather, stirred up by traffic and clogs, hung in the air. There was very little noise from the hundreds of women waiting for news. They stood, alone or in tight groups, clutching the hands of those around them, faces grey with tension and fear, watching the motionless wheels above the shaft.

John climbed up onto the fence to see over their heads. 'Violet!' he called. 'Vi McSherry!' There was disturbance in the crowd to his right, and he saw hands raised.

'John,' came Violet's voice, echoing across the silent road. 'Our Tom's down there.'

He clambered down, and pushed through the crowd that parted for him like waves cleaved by a prow. She was in front of him now, one arm stretched towards him, one hand at her mouth. He took her arm and led her unprotesting, quiet, along the road to where there was space to sit together on a low wall.

'There's nothing we can do here,' he said. 'The rescue teams are going in. They'll be down there for hours, digging their way out under the sea. You know long those tunnels are. It doesn't look good, Vi. But if Tom's there, the men will find him. If he's alive, he'll need you.'

'I'm all 'e's got, John. Just another year or two, he said, then 'e'd pack it in. That's what 'e said, if it didn't get 'im first.'

'I know, Vi,' said John, as she leaned against him. 'Come on, I'll leave the bike here and we'll walk up. Do us both good. Get up on the hill away from this dust. Breathe free.'

'I'll do the 'ouse,' said Violet. 'Has to be clean when 'e comes 'ome.'

All over the town, wives, mothers, sisters went home to clean their houses and wash their bedding, making ready for the return of men who were already dead.

Few people slept well in Whitehaven that Friday night. Underground, shifts of miners and rescue teams from pits all over Cumberland were joined before nightfall by men from Durham and Northumberland. More men were on their way from the Lancashire coalfield, and Scotland. They worked till they were almost too exhausted to get back to the surface, and staggered off to eat and snatch some sleep before going down again.

At the McSherry house, only Judith slept with the innocence of childhood, wrapped in her mother's wakeful arms. Violet fussed and fretted, dusting, polishing, ironing. 'Leave 'er,' said Frank to John. 'It's what she 'as to do.'

For most of the short August night Frank and John sat together in the front room, looking out at the mindless ocean, aware of the men, dead and alive, in the tunnels that stretched out for a mile and more under the sea.

'Fucking coal, and fucking owners,' said Frank bitterly, whisky in his hand. 'Killed thousands of good men in this town. Coal's down there but it's too 'ard to reach, John. Can't ventilate well enough.' He jerked his hand towards the window. 'Gas just builds up, then a stray spark – And for what? These pits are doomed, won't last much longer.'

'Then what happens?' said John, thinking about Whitehaven without the pits. 'What'll folk do for work?'

'God knows,' said Frank. 'Young 'uns are getting out already if they can, pits on t'other side of Canada. Or down south, Yorkshire way, but they've their own men to think of.'

'Courtaulds are starting aren't they, down at Drigg?'

'What kind of job's that?' said Frank, sucking the last drop out of his glass. 'Fit for lasses, not real jobs.'

Just an hour or two into the cloudless day, John left the house and walked first down to the Haig, and then on to the William. They'd asked for help managing the influx of men and equipment as the rescue teams arrived, and Arthur Curran sent his best man down to help. 'Stay as long as ye can,' he said to John. 'They need you down there more than we do.'

They were expecting him, and John began to sort out the chaos in the pit office. He talked briefly to a young miner who'd volunteered to go down at midnight to take plans of the pit to the rescue teams who were trying to find their way through the maze of tunnels to the site of the explosion.

'It were 'ot as 'ell down there,' said the lad. 'Smoke and gas and rockfalls everywhere.'

Just after seven in the morning, the first body was brought to the surface. Rescue teams, filthy and exhausted, bared their heads and stood in silence in the bright early morning sunlight. Throughout the morning a steady procession of bodies continued and all hope slowly faded that anyone would be found alive.

Ministers and priests from all the churches, the Salvation Army too, moved among the crowd at the gate, helping pitiful family groups through to identify bodies. Grieving was quiet; few tears were shed in the glare of the sun.

Violet, Frank and Maggie went through the motions of life, waiting for the knock on the door, and the summons to the pit to identify what might remain of Tom Pickthall. Some of the bodies were burned or scarred, others were unmarked, as if in sleep.

John worked in the office all day, logging the arrival of the teams, finding food and places for them to get some rest. He took control of the flow of money, too, as people in the town and beyond responded to tragedy in the only way they could, with help for bereaved families.

By mid-afternoon he was unbearably tired, and wondering

how much longer he could stay awake. There was a noise in the yard outside, not the usual noise of shuffling feet and murmurs of wives and mothers facing the unthinkable. This was a different noise, excited, breathless. He ran outside.

'They're alive,' someone was shouting, 'just walked out, four of 'em! Coming up!'

Outside the gates, the news flashed round the crowd, and every wife, every mother, hoped against hope that it was him, their man, who might walk out. They clamoured against the gates, calling, crying, praying. John ran to see the men arrive. They leaned on their rescuers, blinking in the light. John searched their faces, and found one he knew.

'Tom,' he cried, 'Tom!'

CHAPTER 28

'THE AIR KIND OF FLUTTERED,' said Tom. He was sitting up in freshly laundered bedsheets upstairs in the West Row house, a bottle of stout in his hand. All the family and Robbie from next door were crowded into the small room. Gulls wheeled and screamed outside. Robbie's mam was at the pit, identifying the burned and broken body of her husband.

'Sounded like a wall collapsed somewhere. I thought my eardrums 'ad burst, it were that loud. There were twelve of us to start with, and we'd one oil lamp. Air were terrible thick, and it were red 'ot. We took us coats off. Some of 'em went off one way but Jack said nay, we're going to face it, come along the face like. We started to crawl. Couldn't breathe, they pulled me through. I 'ad to lie to get me breath and let me heart slow down, then we carried on.'

'What about the others?' asked Violet. 'Where did they go?'

'They went off, don't know where. I called the last of 'em to come wi' us, but 'e didn't. Don't know why. We didn't see 'em again. They didn't come up. When we got out, up th'ospital like, we asked where they were but … it were bad down there. Smoke. 'Ard to breathe.'

'Did ye 'ave water?' said Maggie.

'Aye, two bottles or so. We knew they'd be coming to find us. Jack said, God is good, we will get out.'

'Amen,' said Violet from the doorway.

'We just followed t'face, for hours, felt like. Dinna know 'ow long. Twice we tried to get o'er a rockfall, then the lamp went out. We were stuck. Bert said, if we go back, we go under, so we tore our shirts and wet the pieces and tied them round us faces and went again, and found the air crossing. We saw a body under rocks, and took the lamp. We smelt fresh air and followed it. We knew we'd get out. Bert said it were better than winning Irish Sweep.

'We kept on climbing over falls. Heard knocking on a plate and knocked back but they couldn't 'ear. But we knew we were close. I pushed Jimmy up the top of the last one, and then we saw men, down t'road. And they saw us. We were shouting and carrying on. We were th'only ones they found. How long were we down there?'

'Twenty hours, Tom,' called Frank from the bottom of the stairs, where he sat in his chair listening to the story. 'Twenty bloody hours, we thought you were dead.'

'We never thought we were gone,' said Tom. 'All that time, we just kept going, kept each other going, thinking about which way to go, using all those years to figure it out. We knew we couldn't just rush to nearest way out. God knows where t'others went. Poor buggers. How many all told?'

'Hundred and more,' said Maggie. 'All with wives and mothers and kids.'

258

'And sisters,' said Violet. 'God protects ...'

'Nay, Mam,' said Maggie. 'God doesn't. No one does, not down there. You'll not go back, Uncle Tom, tell us you won't go back.'

'Job's a job,' said Tom. He was quiet for a moment, taking a sup from the bottle in his hand.

'Why me?' he said. 'What did I do, to be spared?'

* * *

Rumours had spread all over town about more men being alive, but the rescue teams knew there was no chance. They were all exhausted and had been stood down to rest before they started to recover the bodies.

When it went quiet, John picked his way through the smaller crowd at the gate, and walked round the harbour. He stopped a while to breathe the salty-sweet sea air and listen to the regular swish of tiny waves on the beach, like the last breaths of a dying man. He hoped the dead far beneath his feet had died quickly, not gasping with seared throats and lungs. He remembered coming so close to death himself, only a few miles south of where he now sat on the harbour wall, drowning in the sea with his waders full of water, and then the pneumonia, although he couldn't recall much about that. And now fate had made another twist. He could have gone his whole life and never found a woman like Maggie. Tom had said, if you find her, don't let her go. And Jessie? Would she marry the doctor? Had she told him the truth? Was that the end of pretence? God, he hoped so.

The bike was where he'd left it. Was it only yesterday? It seemed like a week had passed since then. The noise of the engine bounced off walls and rocks, echoed by the throb of a fishing boat that was puttering into the outer harbour with the tide. Life goes on, he thought.

He stopped off at West Row to see Tom, but he was asleep in

the upstairs bedroom. Violet was out sitting with Ivy Turner at number 17, whose man would never come home. John hugged his wife without words.

Together they put Judith, exhausted by the events of the day, into the new sidecar and they drove slowly back to Sandwith. As Judith slept in her own new room, Maggie and John opened all the windows of the little house and sat together on the back doorstep, watching the last of the light fade to the north, until John was too tired to sit any longer and they climbed the narrow stairs to their bed.

* * *

All through Sunday, silent, stoic people crossed the William pit yard to the makeshift mortuary to identify those they had known and loved. Others went down into the pit themselves to bring out the bodies. On Monday, the coroner's court began its work. There was no weeping. Men were tight-lipped and women beyond tears. The coroner heard all the evidence available at the time and then adjourned for a month. On Tuesday, the first funerals were held at churches across the town and continued with relentless regularity for two days.

It was Wednesday morning. John and Maggie went with Tom to the funeral of one of his closest friends. They'd been at school together, then down the pits as lads, and now Harry was dead. It had taken a while to identify his mangled body.

Moresby Church stood proud on the hill to the north of the town. On the beach below, the Romans had come ashore two thousand years before and built a fort on the high headland, commanding the natural harbours and estuaries to the north and south. It was on this headland that hundreds of mourners assembled. The huge church was packed, and the crowd spilled out onto the grass, standing quiet, singing the hymns whose familiar tunes reached them through the open doors. It was a high, bright, breezy day. Men sweated in their unfamiliar suits. Later, as they stood, dozens deep by the gravesides, a shower swept in from the sea. Rain fell unheeded onto heads, hair and faces, covering the tracks of tears.

They walked back into town when it was all over, leaving Tom behind to see his mates and tell his story one more time. Maggie and John walked slowly, arm in arm, through the mourning town. 'It must have been like this in London, in the Blitz,' he said. 'But whole families, children, not just the men. Imagine.'

'That was war, though,' said Maggie. 'This is about wages.'

'And profit,' said John. 'These pits aren't safe, love, they never were. The price of coal is too high.'

Maggie was quiet for a while. As they climbed the hill towards Kells she held his arm. 'Before we get in,' she said, 'I want to talk to you, without Mam and Judith and Dad.'

He felt suddenly sick. He turned towards her, holding her face in his hand.

'What is it? Are you ill?'

She smiled. 'Not ill,' she said. 'I'm pregnant.'

He stared at her. 'Are you sure?'

'Certain. I thought I was, and the doctor thinks so, too. Nine weeks gone, summat like that.'

'But when?' he said.

'June. D'you remember? We were at it all the time, any chance we got.'

'I remember that cuckoo, watching us.'

'When was that? The day Mam and Judith went to Silloth, wasn't it? No. It was earlier than that.'

'So when that cuckoo was watching us, the baby had already started?'

'Aye.'

'Oh God,' he said, pulling her towards him. 'A baby.'

He let her go and stepped back away from her, looking at her belly, and put his hand against it.

'John,' she laughed, 'Folk 'll see.'

'It looks just the same,' he said.

'Of course it does, for now, but there's things happening in there. It'll show in a few weeks.'

'A baby,' he said again. 'Our baby, yours and mine. When are you going to tell Judith, and your mam?'

'Not yet, not now, not with all this sadness everywhere. Can we leave it a bit, a week or two?'

* * *

It was the first Sunday in September. John saved fuel by taking the train down to Newton to see his mother. He still wasn't sure who knew the truth about him, but he didn't care any more. He wanted to tell her about the baby, that she was going to be a grandmother. It felt as if the baby made everything real, Jessie as his mother, him as her son.

Jessie was in the garden. Later August rain after all the warmth had caused a glut of everything and gardens hung heavy with plums, apples, beans, and tomatoes ripening in the porch at the back of the house. Maybe it was the need for another pair of hands that made her so pleased to see him.

For an hour or two they picked and harvested, until their fingers were sticky and their mouths dry. John was in no hurry to share his news. As they sat finally with cups of tea in the cool of the kitchen, she asked him about Tom, and how John was managing the relief fund that had burgeoned like the garden over the previous weeks.

'It's an honour to be trusted with all that money,' she said. 'They must think highly of you.'

He shrugged. 'I'm an offcomer, married to a local,' he said. They'd rather have me than someone from outside. And I've always been good at sums.'

'Your dad was good with numbers,' she said. 'A clever man, like you.'

He thought about that for a while, the talents that get passed down through families.

'There's something I want to tell you,' he said. 'Maggie and I, we're having a baby.'

Jessie caught her breath. 'A baby,' she repeated. 'So soon.'

'We jumped the gun a bit,' said John, suddenly embarrassed. Jessie smiled at him. 'Like mother, like son,' she said.

'You're going to be a grandmother,' he said.

'I'm too young,' Jessie protested. 'I can't be anyone's granny! My granny was so old.'

'You've got time to get used to it, and get the knitting out,' he said. 'Find the rocking chair and the shawl.'

'A baby,' she said again. 'How wonderful. I'm so happy for you. Is Maggie pleased?'

'Delighted,' he said. 'And Violet and Frank! They've got grand-kids all over the place, but you'd think it was the first.'

'First for me,' said Jessie. 'And Maggie's well?'

'Blooming. Nothing much showing yet. But she knows what to expect, after Judith.'

'Things are much better, much safer, for women now,' said Jessie. 'When I had you …'

'Was it bad?' John had never really thought about it before, about the fact of Jessie giving birth.

Jessie covered her eyes. He saw the tears come.

'I've tried to forget it, but now, just the past few weeks, it's all come back to me. That awful place, the other girls, how the doctor treated us. And then they came, and just took you away.'

'She talked about it,' said John. 'Enid, before she died. Did I ever tell you? She talked about that day, when they came and took me back to Barrow with them. That's when I knew I had to find out, to know what happened.'

'And you found me,' she said. 'And all these years, we've had to lie.'

'We chose to lie,' he said. 'And now we choose to tell the truth.'

Jessie blew her nose, and smiled at him.

"I was so shocked when you told Matthew,' she said, 'but it had to be said. He had to know.'

'Has he asked you to marry him?'

'We've talked about it,' she said. 'I'm not sure I love him like I loved your father, but I'm older now. Maybe love is different. How do we ever know these things?'

'Tom, says if you find someone, you should hang on to them. He lost his wife, and his child, both together. Did you know?'

'No. How dreadful for him.'

'It was a miracle that he and his mates survived,' said John. 'We all cried, the place was awash. And we felt guilty, Maggie and I, about being so happy when all those other people …'

They went back to the garden for a while, working together quietly in the fragrant afternoon.

CHAPTER 29

NOT LONG AFTER JOHN HAD LEFT, the telephone at Applegarth rang for a long time. When Jessie finally heard it she had to shake off her gardening shoes and run into the hall to catch whoever it was before they rang off. It was Agnes, calling from the station at Barrow to say she was on her way home. She planned to visit a friend on Abbey Road, and get the mid-afternoon train up the coast to Newton. Jessie had just got back to work in the garden, when the telephone rang again.

'Damn the thing,' she said before deciding that she had better answer it.

'This is Applegarth', she said, a little crossly, and out of breath.

'Jessie,' said Matthew, 'Is that you?'

'Yes, it's me, I've just run in from the garden. Where are you? Did you have a nice time down south?'

'We're just about to leave Milnthorpe. We stopped to have some lunch.'

'We? Is there somebody with you?'

'Yes, dear. Ann is with me. She decided to come home for a few days, before term starts again you know.' He hesitated. 'Would it be alright if we called in on you later this afternoon, before we go back to Cockermouth?'

'That's fine,' said Jessie.

But it wasn't fine. Ever since that difficult Christmas lunch, Jessie had avoided any chance of meeting Ann. Being patronised so blatantly, and in your own home, was something Jessie didn't wish to repeat, and Ann had kept away, until now. This was the first time she had seen Matthew since they'd talked of marriage. Why did Ann have to be there?

The prospect of visitors, and Agnes's imminent homecoming, reminded Jessie that she had work to do inside the house, especially now she knew Ann was coming. She tidied and dusted the sitting room, using just enough polish to make the room smell good. Nellie would do a proper job when she came the following week. In the kitchen she washed up and swept the floor, storing fruit and vegetables in the pantry to be dealt with later.

She sat at the kitchen table for a minute, and thought about what might unfold. She had been a single woman all her life, fifty years. For much of that time she had been acutely lonely, using work and busyness to fill the space. Now she had a son, and a daughter-in-law, and a grandchild on the way. But still there was no one in the world to whom she mattered more than anyone else, except Matthew. He was a good man, he loved her and they would be comfortable together. Passion might grow, she had decided. She so wanted this to work out.

The car horn sounded in the drive as she was brushing her hair, having washed her face and changed her clothes. Glancing at herself in the round mirror above the washbasin she decided that she looked quite presentable, and perfectly suitable to be the doctor's lady. She opened the door to her guests.

'Hello, Jessie,' said Ann, walking past her into the hall.

'How are you, my dear?' said Matthew. Jessie moved to kiss him, but he moved his head away and there was a slight clash of heads. 'Sorry,' he murmured.

Jessie ushered them both into the sitting room, and left them there while she went through to make tea. She thought Matthew might follow her, but he did not. She could hear that they were talking but could not hear what was being said.

'Here we are,' she said, returning to the sitting room. 'So you've had a good time?'

'Excellent,' said Ann. 'So good to spend some time with Dad.'

A few minutes silence ensued. Jessie busied herself with being hostess, and wondered why Matthew was saying nothing. Something was being left unsaid.

Jessie needed to break the silence. 'John's wedding went well,' she began, 'although the dreadful business at the William pit has pushed it well to the back of our minds since then.'

'We read about it, of course,' said Ann, 'and it was even on the Pathé news when we went to the cinema in Farnham. Only a few minutes. It looked pretty grim.'

'It was,' said Jessie. 'So many men lost.'

'Places like that must get used to it, I suppose,' Ann went on, stirring her tea. 'You wonder why people want to work down those horrid pits, why not just pack up and move somewhere else, somewhere not so dirty and dangerous.'

'Well,' Jessie began, but Matthew interrupted, sensing a difference of view was about to erupt.

'Let's not talk about that now,' he said. 'Too depressing on such a lovely afternoon. Would you like to show us the garden, Jessie? It must have kept you really busy.'

'You carry on,' said Ann. 'I'll go and powder my nose.'

Jessie changed her shoes at the back door before taking Matthew out to see the garden in all its abundance. The smell of ripe plums lingered in warm shade of the spreading tree.

'Is everything alright?' she said. 'You seem a little tired.'

'Quite a long drive,' he said. 'And it was busy in Farnham. We don't see Emily and the children very often. Lots to catch up on.'

Jessie smiled. She wanted to tell him about John and Maggie's baby, but it was too soon.

'I hear the wedding went really well,' she said. 'In the end, they were married by Father O'Toole in Millom.' Surely he'll ask more about that, she thought, but he did not.

Matthew picked a plum from the branch hanging close to his face.

'You missed one,' he said, handing it to her. He looked down at his feet. 'The girls wanted to talk about, you know, us,' he said.

'I'm sure they did,' said Jessie.

'Emily wanted to know all about you.'

'Naturally.'

'She, and Ann too, were a bit puzzled, by, you know, the business with John. Passing him off as your nephew and so on. All rather confusing.'

'I suppose so,' said Jessie.

'I told them all that you've told me, and what great success you've made of your life, despite it all.'

'Successful? You think so?'

'Certainly I do,' he said. 'To be headmistress of the school all those years, helping generations of children, and all those evacuees. I know those families, not an easy business.'

'Well, thank you, Matthew, for saying that. It's a relief, actually, to move on after all those years of responsibility.'

'I said all that to the girls, you know,' he added. There was a short pause. He coughed. 'It's been difficult for them, of course.'

Jessie waited. She wasn't sure what he was referring to.

'Hard for them to think of me, you know, marrying again. They want to be sure, sure that I'll be happy.'

'Of course,' said Jessie.

'Ann and I discussed it first, and then there was Emily, and Robert, her husband. Everyone had to have their say.'

'There's no need …' Jessie began, not wishing to hear much more about it.

'But I told them all,' he said, smiling at her, 'I told them that you'd had a difficult start in life, but that I forgive you.'

'You forgive me?'

'Yes, of course I do, I must forgive the mistakes you made when you were very young. It'll take the girls a little while to feel the same, but in time, I'm sure …'

'So what are you saying, what does this mean?' she asked. Her mind was buzzing.

'It means that we should get married, my dear, in a little while, when the dust has settled, so to speak. Maybe next year, in the spring perhaps?'

'Just a minute,' she said. 'Before we go in, can I ask, what exactly do you forgive me for?'

'All of it,' he said, taking her hand. 'For having the baby, and giving it away, and having to lie about it all these years. It's all forgotten. We start afresh, you and I.'

Jessie stared at Matthew, who smiled at her cheerfully in return.

'Let's go in,' she said, turning toward the house.

'Ann and I need to get away,' said Matthew, glancing at his watch. 'Still another hour or so on the road, and I have a few things to do before it's back to work tomorrow. Ann will stay a week and see me settled and then go back to London.'

'That's nice,' said Jessie.

Ann appeared in the kitchen as Jessie was changing her shoes.

'Are we ready, Daddy?' she said. 'Can't wait to get home. Seems like we've been away for weeks.'

'Right you are, dear,' he said. 'Jessie and I have had a little chat, and I'm ready when you are.'

'So nice to see you again,' said Ann. She leaned down to touch Jessie's cheek with her own.

'Yes,' said Jessie.

'Off we go then,' said Matthew. 'I'll call you when we get home, dear, and see you in a week or two?' He squeezed her hand and kissed her on the cheek.

'Goodbye,' said Jessie. She watched at the porch door as Matthew turned the car round, drove slowly up the drive to the road, and was gone.

Jessie closed the front door and sat down on the little chair by the telephone in the hall. For a few moments she sat with her head bowed and her eyes closed, quite still, although her heart was racing and her mind a blur. Suddenly she raised her head. In that instant she realised that she could not marry Matthew Dawson – not in the spring, not ever.

CHAPTER 30

'HELLO, I'M BACK,' Agnes called from the front door.

Jessie heard a car door slam and saw Mr Baines from Bootle drive away, before Agnes came into the house.

'I decided I couldn't face the hill with this heavy bag. I bought some gorgeous pear brandy in Harrods, and then Jocelyn insisted on giving me four jars of jam, and now it weighs a ton,' said Agnes, talking into the empty space while she took off her hat and shoes. 'So I hopped off at Bootle instead and got Mr Baines to bring me the rest of the way. Cars are so useful sometimes, don't you think?'

Jessie came down the stairs, happy to see a truly friendly face.

'Lovely to see you, dear,' said Agnes, giving her a hug. 'Sorry I'm a bit late. Jocelyn and I got talking, you know how it is. I'll put the kettle on. Do you want tea?'

'The water should still be warm,' said Jessie. 'I made tea about an hour ago.' She decided not to mention her previous visitors.

'Splendid,' said Agnes. 'Let's sit in the front room. I've got something to tell you.'

After the day's revelations, Jessie wasn't sure how much more news she could deal with. She sat, thinking, as Agnes bustled around, finally settling down in her usual chair by the fireplace.

'They've finally made the decision,' said Agnes.

'Who has, and about what? Go back a bit, Agnes.'

'Right. Well. You remember Mr Bennett, from the Ministry, who came to stay for a few days? He was charged with looking at various sites around the country for the new nuclear plant they want to build.'

'I gathered that, yes,' said Jessie.

'Well, the choice is made, and it will be near Drigg, at Sellafield actually. They're not sure what to call it yet, but that's where it will be. Isn't that exciting? They've actually started the building already.'

'I saw the piece in the *Whitehaven News*,' said Jessie, 'reassuring people about safety. Nellie told me last week that the cows will grow two heads. Not going to be easy to convince her, I should say.'

'Anyway,' said Agnes, 'this means they'll be looking for people to work on it, now that construction has started, people in the office, management, that kind of thing.'

She sipped her tea, looking across at Jessie, her eyes bright. 'Of course I've been thinking of something for you, dear, but now you're going to be "the doctor's wife" you won't be needing a job after all. A life of luxury lies head for you, coffee mornings and bridge, I can see it all.'

She laughed, more loudly than usual, Jessie thought. Agnes put down her cup and took Jessie's hand. 'I'm sorry dear, for prattling on when you've all been having such a sad time with that dreadful accident. The price of coal – that's what they were talking about at the Ministry. It must have been awful.'

'All those funerals,' said Jessie. 'One after another. Some families lost two or three men, you know. Whitehaven's been used to tragedy over the years but this was the worst. John was in the middle of it. They put him in charge of all the donations that came flooding in, money from everywhere. It all has to be recorded and banked and divided up. A very important job, and they gave it to him. I was very proud, I told him so.'

Agnes nodded in agreement. She let go of Jessie's hand but continued to look at her. 'And how is Matthew?' she asked. 'Is he back from seeing the girls? Have you named the day?'

Jessie looked across at her old friend. She didn't want to say anything to her, but she knew that the questions would persist until she did.

'Matthew was here this afternoon,' she said.

'That's why the cups were in the sink,' said Agnes. 'I wondered if you'd had visitors.'

'Matthew wanted to tell me about their trip.'

Agnes waited. She could see that Jessie had more to say.

'Ann was with him,' said Jessie.

'Oh dear, is she still being difficult?' Agnes jumped to the problem of Ann and began to talk more freely. 'I never liked her, you know, even as a child. She was so bossy. Joan never dealt with it properly, and she wound Matthew round her little finger. Daddy's girl, all that.'

'Nothing's changed much,' said Jessie. 'Matthew still seems almost afraid of her.'

'What did she say, dear?' Agnes asked, leaning forward expectantly.

'It was more what he said, actually.'

'Well then, what did he say?'

'He told me how worried "the girls" are, about me trying to replace their mother, I suppose. They'd obviously asked a lot of questions about me and not liked what they heard.'

'What kinds of things, for heaven's sake?' said Agnes.

'Right back to the beginning. About me and Clive, and John being adopted, everything.'

'But Matthew defended you, didn't he?'

'That's just it, dear. I'm not sure he did defend me. He said he forgave me. His very words: *I forgive you.*'

Agnes sat back in her chair. 'Forgiven? Sounds as if you're a criminal,' she said.

'Exactly. I don't want to be forgiven. I want to be understood.'

'Of course you do, dear, of course.' Agnes closed her eyes. 'I judged you like that once, I know. But that was in the heat of the moment, in shock. You can't love someone, and carry on loving them, if you have to *forgive* them.'

'I know that, and you know that, but I'm afraid Matthew doesn't.'

'He's not worthy of you, Jessie,' said her friend. 'What did you say to him?'

'I didn't say anything. I was shocked, and he seemed to think everything was fine, and how we should wait a while, something like that.'

The telephone rang in the hall, loud and insistent.

'That might be him,' said Jessie. 'He said he would ring when he got back. Can you answer it, Agnes? I don't want to speak to him. Tell him anything, I'm in the garden, or out somewhere.'

Agnes hurried to the phone, her finger to her lips.

'Hello,' she said, 'Applegarth ... Yes, hello, Matthew, how was your trip? ... Good, splendid ... Jessie? ... she's not here I'm afraid ... maybe in the garden, I could try – no ... alright. Yes, I'll tell her. Goodbye.'

'Thank you, dear,' said Jessie. 'Good thing you were here. I was thinking I'd have to let it ring, and then he would have worried. What did he want you to tell me?'

'Nothing, just that they were home,' said Agnes. 'What are you going to do, dear?'

'Nothing at all, just now. I need to think.'

'About whether to go ahead with it?'

'I don't think I can go through with it, not like this. I have to think about it, but he's in no hurry, so neither am I!' She jumped

274

up from the chair. 'Are you hungry? All of a sudden, I feel terribly hungry. Let's make a lovely meal together, and drink some of that pear brandy.'

It was the happiest evening either of them had enjoyed for a long time. Talking, laughing, and making their food, Jessie was reminded of the joy of good friendship. They started with a sherry or two, had a generous gin and orange each with the meal, and the pear brandy afterwards was just as good as Agnes had promised.

It was late when they were finally clearing the table and washing up side by side in the kitchen. The bottle of brandy was alarmingly depleted and Jessie felt a little unsteady.

Agnes's voice was slightly slurred. 'You know, dear, I think you've made up your mind about Matthew, and I have to confess I'm glad about that. He's not the one for you.'

'I think you're right,' said Jessie. 'After all these years, I can't settle for marriage on those terms.'

'There's nothing wrong in being single,' said Agnes. She finished her brandy and poured herself some more. 'I've never been tempted, never. There's something so base ... knowing what they want, knowing that it's your duty.'

Jessie smiled. She'd often wondered about how Agnes really felt about men and the physical side of things.

'But you and I,' Agnes went on, 'that's different isn't it?'

'Of course. We're just friends, aren't we?'

'It's more than that,' Agnes whispered, drying her hands. Suddenly she turned to Jessie and pulled her close, stroking her hair with one hand. She bent her head and kissed Jessie's neck, murmuring into her ear.

Jessie stood quite still for a moment, feeling the pressure of Agnes's body. She could smell the brandy on her breath. Then she pushed her gently away. Agnes stood back, smiling, stretched out

275

her hand and smoothed Jessie's hair away from her flushed face.

'I knew it all along,' said Agnes. 'I knew you didn't really want him. You were just stringing him along, like you did with Andrew. Deep down, you're only really happy when you're with me. That's right isn't it?'

Jessie stared at her friend, speechless.

Agnes continued to smile. There were tears in her eyes. 'And it's alright now, dear, we can be together. The school doesn't matter any more. People can say what they like.'

Jessie found her voice, but she couldn't move. 'What are you talking about? What will people say?'

'That we're just a couple of middle-aged ladies sharing a house. But it'll be more than that, it'll be our secret.'

Jessie stepped back, and Agnes moved towards her again, smiling, her arms outstretched.

'No,' Jessie shouted. 'Stop. I never – that's not what I want. We're friends, we've always been friends, but that's all, Agnes. How could you think, after all these years, after all you know about me?'

'Yes, I know you,' said Agnes, 'and I know you've never really wanted a man, not to live with, not to love.'

Jessie shook her head with all the force she could muster. 'You're wrong! Listen to me, Agnes. You're my oldest friend and I love you dearly as a friend, but that's all. Believe me. You've had too much to drink, and you're being silly.'

'Silly?' Agnes cried. 'I love you Jessie. I've always loved you, and now it's time for us to be together.'

Jessie put up her hands to ward off the words, to hear no more. 'That's enough. Stop. You're drunk. Don't say any more.' She turned away towards the door and escape. 'I'm going to go to bed, to sleep, and you should do the same. In the morning, when we're sober, we can forget this ever happened. I'm going. Don't follow me.'

Jessie left the room, closing the door sharply behind her. For a moment Agnes stood quite still, until her knees crumpled and she leaned against the sink. Then she covered her face with her hands and began to cry.

Chapter 31

JESSIE LAY AWAKE IN HER BED for a long time, upset and confused. How had this happened? Surely she'd given Agnes no sign, no encouragement? She remembered Andrew's letter about Agnes from months before. She'd always put that down to spite on his part; he and Agnes had never got on well. But had he seen something in Agnes's behaviour that Jessie had missed? Finally, she slept, and woke with the light. For a moment, before she remembered, she was comfortable. But only for a moment. Then she heard Agnes moving around downstairs and the memory hit her. What would they say to each other? They could pass it all off as the brandy talking, and not mention it at all. But that couldn't work, not if they were going to share the house. She wished she could remember exactly what had been said. All she could recall with painful clarity was that suffocating embrace, the smell of brandy, the look of triumph on Agnes's face as she spoke her truth for the first time.

A sound. She caught her breath. Footsteps came softly up the stairs, but her door stayed closed, and it was Agnes's door she heard, open, close and then the turn of the key in the lock. She breathed again. It was unbearable. She got up, dressed and crept downstairs. Agnes had tidied the kitchen and everything was as it should be – although of course nothing could be the same now.

Early morning mist was clearing when Jessie left the house. As she walked down towards the river, the sun was beginning to warm her, and just a thin veil of white clung to the river banks. She decided to climb, up the hill to the old monument on the highest point where the view of the sea and the mountains spread all around.

A grazing deer by the side of the path looked up, then skittered away into the undergrowth. Jessie walked on, taking off her cardigan to feel the cool air on her arms. She needed to think, away from the confines of the house and the village. When she reached the summit she stood and turned in a full circle, taking in every crease of the landscape and the tops of fells and mountains receding to the north: shades of green, grey and brown, and the pale blue of the sky overhead. A jackdaw croaked nearby. On the road far below, two horses were pulling a wagon between ripening fields of barley.

Poor Agnes, she thought. Kind, hard-working, generous Agnes. What a risk she had taken, and for nothing. Their friendship couldn't end like this. There had to be words they could say that would mend it. But Jessie knew she could not stay at Applegarth. She had been happy there while Agnes was away in London, and Agnes might be away for longer still, but now it was impossible to accept her hospitality. When you live in someone else's house, she realised, it's a compromise and you owe them something, and she could not be beholden to Agnes, not now. She would have to find a place to live on her own, and to do that she would need a job. Not just for the money; she wanted something to do that gave her life structure and purpose, but with less responsibility than she had carried for the past twenty years.

She sat on the flat rock already warmed a little by late summer sunshine and looked out at the sea a mile or so away, flat and glinting at the rim. As it always did, the sea reminded her of Piotr, and his death, and how angry John had been with her. She should have gone to his wedding celebration, she knew that now. I will go and see them, she told herself, in private, just me and them, not the rest of the world looking on. And there are other things I must do too, she resolved, soon, but not yet.

When Jessie got back to Applegarth, there was no sign of Agnes. The car was still in the garage and the front door unlocked as Jessie had left it. She felt the kettle; it was cold. She filled it and put it on the range to heat.

Agnes woke with a start when she heard the tap on her door. Her head ached and her eyes were puffy and sore. She lay still, hoping Jessie would go away. In vain.

'Agnes,' said Jessie quietly. 'I've brought you some tea.'

'Leave it there. I'll come down.' When the footsteps had retreated down the stairs Agnes got out of bed, unlocked the door, picked up the tea from the floor and took it back to bed. Unhappiness weighed her down, blocking her mind.

She had been so sure that Jessie felt as she did, but now everything was ruined. She would have to say something. She got up, dressed with care, put her London things into her bag, and opened the door. There was no sound, but she knew that Jessie was there, waiting. She went down the stairs, carrying the bag and the cup. As she reached the foot of the stairs, the bag was lifted from her hand and Jessie walked ahead of her into the kitchen.

'Sit down, dear,' said Jessie. 'Would you like more tea?'

Agnes shook her head.

Jessie leaned across the small kitchen table and took her friend's hand. Agnes did not respond, looking down, avoiding Jessie's eyes.

'Last night,' said Jessie. Agnes shook her head again. 'We both drank a little more than we should. I think the best thing would be to forget whatever was said. I can't remember everything, but I think that would be the best thing to do. Do you agree?'

Agnes nodded wordlessly. Jessie felt the slightest squeeze of her friend's fingers, and saw a tear fall onto the table.

'We will be friends, as we have always been, but I cannot live here with you. Not now. It may take me a little while to find somewhere, but by the time you come back from London, I will be gone.'

Agnes didn't move.

'Did you hear me Agnes? I will be gone.'

Agnes nodded, pulled her hand away and stood up, turning to look out into the garden. She took a handkerchief from her sleeve and wiped her eyes. 'Where will you go?' she whispered.

'I'm not sure yet.'

'Will you go to Matthew?'

'Perhaps. I don't know. He and I need to talk about it.' She watched Agnes's narrow back, and the slight movement in her shoulders. 'Don't let's say any more now. Let it be for a while. When you come back from London we'll do something together, a walk or some shopping, and we can talk then.'

Agnes nodded. She blew her nose. 'I have to get some more things and telephone for the car. I'm getting the earlier train.'

'Is there anything I can do?' said Jessie.

'No,' said Agnes. 'Nothing.'

No more was said. The car came, Mr Baines loaded Agnes's bag into the boot and they drove away. Jessie watched from the sitting room window but Agnes did not look back.

Jessie turned away and sat down at the little desk on the sunny side of the room. 'My morning room' Agnes called it as she always wrote her letters there. This morning it was Jessie's turn to take the creamy writing paper from its holder in the desk and take up her favourite pen. There were two letters she needed to write.

The first was to Andrew; it was short and deliberate. Jessie chose the fewest words she needed to explain that she had loved him once, briefly, and no more. She would not be going to Canada and he should accept that and get on with his life. It should have been said years ago, she said to herself. Then she went upstairs, found the bundle of his letters in the drawer in her bedroom, brought them down to the cold fire grate and set fire to them, one at a time, watching the burning scraps disintegrate.

The second letter needed some careful wording, and an address that Agnes had given her some weeks before.

Dear Mr Bennett,

You will remember that we met some weeks ago at the home of Miss Agnes Plane while you were investigating the new site at Sellafield.

I understand that the new works there have now been started and I am writing to you to ask whether you are still interested in employing local people to help on the organisational side of things.

You will remember that I have been the headmistress of the local school for many years until very recently, and I am now available for other work.

I would be happy to send a full curriculum vitae if that would be appropriate.

I look forward to hearing from you.

Yours faithfully,

Jessie Whelan (Miss)

The final thing that Jessie had decided to do would have to wait until later in the day. As she swept the kitchen floor, and pottered in the garden, picking the last of the runner beans, Jessie thought about what she would say. At five o'clock, she poured herself a glass of sherry and drank it straight down. Then she stood looking at the telephone in the hall for a while before she picked up the receiver and dialled the familiar number.

CHAPTER 32

FOR A MOMENT, JESSIE DIDN'T RECOGNISE HIM. The autumn day was warm and still, and steam from the train lingered in clouds on the platform at Seascale as she stepped down from the train and looked for him. She caught sight of him at the far end of the platform, and watched him unseen until he turned and waved and walked towards her. He was bare-headed, without the usual wide-brimmed hat, and held his jacket over his shoulder. His shirt-sleeves were rolled up a little and his tie pulled down. He looked like a boy on his way home from school, not a respectable middle-aged doctor meeting his lady friend.

They stood awkwardly for a minute as a group of boy scouts streamed past them, and then he leaned forward and kissed her cheek.

'I've been worried about you,' he said, taking her arm. 'You never seemed to be at home when I telephoned. I thought you must be avoiding me.'

'I had some thinking to do,' was all she said. 'Do you want to walk on the beach? The tide's out. So much space out there.'

She had said very little on the telephone, except that she thought they should meet and talk. He wanted to drive down to Newton, but she'd suggested Seascale, which they could both reach on the bus or the train, and there was less chance of being noticed. It was quite early on the following Saturday morning, and the weather had changed again. The breeze was slight and from the south-west; far out at the edge of the ebbing tide benign waves creamed over the sand.

'Has Ann been in touch?' she asked, as they walked the few yards from the station down towards the beach. Above them the arc of the sky soared uninterrupted, from the low rise of Black Combe in the south out to the shadow of the Isle of Man and then north towards Sellafield. Imposing houses on the seafront hid the higher mountains from view.

'No,' he said. 'She's very busy in London. I'm on my own again.'

'Lonely?' she asked.

'Not really.' He looked down at her walking beside him, 'Are you?'

'I'm used to living alone,' she said. 'Agnes is back in London, for several weeks this time. It feels odd, not starting the school year as I normally do, but the routine of all that is fading actually as time goes by. After I left at Easter I couldn't understand why certain times of day made me feel alert, or tired. It was all down to the routines of school. Funny what your body gets used to.'

'Do you miss the schoolhouse?' he asked. He was still holding her arm as they crossed the road to go down onto the beach, and she was happy for him to do so.

'I do miss it – more than I expected to. Applegarth is very comfortable, but it's Agnes's house and always will be. No matter how hospitable she is I still feel like her guest. Like a lodger, almost.'

'There is another alternative,' he said, squeezing her arm a little. 'My house is quite big enough for two, with plenty of space for each of us.'

Jessie didn't respond. There was more she needed to say. A wooden seat looked out over the beach. Matthew sat down still holding Jessie's arm, and she sat down next to him.

'I'm sorry,' he said. 'Sorry I was so ... formal with you that day, when Ann and I called in. She and her sister had been, well, difficult, and I didn't want to start her off again. I'd been telling her that you and I are just friends, you see, so I had to make it look ... well, you understand.'

Jessie wished she did understand. She hadn't expected an apology. 'Shall we walk on the sand, out to the tide?' she said. 'We can take our shoes off.'

They did so. Jessie put her shoes into her bag, but left her stockings on. He undid his polished brogues, took them off and tied the laces together so he could hold them in one hand. Then he pulled off his socks. She noticed the hairs on his forearms and his pale feet. She felt suddenly attracted to him; things were not working out the way she had anticipated.

'It must be difficult for Ann,' she said. 'Emily has her family, but Ann only has you.'

'She's a grown woman,' said Matthew. 'She doesn't need me, nor I her come to that.'

'But you must care what she thinks.'

'Of course, but I'm free to make my own decisions.'

They walked on towards the sea across the wide bank of ridged sand. The breeze had freshened, and she had to listen carefully as his voice was whipped away towards the village.

'I thought I was clear about ... about us,' he said, 'but now I don't know. Have you been avoiding me, Jessie? It's felt like that. Have I upset you? Has something happened?'

It was time to tell him. She didn't know how he might react.

'I was upset, yes,' she said. 'It was something you said.'

'What? Tell me.'

'You said that you forgive me.'

'And I do, really,' he said, putting his hand on her shoulder. 'You've been through so much. We can make a fresh start.'

'But why forgiveness?' she persisted. 'Do you think I've done things that need forgiving?'

He stood still again, watching her face. 'But – you told me yourself, about the baby, and giving him away, and then pretending ...' He looked away for a moment, towards the sea. 'I thought you wanted me to react to all that, to say something.'

'I did,' she said. 'I wanted you to understand.'

He looked at her. 'But how could I, with everything you've been through? My life's been so easy compared with yours. I married the first girl I fell in love with, we had a comfortable life, two wonderful children. When Joan died, that life fell apart but I've never had to struggle, and make such hard choices, not like you.'

Jessie would not soften. 'I gave John away because I had to,' she said. 'Clive and I were going to be married. When he died, what choice did I have? I made a life for myself, through my own efforts, in spite all the pressure to move over and let a man have the job I'd worked so hard for. When John found me, it could all have been lost. He understood that. It was something we agreed between us, that he would be my nephew. And it was alright, until he wanted to be honest with his fiancée, with Maggie. Once she knew, I knew it would come out.' She grasped his arm, and tugged at it until he looked at her. 'So what is it you're forgiving me for? I never asked for forgiveness.'

286

He didn't reply, turning away again.

'It was Ann's idea,' he said. 'She said that if I was serious about being with you, we would have to put the past behind us, and I would have to forgive you for everything that had gone before. She said that you had gone astray.'

'Gone astray! How dare she?' said Jessie. 'And you agreed with her?'

Matthew squirmed under Jessie's anger. 'I didn't know what to think,' he said. 'I just want to be happy again.'

'Like before,' she said.

'Yes. Is that so terrible?'

'She knew,' said Jessie. 'Ann knew how I would react to being *forgiven*. She knew it would drive us apart.'

'That's an awful thing to say,' he said, angry himself now. 'She loves me. She just wants the best for me.'

'And for her that means you have to get away from me, don't you see? She's never approved of me, and this was her way of saying so.'

Jessie walked on, leaving Matthew staring miserably after her.

She stopped and walked back towards him. 'It would never work,' she said. 'You want to be married because that's what you're used to, what feels natural to you. It's completely different for me. I'm used to being alone, being in control of my own life. I've tried to see myself as a married woman, as the doctor's wife, but it would feel like a trap, a prison.'

Matthew could feel his hopes slipping away. 'But where will you live?' he asked. 'You've no job. If we were married you wouldn't have to work, and you would have a home. The house in Cockermouth is big enough for us both. I wouldn't bother you.'

'Bother me? You mean sex? It's not the sex I'm afraid of, Matthew, it's the marriage.'

Jessie stood facing him. Her eyes were bright, her mind

287

suddenly sharp. At last, she was clear what she wanted, and what she didn't want.

'I'm sorry, Matthew,' she said. 'You've been so kind. I know you want to care for me, but I'd feel like a caged bird.'

'You can't marry me, ever?'

'I can't. I'm sure now.'

'But why are you crying?' he said.

She brushed the tears from her cheek.

'I'm not crying,' she told him 'It's just the wind.' He stretched out his hand towards her, but she stepped away.

Above their heads a seagull wheeled on the wind, its scream lost in the rushing air. Jessie looked up, watching the bird, before she turned and walked back alone towards the shore, dwarfed by the sweep of water, sand and sky.

JESSIE WHELAN has always been a good liar, trying to protect her independence and her career as a teacher. But she risks everything when, after years of discreet loneliness, she embarks on a love affair. In the meantime, her secret past draws ever closer.

Ruth Sutton's powerful novel is the first part of her trilogy – *Between the Mountains and the Sea*. It is set in Cumbria, the north-west corner of England.

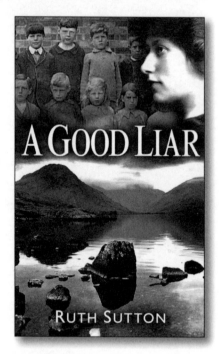

If you've enjoyed *Forgiven*, you may want to...

- Order another copy of *Forgiven* to pass to a friend

- Order a copy of Part 1 entitled *A Good Liar*

- Learn more about Part 3 of the trilogy *Between the Mountains and the Sea*

- Find out more about Ruth Sutton, the author, and read her blog

For all of these, check out the publisher and author's website <u>www.ruthsutton.co.uk</u>